Acknowledgements

I would first like to thank my Lord and Savior for bringing me through all the years of my life. I now know that through Him all things are possible.

My mother Theresa Jackson, I want you to know that you are definitely the wind beneath my wings. You're the greatest mom ever, and I love you so much!

To my daughters, Sakiah and Tiana. I know I was absent when I should have been present. I missed out on parts of your lives that I can never get back. For that, I truly apologize. I promise with all my heart to make the future a better one. I will not only put my all into being a mom, but also into being a grandma to your children. I love you guys!

To my brother, Hareef, thirteen years and it's all over. Let's leave those bars for the animals, Bro. I love ya!

My sisters: Doreen, Marion, Deborah, Smooth, Renee. I love you all for many reasons. Thanks for always loving your "lil sis." Told y'all I was going to blow!!!

Shakirah, Janelle, Nay-Nay, B.J., Yasin, Yasmin, Yamarrah, YII, Tanisha, Theresa, Tyrell, Paris, Lamar, Ayesha, Al-Nisa, Jimmy, Gerecia, Gerard, Javonna: I love you all. Focus on a dream and grab it!

To all those who read this in the raw while I was locked up in Clinton: Carla B., Tiajuana C., Keisha H., Kay-Kay, Miseka.

Thanks for the encouragement.

To my publisher Wahida, you are simply the best! Thank you for giving me the opportunity to let others know I'm more than my past.

To Keisha, thanks for the editing. You are great!

To my original typist, Keisha Brown, you are the best friend a person could ever want. Love ya!

Cambus S., Yaruba P., Sabrina W., Vanessa Clark, thanks for the letters, money, and visits while I was locked up. I could never forget the love.

To anyone I've harmed during my struggles. I apologize. I was caught in the grip of addiction. The sober me wouldn't hurt a fly.

To anyone still caught in any addiction, I will tell you that if "nothing changes, nothing changes." One day at a time is worth trying.

Kristina, we almost made it beyond there. We almost got to the end of the Rainbow, we almost found that pot of gold. We almost got off at that last stop. But almost doesn't count. And it's a shame because through it all I never judged, just loved. My fist is still tight. Reason or season? I haven't figured it out yet. Best to you and yours. Remember real love is felt in all things, it doesn't have to be proved over and over. And the key is to continue to love even when it hurts….To my extended family, the Jacksons, Winchesters, Proctors Hobbs…I love you all.

To my Dad, Harry Jackson, even though we were separated, my love always stretched through the miles.

Oh, yeah, to all my haters. You see me!!!

Love is love,
T. Missy Jackson
April 2, 2009

This one's for Tyrique, Ti-asjah, and Sakyi:
The world is yours.

R.I.P. La'mar N. Prim I love you nephew
and will miss you always!

CHAPTER 1

The Robbery:
Memorial Day 2002

C heetah awoke late in the afternoon, groggy from all the weed she smoked last night. She had smoked about four blunts to head. That weed was a new blend, and the first blunt was so tasty, before she knew it, she had rolled the whole quarter pound she bought. She searched the ashtray, hoping that a tail was still there. Empty. Before brushing her teeth, she had the urge to smoke. Her weed habit was worse than a crackhead on crack. She had to have it. In her mind, her day couldn't start without it. The room she rented at the boarding house was so small you could turn around once and be out. The bed sat next to the kitchen table. A small partition separated the bathroom from the rest of the room.

Dragging herself out of the bed, Cheetah staggered to the bathroom. She threw some water on her face before she started brushing her teeth. She went back into her bedroom and threw on the same clothes from the day before.

Cheetah peeled thirty dollars off her bank roll, slipped on her jacket, and walked out the door.

She headed down the block to cop some weed. She usually copped some weight in New York whenever she and her friend

Naj went to re-up, but Naj had done the last pickup from their connect in Elizabeth. She was out of weed but not out of luck. There was always a nigga posted up on the block advertising his goods. Today she would be forced to test it out.

Just as Cheetah thought, the same little nigga she had passed yesterday was on post in the same spot. Not knowing him personally, Cheetah approached him cautiously. He was leaned back against the side of an abandoned grocery store puffing on a blunt. Cheetah walked within three feet of him and stopped.

"What's up? I'm tryna smoke." Cheetah said, holding out her fist to give him a pound. He eyed her for a second, rose off the wall, and tapped her fist with his.

"What you tryna smoke? I got it all from A to Z," he said taking another pull off his blunt.

"I'm tryna get a quarter of piff. You good?" Cheetah asked for the blend of weed she had smoked the night before. It was a light green in color with red lines that ran through the buds like veins. It had a mild taste and an instant affect.

"Fo' sho, Ma! You wanna hit this?" he asked, offering Cheetah the blunt. Did she wanna hit it? Hell yeah she wanted to hit it!

"Aight," Cheetah said, taking the blunt out of his hand. He walked to his stash while Cheetah hit the blunt. As soon as the smoke filled her lungs, she knew it was laced with something. The mint taste and the slight tingle on her tongue was different than any other taste she ever had. Cheetah held the smoke and the tingle spread throughout her body.

As he approached her, he noticed the funny look on her face.

Blowing out the smoke, she looked at him and said, "My nigga, what the fuck is this?"

"Just a little gank, Ma, nothing much. Go 'head. Hit that shit again," He said, assuming she got down since everybody in the hood smoked gank.

Cheetah heard about gank but had never cut into it. It was weed laced with PCP. Supposedly, it took a person on a different trip each time it was smoked. If you were a first timer, you were

8

definitely going to be cooking after you smoked it. Niggas from around her way had tried to get her to smoke it before. Weed and little liquor here and there ain't neva hurt nobody. Usually, she wouldn't have tried any new blends. She was cool with her normal piff or chocolate.

Being the daredevil that she was, she took two more long hits and passed it back. A feeling of electricity shot through her body. She felt the sensation like she'd just bit into a York Peppermint Patty.

"A, yo, what's good with this, my dude? Why the taste so potent?" she asked as she let out the next cloud of smoke.

"Ma, that's my double dip special. I laced the weed, then dipped the blunt after it was rolled. Let it dry and dipped it again. That's a head cracker, Ma!" young dude said as he passed the blunt back.

Enjoying the tingling feeling, Cheetah smoked the rest of the blunt, copped her a quarter of piff and two blunts of gank. They pounded fists and she bounced.

With each step, she had to focus in order to hold her balance. Halfway up the block, she was hit with a hot flash. Trickles of sweat began to slide down the side of her face. A couple more steps, and her vision got blurry, her mouth cotton dry. Her legs became heavy like boulders. Each step was becoming more difficult to take.

It felt as if everything had slowed down, and the buildings were moving, twisting and bending. She wiped her face, trying to focus.

Trying to figure out what was wrong with her feet, she looked down and her feet were in cement blocks. Her eyes were big as saucers.

She looked up and noticed that all the buildings around her seemed to be leaning. Allowing her eyes to scan her surroundings, Cheetah looked at a man walking, but his face was contorted. Then she glanced at a woman crossing the street; her head was real big, and her body looked very small.

"Oh, shit," she whispered, tripping.

Cheetah looked in the faces of passersby's, seeing slanted eyes and scales on their faces. Everyone looked like aliens. She couldn't believe what was going on around her. She wanted to move, but she couldn't. She just stood there, transfixed, feeling like she was out of her body. Tears started to roll down her face.

The more she tried to move, the harder it was. Just as paranoia was setting in, she felt a hand on her shoulder.

Turning around in slow motion, she came face to face with someone she recognized, but couldn't place because they too had a face like everyone else.

Another alien!

She threw her hands up as a defense mechanism to protect her face.

Concerned by the way Cheetah was just standing there, her best friend, Naj, grabbed her by the shoulders and squared her up, nearly causing Naj to drop the backpack she was carrying. Pulling Cheetah's hands away from her face, Naj looked her in the eyes and saw that something was definitely wrong.

Naj met Cheetah five years ago at an annual gay pride two-on-two round ball tournament at Branch Brook Park back in '97. Even though they only knew each other for a few years, it seemed a lifetime. Both of them were in the "life". Cheetah looked like a cuter version of Chris Brown with dreads. Naj looked just like a thugged out nigga. It would take some ID to know they were women.

Naj shook Cheetah and asked, "What the fuck is wrong wit you?"

"Ahhh. Uhhh," Cheetah was trying with all her might to get some words out but couldn't.

Naj grabbed her again with a little more force. Yelling this time, she said, "Cheetah, did you take something?"

Duh, that's obvious, Naj thought, answering her own question.

Cheetah took a deep breath speaking, she slurred, "Naj... home. Take...me... home."

Not wanting to cause a scene, Naj grabbed Cheetah by the arm and helped her home. Reaching into Cheetah's jacket pocket, Naj found the keys and unlocked the front door. It took them more time than usual to reach the room because Naj practically had to carry her up the steps.

Naj told Cheetah to sit down on the bed while she went to wet a wash cloth. Cheetah fell back on the bed. The room was spinning. Naj placed the cloth on her head.

This is not working, Naj thought.

Going back to the sink, she filled a glass with cold water.

"Here, drink this."

She held the glass to Cheetah's chapped lips. Sweat dripped down her face.

"Take this hot ass jacket off."

Naj helped her out of the leather Avirex jacket and took off the Timbs she had on. Cheetah tried to stand, but lost her balance.

"Sit down. What is it? I'll get it," Naj told her.

Minutes passed before Cheetah turned toward Naj and spoke.

"Naj…man…get…me…a…glass…of…milk…please."

Her words were still coming out slow and broken. She knew what she wanted to say and the thoughts registered in her mind. She just couldn't make them come out right.

Naj was truly upset at Cheetah for pulling this stunt. To her, people who used drugs were weak minded. She was totally against the use of drugs. She didn't even like the fact that Cheetah smoked weed. Although she sold drugs on the reg', she didn't believe in someone being a user and baller at the same time. Sooner or later, the drugs were going to either cloud your judgment, or cause you to slip. Cheetah was a hardheaded mafucka, and Naj was getting tired of telling her the same thing over and over.

After filling the cup up with milk, Naj went back in the room.

Cheetah guzzled down the drink in one gulp. They sat there for a few minutes, both lost in their own thoughts.

You trippin' Cheetah. Get yourself together, she thought. Cheetah was trying hard to shake this high.

Naj was sitting in the chair beside the bed that Cheetah was stretched out on. She kept her eyes focused on Cheetah's face. Finally, after what seemed like forever, Cheetah sat up, looked at Naj, and had the nerve to smile.

Cheetah was the wild one. She stayed in some shit. Ever since high school, she dressed like a nigga: jeans sagging, extra large t-shirt, and her staple white on white Air Force Ones. She kept her fire red dreds that complimented her butter brown skin, nice and neat with a sharp shape up. Her light brown eyes made her baby face appear sexy, and the deep set of dimples kept the girls smiling. She may have looked like a man, but whenever she spoke it revealed that she was a girl. Early on she learned it was better to just be yourself. If a bitch didn't like it…oh well. There were plenty of them that would. She didn't get down with trying to fool hoes.

Even though Naj was the calm one, she always stayed in drama. She had more hoes than pimps in Chicago. Besides being two years older than Cheetah, the only difference between them was that Cheetah never had no dick. Naj tried it once when she was thirteen, thinking that it would make her stop loving girls that way. Her straight back braids, and chiseled face with the scar that ran down its side made her look hard. At six feet tall, she had no shape at all, just straight up and down. It was as if the chromosomes should have been XY. She had the thugged-out look on the money.

Naj could not believe that Cheetah was now sitting up in the bed, smiling like a Cheshire cat.

"Don't be smiling at me, nigga!" Even though she already had her suspicions, she asked anyway. "What the fuck you been dipping into, Cheetah?"

The smile that had just etched Cheetah's face vanished. She now looked at Naj and thought, *don't start that preaching shit.*

"Chill, dawg. I smoked a blunt with that little nigga that be on the corner down the street. His ass ain't even tell me that shit was laced wit some gank."

Naj's grill was twisted.

"Breathe easy, my nigga. I'm alright now."

"Some gank?" Naj yelled. "And you want me to breathe easy. You know that shit be making niggas go crazy, right?"

Cheetah knew Naj would act this way. To be honest, she was not in the mood to hear any lectures. She also didn't want to get into a confrontation, so she kept her calm and chose her next words carefully.

"Look, Naj, I'm not going to go crazy, so just chill out okay? I just had to get over the initial shock because it was my first time. I'm high as hell now! Cooking! I can handle it. Stop acting like I'm a young ass teenager or something," Cheetah said with finality.

Naj wanted to get at her with some other shit right now. She made a mental note to talk to her later. Before she got down to the business at hand, she sucked her teeth and said, "Yeah alright, whateva. You grown right? But your stupid ass was just stuck in the middle of the street crying like a baby!"

Cheetah swung her feet over the side of the bed and ran her fingers through her hair.

"I'm good, Naj. I kind of like this shit."

Naj was tired of this pointless conversation. She had come to talk business.

"Okay, whateva, nigga. You ready to ball? Can you work out now, or do you have to let this shit wear off? I need you to do this drop off by yourself. I got Ja'nise and the kids waiting to go to Chuck-E-Cheese. I'ma probably be there 'til about eight."

Cheetah stood up off the bed and stretched.

"Yeah, I'm good."

"Okay, look then," Naj said, slinging an oversized backpack onto the bed. "It's a hundred bricks of heroin in this backpack, fifty individual bags in each one. This that fire right here, my dude. This shit got a DOA stamp on it and it's definitely gonna be putting niggas on their ass. I gave Scabs and a couple of his dopefiend friends some samples. They put the official on it.

"I want you to hand 'em out as usual, and when I get in later we can start to collect from whoever is ready to turn in some money. Nigga, this right here should put us way over the top! I just spent twenty thousand on this pickup. All we had left was a few thousand saved to get us whatever we may need. No shorts!" Naj stressed.

"You know the dope man don't take no shorts. Tell them knuckleheads you want four hundred off each brick. If you pass out ten bricks on each block we should be getting four thousand from each set. That's forty thousand in total. That will put us right where we need to be. You can get out of this room and we can get our shit straight, aight?"

Cheetah twirled her dreds as she stood in the middle of the floor. She always did this when she was in deep thought.

"Yeah, that's what's up," she said as she stopped jumping. "But as far as me getting out of this room, you know how I do. I'm not trying to be all flashy. When I'm able to cop me a condo or house then I'll bounce. Until then, I'm staying here."

"Aight, then I'm out. Beep me to let me know you aight, or hit me on the celly, okay?"

"Aight, Naj, one!" Cheetah said tapping her middle finger over her heart.

Naj copied the gesture saying, "One" as she walked out the door.

It was Naj's play sister Brandi who hooked them up with their connect three years ago. Brandi was really a man that used to trick with Papi on the down-low. He helped them get on. The streets of Newark was a hustler's pot of gold.

The milk made Cheetah feel better, but she was still high as hell. In fact, she felt like she was floating on air. She walked to her bedroom mirror and stared at her reflection.

"What the fuck!" she said out loud.

The reflection in the mirror looked like she was at a carnival in the fun house. First, her face looked long and thin. She blinked and the face in the mirror changed. Now it looked small and fat. She looked for a while longer then vigorously shook her head as if to make it all disappear. When she looked back in the mirror and things remained the same, she looked away. She went into the kitchen and drank two more cups of milk. She had heard on the streets that if you went on a trip from gank, you needed to drink milk to subdue the high. The way she was feeling, she hoped it would do just that.

Cheetah went back into her room and put her jacket and boots on. She checked the contents of the backpack and headed out the door.

Her initial thought was to catch a cab, but since it was so nice and she had her groove on, she decided to take the bus instead. She headed toward the bus stop on Avon Avenue. She hated walking this way because she would have to cut through the notorious Stratford Avenue.

Now if ever there was a street that held a name for being truly gangsta, Stratford Avenue was it. The young cats that *repped* the block were crazy and deranged. The street held a rep of its own, for murder, mayhem…all kinds of wild shit went down on Stratford Ave. Cheetah tried to avoid it by any means possible.

The last time Cheetah walked down Stratford, some dude said to her, "What's poppin'?" fucking with her.

Cheetah wasn't down with the "What's poppin', what's crackin'," gang lingo, so she continued to walk on by as if she didn't hear him. The next thing she knew she felt something whizzing by her head, then heard a loud crash. The boy had thrown a forty ounce bottle of King Cobra at her. She didn't stop to beef because she knew she would have to kill someone in order to get out alive.

Now walking up Stratford, she had a feeling of deja vu. She felt her waist and realized that she had left her gun at home. So she put a little pep in her step and tried to block out her surroundings. Had she really paid attention to the people and cars around her, she would have noticed the black Escalade turning up the one way street, following her.

Cheetah heard a familiar voice holla, "What's poppin', Ma?"

Instead of looking toward the source, she started to run, but two guys jumped out of the Escalade, grabbed her, and dragged her into an alleyway. Using her street senses, Cheetah began taking in as much of the scene as she could. She noticed that one of the guys was tall and medium built, while the other was more on the muscular side.

"Bitch, you know what it is," the taller one said, pushing the gun to her temple. Her high went straight out the window; she was sobering up real fast.

They were both dressed in all black, complete with ski masks. Cheetah tried to distinguish the voice that boomed from behind the mask, but she couldn't place it. She knew it had to be someone from that block jacking her because she had just passed a parade of people. No one came to give her a helping hand or even to see what the hell was going on.

"Bitch, take the back pack off and strip," the heavyset one yelled, pushing the gun harder into her temple.

"Fuck you!" Cheetah spat. "I'm not stripping and I'm not giving you niggas shit!"

"Oh, bitch, you tough, huh? Now you gonna strip and get fucked!" Too Tall said as he grabbed his nut sack and began to unzip his zipper.

Cheetah threw the bag on the ground, spitting in the fat robber's direction. As he bent down to pick up the bag, the second robber punched her hard in the temple. She stumbled a bit, but held her balance. Her first thought was to hit him back, but she knew that she couldn't go up against him. She attempted to run, but not before the leader of the two snatched her by the dreads, hitting her in the head with the butt of his gun. The blow dazed her. The tall one got angry and hit her square between the eyes. As soon as she hit the pavement, they began stomping her.

"Fuck this bitch. Let's roll," the leader told his partner.

Too Tall walked around Big Boy to the other side of Cheetah and bent down for the bag. Cheetah made one last feeble attempt to fight. Reaching out, Cheetah grabbed his leg, and with all the strength she could muster, yanked it. Too Tall lost his footing and landed on the ground. Big Boy, not believing what just happened, went loco on Cheetah. He started stomping her. Cheetah curled up in a fetal position trying to protect her face and chest.

CHEETAH

"Oh, so you want to be a tough little mothafucker, huh? You bad, huh?" he said as he kicked her in the back of the head.

"I was going to go easy on your ass, but you done brought the beast out, son!"

"You are a son, right?" he asked, now laughing. "At least I know that's what the fuck you walk around here acting like. Now I'm going to beat you like one!"

He brought his foot up high and tried to stomp a mud hole in Cheetah's back. One kick caught Cheetah between her shoulder blade and neck. Her eyes rolled up into the back of her head and everything went black.

"Get the fuck up!" he yelled over his shoulder to Too Tall who was still lying dumbfounded on the ground. "Get up and get the bag mafucka!"

Too Tall scrambled to his feet, grabbing the bag on his way up. Big Boy reached down and snatched her chain off her neck. He then pulled the diamond stud out of her ear, and took the diamond pinky ring off her finger. Too Tall stripped her of her jacket and boots as Big Boy headed out the alleyway.

"Hold up. Hold this," Too Tall said, handing Big Boy the book bag along with her personal items. "I got one last thing to do, son," he said as he unzipped his jeans and pulled out his already erect dick.

"Man, fuck that bitch! Let's be out," Big Boy said.

"Hold up, dawg," Too Tall said, his dick now aimed at Cheetah. "I ain't trying to run up in her. I just gotta do somethin'."

Stepping closer to Cheetah, Too Tall looked down at her still body. "Bitch, this is for pulling me to the ground," he said as he let off a stream of piss. He zigzagged his dick, so the urine hit every inch of her body, spelling out his name on her. After relieving himself, he put his dick away, kicked Cheetah one last time, and ran out the alley with Big Boy on his heels.

Cheetah felt cold water dripping on her face. She opened her eyes and saw a young boy, who appeared to be no older than fourteen standing over her, holding a bottle of water.

17

"Yo, you aight?" he asked with a concerned look on his face.

Cheetah didn't know how long she had been lying in that alleyway. The last thing she remembered was being punched.

"Can you talk? You good?" the young kid asked again, kneeling down beside her. Cheetah tried to move and pain shot through her like an arrow.

"How long I been here?" she asked as she mustered up the strength to get into a sitting position.

"Not long. I was on the fire escape of my building and I saw when them dudes was stomping you. They peeled out like five minutes ago. That's when I came down to check on you. You need to go to the hospital. You don't look too good."

"Nah, I'm good. I just gotta make a call. You wanna help me to my crib?"

"Yeah, I got you."

Cheetah pulled out her cell phone and called Naj.

"Yeah, who dis?" Naj answered after the first ring.

"Naj, it's me, Cheetah. 'Oh no!' at my house," Cheetah said, and then hung up the phone. "Oh no!" was the code for an emergency. No matter what the other was doing, that code meant to drop everything and get to the destination.

Cheetah stood up, and the pain was so excruciating, it doubled her back over. The young kid helped her up and together they made it back to Cheetah's place.

"Yo, my money fucked up right now," she began saying to the young kid. "Hit me up later and I got you for helping me out."

"Nah, I'm good. You just go get yourself fixed up. My sister got murdered in that same alley a few years back. I wished I could've been there to help her out," the young kid said.

Cheetah was touched and beyond grateful.

"Yo, you ever need anything come holla at me, okay? What's your name anyway?"

"Justice, but they call me Lil' J." With that said, he turned and walked away.

Once inside her room, Cheetah went straight to the mirror.

Looking into it, the person who stared back looked a hot mess. She was fucked up! She had at least five knots on her head the size of small grapes, one eye was swollen shut, and blood was dripping from her bottom lip.

She coughed again and blood splattered onto the mirror. The pain at her side was excruciating. She made her way to the bed and laid there until Naj came.

As soon as Naj hung up from the call with Cheetah, she turned around on the highway, nearly forgetting she had Ja'nise and her two children, Malik and Malikah, in the car.

Ja'nise was Naj's "wifey." They met back when Ja'nise danced at a club called Flowers. Each time Naj visited the club, she always made it rain whenever Ja'nise took the stage. Ja'nise had noticed Naj and was very interested in meeting her. Everything about Naj's swagger turned her on.

It wasn't until Naj commissioned Ja'nise to the VIP room that she found out Naj was in fact a woman. Ja'nise was shocked. If she wouldn't have brushed up against her breast, she wouldn't have believed her. This didn't change anything because Ja'nise was bisexual. She had been with many women, but never in a relationship.

Naj was a solid build at five-eleven and weighed one-ninety. From years of playing basketball, she was in great shape. She kept her braids fresh with a clean shape up. Dressed in a New Jersey Nets jersey, Sean John jeans, and a pair of Jordans, she looked as good as any man.

Ja'nise was very surprised when Naj didn't solicit any sex or a lap dance from her. She just wanted to talk. It was something about Ja'nise that made her want to open up. She told Ja'nise that she had lived with her grandmother since she was five. Both of her parents were gone. Her mother was killed in a drive-by shooting, and her father was serving a life sentence for killing the niggas who murdered his wife. Naj's life wasn't simple. She hustled day in and day out.

Ja'nise figured Naj would react like most niggas once she revealed that she had two children, and wouldn't want nothing more than to trick. To Ja'nise's surprise, Naj had said, "Good 'cause I wasn't having any."

It didn't take long before Naj was wide open. Naj let her playa card go to be with Ja'nise, and be a family. Naj turned out to be better than any man Ja'nise had ever been with. She took care of her kids as if they were her own.

Driving like a maniac, Naj made it to Cheetah's in ten minutes flat. Leaving Ja'nise and her two children in the car, she ran up the steps to Cheetah's place two at a time. Using her own set of keys, she entered the room. Cheetah was lying on the bed all beat up and bloody.

Naj walked over to Cheetah and turned her over.

"Ouch, be easy, man!" Cheetah yelled out in pain.

Her eyes were wide. "What happened? What the fuck happened, Cheetah?" Naj screamed.

"Them Stratford niggas jacked me. Ahh, shit, it hurts," she said holding onto her side. "They took the backpack, Naj, and everything else. Ahh, shit! I think my ribs are broken," Cheetah said as she coughed up more blood.

Naj got a towel and held it to Cheetah's mouth. Cheetah needed to get to the hospital. Even though the fact that they had just lost out on practically everything they had made her sick, she had to get Cheetah some help real quick.

"Aight listen, Cheetah. Can you walk?" Naj asked.

"Yeah, but it hurts real bad, man."

"Okay then I guess I got to carry you then."

That's exactly what she did. She picked Cheetah up, and carried her to the car even though Chettah weighed one hundred seventy pounds. Naj picked her up as if she were a baby.

Ja'nise saw them coming and got out. Naj put Cheetah in the front next to her, and Ja'nise hopped in the back with the kids.

"Baby, what happened to her?" Ja'nise asked from the back seat.

"I'll tell you later, okay? Right now we have to get her to the hospital fast!"

Naj did ninety-five all the way to the hospital, avoiding as many lights as she could. By the time they pulled up in the emergency room parking lot, Cheetah was blacking out from the pain. Naj parked and ran to the desk to get some help.

Sitting behind the desk was a *Throw Mama from the Train* look alike. Naj slammed her fist down hard on the desk, and the receptionist looked up.

"May I help you, mister?" she asked.

"Yeah, you can help me by getting a gurney for my friend and you can help yourself by not calling me no damn mister!" Naj yelled.

The nurse looked confused because from the looks of the person in front of her, it had to be a man. Instead of questioning any further, she just shook her head, got up, and got an intern to assist Naj.

By the time they got to the car, Cheetah had fainted. Quickly, they rushed her inside the hospital. She was taken back behind the curtain and Naj took a seat. No sooner had her butt hit the coldness of the hard plastic chair did the same dumb ass receptionist come up to her with a pile of papers for her to fill out. She immediately began asking questions about insurance and shit. Naj, not really feeling this bitch, just ignored her. Catching the drift, the receptionist walked away mumbling something under her breath.

Naj had more important things on her mind at the moment. First and foremost, she was worried about Cheetah, and was praying she would pull through without too much damage. She knew that if a person coughed up blood that it could mean internal bleeding. She hoped that wasn't the case this time.

Secondly, she was thinking about her money. Their money! She had just spent twenty thousand on that pick up. All they had was the four thousand she had saved for pocket cash.

They made a nice amount of money on a weekly basis, but somehow they always recouped the same amount. Splurging on unnecessary things kept them at a steady level. Naj wanted to come up. It was time to master the game, not just play it. With the territory and the clientele they had, there was no reason that in the past five years they didn't have at least a million dollars saved.

Naj felt that if she dug deep, they would be set by the end of the year. She wanted to take five hundred stacks and bounce to Atlanta. She was tired of the city. She wanted to get a house built from the ground up, open up her own clothing business, and leave the hustle behind. However, with the loss of the bricks of dope they were back at square one. She knew that eventually they would get back on board, but first Cheetah had to pull through.

Naj got up and walked out to the car. She told Ja'nise to take the kids to Checkers, a fast food restaurant up the street while she waited. She went back in and waited at least another hour before the doctor came out to speak with her. He told her that Cheetah had been severely beaten. She had four broken ribs, a broken blood vessel in her eye, a concussion, and a fractured collar bone.

Relieved to hear that she would be okay, Naj asked how long before she could leave. The doctor wanted to keep her until her ribs healed up, but in order to admit her, he needed the information the receptionist tried to get earlier.

Naj gave it to him and asked if she could see her.

The doctor said, "Yes," but warned her that Cheetah was heavily sedated and it probably would be better to come back later.

Naj agreed with him and left the hospital. She took Ja'nise and the kids home, and tried to eat a burger Ja'nise had gotten for her. Her mind was so focused on Cheetah and the robbery that she couldn't stomach any food. She got up and headed back to the hospital.

Cheetah was fast asleep. Naj walked in quietly and sat in a chair next to the bed until Cheetah woke up. Cheetah looked at Naj and tried to sit up, but she couldn't. She was heavily bandaged, and in so much pain she whimpered in agony. Naj jumped up and went to get the nurse. She came in and gave Cheetah a shot of Demerol. Cheetah, now feeling no pain, was ready to talk to Naj. Naj didn't want to pressure her, but she needed to find out what happened on Stratford Avenue and who did this.

"Hey, you okay?" Naj asked, noticing how relaxed Cheetah's face looked now.

"Yeah, I'm good."

"Aight cool. You want to tell me what happened now?" Naj asked, pulling her chair as close as possible to the bed.

Cheetah picked up the remote hooked to the bed and raised herself up to a sitting position. She took a sip of water from a cup that was sitting next to her bed and started talking.

"Naj, I left right behind you. I was going to get on the bus and go up the block to meet up with the runners. When I turned up Stratford Avenue, this black Escalade pulled up right behind me. Two jokers jumped out and forced me in the alley."

Tears started rolling down Cheetah's face as she continued. "Naj, they wanted me to strip. I told 'em, 'hell no!' and started swinging on those niggas! I caught one in the stomach, and he dropped me. They beat me until I couldn't feel shit, man. This is the shit though, Naj, it was mad heads out on that block and nobody tried to help. So I know it had to be a couple of those Stratford niggas that did this shit! We gotta get them, Naj. They gotta get done!"

Naj was more than heated. The niggas responsible for this would definitely be handled. But first, she had to find out who they were. That shouldn't be a problem, because the streets is always talking. She knew that Cheetah wasn't going to rest until she got her revenge. Naj just hoped she could keep her calm enough to handle this shit correctly.

"Listen, Cheetah," Naj began, "you just get yourself healed and we'll deal with that once you get better. I'm gonna take care of some things and I'll come back tomorrow, okay?"

"Yeah, aight," Cheetah said as more tears fell from her eyes.

"Don't worry dawg, wipe your eyes. We gonna be aight."

Naj got up, and got some tissue from a box of Kleenex

sitting on an end table. She wiped Cheetah's tears away and left without another word.

She had to find out who the fuck did this to Cheetah. She needed info and needed it now!

Once in the parking lot, Naj dialed Esh, Cheetah's niece. Esh answered on the first ring.

"What up, Naj?" she asked breathlessly. She was in her bedroom and had just finished putting in work doing three hundred crunches.

"How you know it was me?"

"I know you heard of caller ID, dumbo. I got ya number programmed in my cell.

"Oh, okay, that's wassup. But on some serious shit, you need to speed down to University Hospital and check your aunt out."

"For what? What happened?" Esh asked, getting dressed.

"She just caught a bad break. I'll let her fill you in on the details. I'm on the move, trying to handle my end. She need some fam' there with her. Don't tell your grandma though. You know how she be trippin'."

"No doubt, I'm already out the door," she said.

Esh was nineteen years old and had three children. She and Cheetah were very close in age, just six years apart. For the most part, they got along like sisters. Cheetah's sister, Dana, was a fiend, strung out on heroin and crack. Esh was raised by Cheetah's mom right along side Cheetah. Even though they argued and bickered nonstop, Esh loved her aunt to death.

She threw on her pink Juicy sweatsuit along with a pair of pink and white Air Max sneakers. Esh was a very pretty girl. Her low cut hairstyles enhanced her sex appeal. Long legs, a flat stomach, and mocha colored skin made her a hot commodity with the young men. She was "ghetto fab'" and knew it.

Her days consisted of seeing which baller was going to spend some of that drug money on her. She never had a job and didn't plan on getting one anytime soon. The streets fed her and her children very well.

She called her grandmother and told her that she would pick the children up a little later. Then she grabbed the keys to her eight year-old Infiniti and headed to the hospital.

Naj rode up and down Clinton Avenue until she saw just who she was looking for. She spotted Scabs standing in front of the liquor store, trying to bamboozle a young lady out of some change. Scabs was an old neighborhood dope fiend. His body was so messed up from shooting dope into his veins. He had abscess marks all over his body; that's why they called him Scabs. He was also a grimey nigga. If you had money or dope he would sell his momma! Naj knew him since she first stepped foot in Newark. He hustled for her every now and then and he always knew what was going on around town.

Naj pulled over and called him to the car. As soon as he saw who it was he started acting like he didn't feel well, hoping he could score some money or drugs. He walked over to the car and leaned towards the window.

"Hey, Naj! What's up? Can you help me out with a little somethin'? I don't feel well," he said holding his stomach as if in pain.

"Look Scabs you can stop with the fake sick shit. Go over to the passenger side and hop in. I got a proposition for you."

Scabs did as instructed. As soon as Scabs got in Naj drove off.

Naj immediately began drilling him about the robbery. Did he hear anything about it? Did he know who did it? Did he see anything? The way she was asking questions, you would have thought he was under interrogation.

Scabs hesitated before saying anything. Naj noticed this, so she offered him some money for his information. Scabs didn't actually know who did it, but he overheard some dudes talking about it. They mentioned the 52 Boys. He told Naj that he would find out more and get back at her. Naj gave Scabs twenty dollars, promising him a thousand if he could get the name of the two who did it, along with the driver. Scabs told her he would holla. She dropped him off.

"Damn!" Naj yelled as she pulled off.

The 52 Boys were the deepest crew in Newark. They had niggas everywhere, all over the city. They repped hard for the crew. Anybody who wanted it could get it, but most niggas thought twice before trying to give it to them.

They called themselves the 52 Boys because the crew was just that deep–fifty-two niggas. Always fifty-two of them! If one got killed or incarcerated, they automatically recruited another. They said they were like a deck of cards minus the jokers. If one card was missing, you couldn't play the game, so they always kept exactly 52 Boys.

They were scattered throughout the Newark, Irvington, and East Orange area. Knowing that they were ride or die niggas, Naj knew this was no small shit if they were indeed the ones who did it. It was going to be a battle fo' sho!

Esh walked into the hospital room and found Cheetah surfing through the channels on TV. She quickly scanned her eyes over Cheetah's body and saw all the bruises.

"Damn, Auntie, somebody fucked yo' ass up," Esh said, strutting towards the bed.

Cheetah didn't even look her way. She just continued to press the remote buttons as if Esh wasn't in the room.

"They must've fucked ya mouth up too, huh? You can't talk? What's good wit ya?"

Cheetah looked over towards Esh and gave her a cold stare. "What the fuck I tell you about your mouth, Esh? You better watch how you talk to me, girl."

Esh pulled a chair up close to Cheetah's bed. She placed the oversized pink and white Cole Haan handbag on the floor. Cheetah looked down.

"Yo, pick that up off the floor. You fuckin' up your money by placing your purse on the floor."

"What? Here you go with that superstitious bullshit. You kill me with that." Esh picked up her handbag, and tossed it at the bottom of the bed.

"So whose chick you done fucked wit' that got to you? You laying up here all beat the hell up and shit?" she asked, kicking her sneakers off and curled her feet up under her.

Cheetah couldn't help but laugh at Esh. Her mouth was reckless. Every other word that came out of her mouth was a cuss word. Cheetah scooted up a little and the pain made her grimace. Esh sat up to assist her, but Cheetah waved her away.

"I'm good. Just hurting like a mafucka. And I wasn't fucking with nobody's girl. These punk ass niggas jumped me over on Stratford. Pussy ass bitches. Word is bond Esh, on everything I love, I'ma murder they ass. They got me for my work and my shine."

"True story, Auntie? For what?"

"How the fuck I know for what? What do people usually rob other people for? Them niggas was beasting. But it's all good. I'ma hit 'em up. Watch!"

"Just be careful, Auntie. You can't be wildin' out without thinking this thing through. You might not even be able to find out who it was."

"Oh, I'ma find out. Ain't no secrets in the hood. Matter of fact, let me get my rest right now. I know you done dropped your kids off with my mother. Go get 'em and take 'em home, and cook them a home cooked meal or something. Just leave me alone right now."

Esh knew when to leave Cheetah alone. She grabbed her purse, put her sneakers back on, kissed Cheetah on the forehead, then bounced. Cheetah grabbed the remote and absentmindedly flipped through the channels.

CHAPTER 2

Payback Time

The doctor kept Cheetah in the hospital for a week. He said that it would be a couple of weeks before her ribs completely healed, and advised her to take it easy. Cheetah was hard-headed. She was ready to get back to the block and get at the niggas who robbed her.

Naj was on it. She had every fiend and nigga she knew keeping their ear to the street, but she kept coming up empty. The only thing she did know was that the niggas responsible were affiliated with the 52 Boys. Naj knew that it would take an army to go up against them. Whatever! Them duded were not invincible. They could get it too!

While Cheetah was in the hospital, Naj took the liberty of moving her out of the boarding house, and setting her up in the spare bedroom in the basement where she and Ja'nise lived. The room was small, but it had carpet and wood paneling. It was livable. She would get Cheetah a bedroom set in the morning.

Naj picked Cheetah up from the hospital. Once they got to the house and settled down, Naj cracked open two Coronas and got comfortable in Cheetah's new bedroom.

29

"Naj, I wanna get these niggas so bad my ass itches!" Cheetah said taking a sip of her beer.

"Yeah, me too, but we gotta be easy, dawg. These niggas are deep. We'll get 'em when the opportunity comes up." Naj replied, opening her beer.

"Fuck opportunity!" Cheetah spat. "Let's just do these niggas. We can spray the fucking block up and show 'em we ain't no suckas!"

"Then what, Cheetah?" Naj asked. "Huh? Man, I got a fucking family to protect so just calm the fuck down. We'll come up with something."

Cheetah wasn't feeling this shit. She sat her Corona down on the floor, got up, and left Naj sitting there. She went outside and walked up the block. She was living in a whole new neighborhood. She didn't know the cats on this end of town, but she was born and raised in Newark. Home was wherever she chose to stomp at.

She was aggravated and wanted to get high. She saw some niggas on the corner and asked them where the weed was at. Everyone was hustling gank. Cheetah thought back to the way it had her feeling on the day of the robbery. She was cooking! High as hell!

Fuck it, she thought.

After the initial trip she enjoyed the high. She copped a bag, went into the bodega across the street, and got a blunt and V8 splash. She walked to the park on the next corner and found a spot under a tree. She twisted the blunt up, sat back, and smoked.

After she was done she sat for a minute waiting for the trip. She didn't experience the feeling she had gotten the first time. With the mixture of the pills and the weed she felt like she was floating on air. She felt like superman. She felt immortal! She felt she could lift a building.

It was at that moment she got the craziest idea. If those niggas could jack her for one hundred bricks that easy, then why the fuck couldn't she jack a nigga the same way? All she needed was her gun and a mask. She went back to the house and fell asleep with a smile on her face. She had plans!

It was five-thirty in the morning when Cheetah woke up. Her adrenaline was pumping. Suited up in all black, she wrapped her dreads in a Rasta style hat and grabbed her .44. She was ready to catch a nigga slippin' early. One thing about dope fiends, they got up early to get their fix. A dedicated hustler could easily make a few stacks by 8am.

Her plan was to ride around and hit up as many one-man hustlers she could find.

Cheetah cruised past Clinton Avenue and 17th Street, and saw three young cats out there. She knew they were hustling because they all kept running to different stash spots. She drove around the block and came back to Clinton Avenue and parked by 15th Street.

From a distance, she watched like a hawk circling its prey. She clocked one of the runners running behind the back of an abandoned building.

"Like taking candy from a baby," she whispered, seizing the opportunity.

When she saw what she needed to see, she crept through a few backyards until she came to the back of a building. One of the cats was running behind. He must have had the best heroin out there because he was getting mad sales.

Cheetah stooped down behind a garbage can and waited. A few seconds passed and he was coming towards her. In one swift move she grabbed both his legs. He fell hard! She jumped on the young dope boy, hit him in the back of the head with the gun, then put the nozzle to his neck.

"Mothafucka don't move! You can make this easy and live 'cause it's damn easy for you to die, your choice," Cheetah whispered in his ear. She had the bandana tied over her mouth and nose right up under her eyes, old western movie style. She put a little bass in her voice, so she wouldn't be recognized as a chick.

"Aight, yo! Don't shoot, aight?" young dude cried, his voice cracking.

"You don't fucking talk, just be still!" Cheetah said, pushing the gun closer to his neck.

Cheetah went through his pockets and got all the money. She then patted him down checking for a gun. He had none.

"Get up slowly and don't look back."

He got up and Cheetah told him to take her to the stash.

She walked behind him with her gun jammed in the small of his back. They walked to the side of the building. He removed a loose brick, pulled a bag out, and handed it to her. She tucked the bag in her pants, and laid him face down on the ground. She took his pants and socks. She took his belt off and pulled his boxers down around his ankles. Then she tied the belt tight around both his legs.

"Nigga, don't try to move. Fuck around, and I'ma blow your top off," Cheetah said as she tightened the belt a little more.

Cheetah got up and left the way she had come. She ran fast and low.

She got to the car jumped in and sped away.

She drove to Dunkin Donuts on Springfield Avenue, and parked in the lot. She was so nervous. It took at least ten minutes to slow the beating of her heart. When she calmed down she went inside, and got a dozen Bowtie donuts and a French Vanilla coffee.

When she got back to the car she put the money and drugs in the donut bag and sipped on the coffee. She turned the radio on, listening to the morning show on 105.1FM with Ed Lover and Monie Love. She had to relax before she drove off. Floetry came on singing *"Say Yes"* and Cheetah drank the rest her coffee.

She was ready for her next vic'. She had to hurry up before the sun came up. She continued hitting corners until she spotted dude on the corner of 18th Avenue. She checked the gun to make sure the safety was off just in case something went down. She put the donut bag under the seat and left the door unlocked. She got out and slipped up the block unnoticed.

She knew this nigga named Get 'Em came out every morning to get his grind on. Get 'Em got his name from niggas sleeping on his gangsta. He was no joke and anyone who crossed him, he *got 'em*. He wasn't no king pin, but the nigga was a baller. He brought out at least twenty bricks with him every morning. He kept good dope and had good clientele.

Cheetah dipped between two houses, watching him go to an abandoned car in the lot where he kept his stash. When he went back to serve his customers, Cheetah quietly walked to the lot. It was more like a junkyard with old tires, chairs, couches and shit. It was easy for her to hide behind something, and lay low until he came back.

Dope sales are rapid early in the morning, so Get 'Em was back in a second. He opened the door to the car and Cheetah sprung. She knew he stayed strapped with a gun so she went at him with force. She hit him four times, and pulled him out of the car. On his way down to the ground, she kicked him in the jaw. He was out cold. She grabbed the stash bag off the seat and emptied his pockets. He had on a Movado watch and a thick link chain with a diamond encrusted cross. She took that too. She kicked him in the head two more times and ran back to her car.

She got in the car, got the donut bag, and put the money and drugs in it. She put the jewelry in her pocket. Her adrenaline was pumping. She started the car and pulled off quick. She was enjoying this shit. It was getting to be fun! She had no idea how much money she had, but she didn't want to stop.

She drove down to the Little Bricks Projects, but there were too many niggas out there. She had to find a little side street hustler. She rode around a little longer, ending up on Astor Street, but the block was empty.

"Must have known I was coming, punk asses," Cheetah said out loud.

The sun was coming up. She decided to head home. Ja'nise would be up, getting ready for work. She needed to get the car to Naj so she could take her. She stopped at the gas station, filled the tank up, and bought another blunt and a V8 Splash. She still had some gank left from last night, and could smoke it while she counted her money. Opening the V8, she took a sip. She glanced at the donut bag and started laughing.

"Fuck the world; I'm out to get mine. Anybody in the way is getting done, ya heard?" Cheetah shouted. She drove up Clinton Avenue with a smile on her face. She passed Stratford Avenue and got a funny feeling in her stomach. Before it was all over, those cats was going to go down. Without a fucking doubt!

When she pulled up in the driveway she saw that Naj's bedroom light was on. She parked and went in the house. Everyone was up, getting ready for their day.

"Cheetah, what's up nigga? What you doing up so early?" Naj asked, standing over the stove, scrambling some eggs.

"I just ran to the store Naj. I couldn't sleep and I got a craving for some bowties," Cheetah lied.

"Oh yeah, bowties? Let me get one."

Cheetah realized she had put the money and drugs in the donut bag, so instead of handing Naj the bag, she reached in, grabbing two bowties and gave 'em to her. She went downstairs to tell Naj all about her morning, but she wanted to wait until Ja'nise and the kids were gone.

Once she got downstairs, she put the bag on the counter and put the gun in a shoe box at the top of the linen closet. She dumped the bag out and knew just from looking at it that she had over a thousand dollars. There had to be at least forty bricks of heroin there as well. She separated the money from the drugs and started counting the money. In total, she had thirty-four bricks of heroin and thirty-five hundred. Not bad for an hour of work. She put the dope in the box with the gun, tied a rubber band around the money and rolled up a blunt.

Naj shouted downstairs telling Cheetah she was leaving and would be back soon. As soon as she heard the door shut she lit the blunt. She was beginning to really like this gank. It made her feel nothing like herself. She felt on top of the world the last time she smoked it. The mint taste was something she could do without, but the results was the banger.

Yeah, she thought, *I found my new high.*

She smoked the blunt and thought back to her earlier days of hustling.

Cheetah was fourteen years old when her hands got dirty in the drug game. Stepping out her door everyday as a teenager was like walking on the set of *New Jack City*. Up and down the block, hustlers and fiends moved around like trapped animals. The same ones everyday, doing the same thing.

Cheetah's mother, Mrs. Marian Johnson, tried to raise her with morals. She bought her girl clothes, tried to teach her how to be a respectful lady, but Cheetah had a different plan. No matter how hard she tried to do right, the streets called her. Mrs. Johnson worked a sixteen-hour shift just to make ends meet, but that still was only enough to handle the bills and provide her daughters with their needs, not their wants.

Cheetah not only needed more, she wanted more. She longed for the Guess jeans, and Air Max Nikes everyone else was sporting. Running sales for the hustlers on the block helped her to get a foot in the door. Not long after, she graduated to packaging and delivering. After strenuous hours of bagging the crack-cocaine, and stuffing it in small multi-colored Ziploc baggies, she would deliver it to the runners scattered throughout the neighborhood.

In school, Cheetah played every sport they had, but on the track team, she was that bitch! She was Country Runner of the Year. Hence, the nickname Cheetah. If her focus was on school and not the streets she probably could have qualified for the Olympics, but the continuous hold of the hustle was too much for her to shake. By her senior year she had stopped all extra curricular activities. More hours on the block meant more money stacked. So she split her days with school and hustling. After she graduated, she had enough money stashed to finally buy her own weight. She copped a half a kilo and beat the streets. Cheetah put everything she had into the hustle.

When Naj got back, she smelt the gank all through the house. She knew it was coming from the basement. When she got down there, Cheetah was laying on the floor with the cross medallion and chain around her neck, the money on her stomach, and the gun in her hand. From the bottom of the steps it looked like she was asleep. When Naj got closer she saw that she was awake.

"Hey, Naj," Cheetah said staring at the ceiling. Cheetah had this big ass smile on her face. She was toasted. She had been lying on the floor staring into space for the past half hour. When she had finished smoking the blunt, she heard noises coming from upstairs. She went to the closet and got the shoebox. She took the gun out and laid it on the floor.

Cheetah was tripping, but in the haze of the high she thought it was real. She had forgotten all about the watch and chain until she reached into her pocket for a light. The chain was thick as hell, and the cross was freezing with diamonds. She put the chain and watch on, and stood in the mirror singing *"What Y'all Niggas Want"* by Eve, enjoying her high until she heard the noise again. She got the gun, money, and drugs out and lay back on the floor. She remained in that position the entire time.

Naj stood over Cheetah, giving off mad attitude. Cheetah wasn't sure if Naj was upset so she just smiled.

"Cheetah, what the fuck you doing?" Naj asked, looking at the gun in her hand.

"Just smoked a blunt, man, that's all!" she said still smiling.

"Man, I don't allow nobody to smoke in this house. I got kids here, man. That ain't no weed anyway, that's that gank shit!" she yelled, getting angry.

"Aight, Naj, be easy. I was just chilling. I got to talk to you about something anyway."

Naj calmed down a little. She had made her point. She couldn't allow Cheetah to smoke in her house, not with the kids there.

"What's up? Holla at me."

Cheetah sat up and put the gun in the box. She then stood and sat on the weight bench.

"Naj, listen, I know we took a big fall and I feel partially responsible. If not entirely, so, man, I sat down here contemplating on how we gonna build back up. I figured, shit, since those cats jacked me, why can't I jack a few niggas and get paid." She paused to see how all this was soaking into Naj's head.

"Uh-huh, go on. I'm listening," Naj said giving her full attention.

"So today I went out and ran down on a few cats that were out hustling. I got eighteen hundred, and enough heroin to make seventeen hundred. "

Naj didn't say anything so Cheetah continued.

"Naj, man, we can either put this shit out on the block to be sold or do it ourselves. I know one thing; I'm out for revenge, and if I can't get to the ones who did this to me, then I'm letting my vengeance out on whoever, feel me?"

Naj felt what she was saying, but she also knew the stickup game was a very dangerous thing. She wanted to get at those niggas who did this just as bad as Cheetah, but it had to be done correctly.

"Cheetah, man, that's all gravy that you went out there and got paid, but yo, you gots to think, man. Newark ain't full of suckas. These nigga's catch wind of us being the stickup people, and we gonna have mad beef. It's just us, man. Then you out there doing some solo shit, you could have gotten yourself killed, man. You know you my dawg, and I'm down with you one hundred percent, but just lay low. We'll make our move. I'm feeling you though. This shit might work but if we gonna do this then we gonna go all out. We could go after the big dogs! The ones that push keys and shit, nah mean?"

Cheetah stood, walked over to the sink, and splashed some water on her face. She dried it off with her t-shirt and sat back down.

"Yeah, I hear you. Aight, I'ma be easy," Cheetah told her.

"Okay, so what's on your agenda for the day? You aight? How your ribs feel?" Naj asked, concerned.

"Man, this gank got me cooking. I don't feel shit!" Cheetah stood up and flexed. "I'm a soldier, man, and this shit ain't stopping me."

"Okay, since you cool, how 'bout we hit the mall or something? We need to get you a bed set and I need some new Timberlands."

"Yeah, that's what's up. Let's go."

MISSY JACKSON

CHAPTER 3

Holla Back, Youngun'

Cheetah took the jewelry off and put the drugs and money away. She changed her clothes, putting on a sky blue Enyce velour sweatsuit and some matching Air Jordons. She met Naj upstairs. She was still a little high from the gank but she was functioning. She needed a relaxed day. The past week had been hectic for her. The mall was just what the doctor ordered.

It was still early. The mall opened at ten, but they didn't plan on going 'till about noon, so they stopped for breakfast at the little hood diner, John's, on Clinton Avenue. After stuffing their faces with fried fish, cheese eggs, and grits, they went to Kings Furniture on Market Street, and purchased a five hundred dollar bedroom set, and arranged for same day delivery. Then they rode up to Marian's, Cheetah's mom's house. Cheetah hadn't seen her mom since the robbery and she usually saw her three times a week.

Marian Johnson was a heavyset, pleasant looking woman. She was one of the sweetest people Naj had ever met, and she loved Naj like she was her own daughter. You could always expect to see her cleaning when you went to her house. As soon as you walked into the door you smelled Pine-Sol and bleach.

Today was no exception. She was in the kitchen on her hands and knees scrubbing the floor. Because the front door was unlocked Cheetah and Naj entered unnoticed. Cheetah walked over to her mother, bent down and kissed her on the cheek.

"Well, well, well. Now what do I owe this visit?" she asked as she got up off the floor, wiping her hand on her pants leg.

"Hey, Mom!" Cheetah said. "You know you my favorite girl. I had to come so you could see I was okay."

"You know you should be taking it easy," she replied sternly.

"Mom, I'm okay. I just wanted to make sure you're okay. I know Esh blew it all up when she told you. That's why I didn't want her saying nothing."

"I'm blessed. You don't worry about me. The Lord will always take care of me. He'll take care of you too, if you get out of those streets. And what you standing over there for?" she asked looking at Naj. "Come on over here, Nichelle and give me a hug! You need to come see me more."

Mrs. Johnson always called Naj by her first name, and she called Cheetah "Stink," a name she gave her as a little girl.

"Hey, Mamma Marian," Naj said hugging her. "How are you?"

"Just fine. How are you? I swear you two look more and more like boys every time I see you. Y'all need to come over here and let me give you a makeover. I'll put the straightening comb to your head and get you a nice dress to come to church with me. Lord knows you could use some of the Word, out there doing God knows what," Mrs. Johnson stated, shaking her head.

"Ma, please. I'm okay. Don't start preaching. I just came by to give you some money. You saw Dana lately?"

"Nah, I ain't seen that child. I pray for her every night. Every time the phone rings, I'm scared it's going to be bad news about one of y'all. Y'all gonna be the death of me I swear," she said trailing off.

Cheetah walked over to the refrigerator and grabbed the container of juice. She opened it up and started drinking out of the bottle.

"Stink, what I tell you about doing that!" Mrs. Johnson yelled at Cheetah.

"Don't worry, Ma, I'm about to down this. There won't be any more to put back in the fridge," Cheetah replied, tilting the bottle back up to her mouth.

Mrs. Johnson shook her head and thought back to the day she knew Cheetah was different. She had gone out school shopping. Cheetah was twelve years old. She bought Cheetah a couple of dresses and a nice pair of dress shoes to match. When she came home and showed Cheetah her new school clothes, Cheetah ran in the room and locked herself in. She wouldn't come out until Mrs. Johnson promised to take the clothes back and get her some sweat suits and sneakers.

Now she looked at her daughter, dressed in the blue sweat suit and sneakers and she knew it was more than just a phase.

"How are Esh and the kids? You heard from them?" Cheetah asked.

"Yeah, I had those babies yesterday. I don't know why she went and had that last one. She could barely handle the two she had already. She's a pretty little girl though. If I was a few years younger, I'd take 'em from her but I can't get around like I use to. I'm getting old," Mrs. Johnson said, sitting down.

"Ma, don't talk like that, you know you gonna live a long, long time."

Naj always enjoyed visiting Mrs. Johnson. She noticed the change in Cheetah around her mother. The thug persona disappeared. She was an entirely different person. Her tough attitude faded around her mom. If she was angry, tense, or bothered, once she got around her mom it all vanished. Just stepping into her mom's house gave her peace. Cheetah loved the hell out of her family. Mrs. Johnson walked over to the sink and started drying the dishes.

"Yeah, I'll live a lot longer if I wasn't so worried about you and your sister."

"Mom, listen, I'm going to find Dana and we going to come over here next Sunday to eat dinner, okay? I love you but I gotta go," Cheetah said handing Mrs. Johnson the last of the utensils.

"I'm going to the mall, you need anything?"

"Well I could always use some white shirts for church. You know I'm an usher now. Also, get me some off white queen sized stockings."

Cheetah dug into pocket, counted out one hundred fifty dollars, and handed it to her mother.

"Here's a coupla dollars for your pocket. I'll get ya stuff for ya. Is that enough?"

"Yes, baby, that's more than enough."

They embraced and kissed each other on the cheek.

"Okay, Mom, I love you."

"I love you too, Stink, and you too, Nichelle. Take care of my baby," she said to Naj.

"Don't worry, I will," she said giving Mrs. Johnson a hug as well.

Cheetah and Naj headed toward the front door.

Cheetah and Naj rode up Avon Avenue. This was their block. They hadn't been up there since Cheetah got robbed. The regular cats were out trying to get their hustle on. Ra'dee saw the car pull up and broke out into a slow trot. He was their number one worker. He thought fo' sho they were coming through to hand out packages.

"What's the deal, y'all?" he asked approaching the car.

"What's up, Ra'dee?" they asked in unison.

Ra'dee leaned in the window.

"Man, ain't shit up! This shit is dry as hell out here. Cheetah since you got robbed it's been dead. When we gonna get back on board, huh?" he asked standing up straight, rubbing his stomach. "A nigga gotta eat!"

"Yo, man, you know I got you," Cheetah said. "We gonna holla at you later, okay? I got something for you, aight?"

"Aight, my customer's fiendin' for that good shit."

Cheetah knew Ra'dee would be there with the crew. He was very reliable. They had known each other since they were in elementary school.

"Aight, 9pm," Ra'dee said, confirming the time.

Cheetah got out of the car and went in the bodega on the corner. She got a handful of watermelon Jolly Ranchers and a V8 Splash. She drank one almost every day. Once she was back in the car, Naj headed to Route 78. They were going to Short Hills Mall. The day was going pretty well so far. Naj turned on the CD player, and 50 Cent's "*Candy Shop*" filled the car. 50 Cent was the hot item at the moment. Naj loved him.

They rode to the mall in silence, both of them caught up in their own thoughts. Cheetah was focused on how she could blow up off of this stickup thing. Naj was trying to figure out how she was going to keep Cheetah from going back out to do another stickup. She knew Cheetah was a ticking time bomb. Now that Cheetah was also smoking gank, Naj was more worried about her. Whatever it was they were going to do for money, they had to do it quick and get out of the game before Cheetah went over the edge.

The mall was packed as usual for a Saturday. Naj and Cheetah knew the mall like the back of their hand. It shouldn't be hard since they went to the same stores every time they came. They hit Footlocker first. Naj selected a pair of Timberland construction boots, and Cheetah stuck to the norm—three pairs of white Air Force Ones. Her motto was: As long as they were crisp, they went with everything.

Next, they were off to Macy's. They went straight to the Polo section, then the cologne counter, and then underwear. By the time they were finished, they had ten bags a piece. Sticking to the routine, they went to the food court. McDonald's for Cheetah, and Olga's for Naj.

They sat near the escalator and shared some small talk. Cheetah let her eyes wander and stopped in mid-sentence.

Naj followed her gaze. Standing by the escalator was one of the baddest bitches Cheetah ever saw in her life. She was tall, maybe five-nine with some long ass legs. She had jet black hair down her back that was definitely bouncing and behaving. She was a caramel color and had a beautiful smile. Cheetah was stuck on stupid, staring at her.

Naj nudged her on the shoulder and said, "Why don't you holla at her, man?"

Cheetah swallowed the food in her mouth and said, "Nah, she probably ain't down with the lesbian thing, man."

"You'll never know unless you try, dawg," Naj replied, popping a fry in her mouth.

What the hell, Cheetah thought, and called out to her.

"Yo, shorty! Shorty! Let me holla at you."

The girl turned around, looked Cheetah's way, and pointed to herself.

"Yeah, you, can I speak to you for a minute?" Cheetah asked pointing back.

"It depends," the cutie replied.

"On what?" Cheetah asked.

"Well, what you wanna talk about?"

"Well, why don't you come over here and find out," Cheetah said, waving her over.

Shorty strutted over to where they were sitting. Cheetah was mesmerized by the way her hips rocked side to side when she walked. She was tall, slim in the waist, with a nice backside that could stop traffic. The Azzure jeans she had on was so tight they fit like a second skin.

"What's up? What's good?" she asked.

"You," Cheetah replied. "What's your name, Ma?"

For a moment she just stood there looking back and forth between Naj and Cheetah. Then she started laughing. Cheetah and Naj looked at each other and hunched their shoulders.

"What's so funny?" Cheetah wanted to know.

"Yo, it took me to get all the way over here to see that you two were bitches," she said still laughing.

Cheetah was upset by her outburst. "Listen, Ma, ain't nothing bitchy about me except my moan, now you gonna sit down or what?"

"I guess so. This may just be very interesting."

When she sat down Cheetah noticed a mole above her lip. Damn! She was sexy as hell.

Cheetah took a drink of her V8 Splash. "So, again I ask, what's your name?"

"I'm Tara, and you?"

"I'm Cheetah and this is my dawg, Naj," Cheetah said pointing to Naj.

Naj was acting nonchalant eating her burger, trying to front like she wasn't paying attention. Tara looked her way.

"Hey Naj, how you doing?"

"I'm good," Naj replied.

Tara focused her attention back to Cheetah. "So, what's up?"

"A nigga tryna get yo' number," Cheetah said, staring deeply into Tara's eyes.

"I'm sorry, boo, I don't get down like that," she replied, letting Cheetah down easily.

"Check it, shorty, I was just trying to kick it. You act like I said I wanna eat yo' pussy or something. Fuck it! You can step. I don't even want your number."

The thug in Cheetah turned Tara on. Tara didn't like the way Cheetah came at her and was at a lost of words. Cheetah's chipped tooth complimented her attitude, reminded Tara of the rapper Nas before he got his tooth fixed. Cheetah's eyes were piercing through Tara.

"Damn, Cheetah! Why you talking all slick?" Tara asked sucking her teeth.

"That's just me, baby. So what's up? Can I get your number?" Cheetah asked pulling out her cell phone.

Tara decided to give her the number just to see how this would play out. After they exchanged numbers, Cheetah asked Tara to go with her to Lane Bryant to pick up the things for her mom. Tara agreed and they all got up and left.

Once they got to the store Cheetah gave Tara her mother's sizes and let her pick out the outfits. After that, they went to DSW and got Cheetah's mother two pair of shoes.

As they walked out of the store, Cheetah asked, "Yo, you

good? You want somethin'?"

Tara wanted the pink and white Wilson's Leather motor-cycle jacket she'd spotted, but didn't have enough money for it. Not wanting to seem thirsty, she said, "Nah, I'm good."

"Listen, I know you came here for somethin'. Since I don't see you with no bags that must mean you window shopping. Let me get you somethin', Ma."

"Aight, it's your money," Tara replied.

They copped the jacket from Wilsons Leather for seven hundred and bounced.

They all walked out to the parking lot together and said their goodbyes. Cheetah told Tara she'd be waiting for her call.

"Why you can't call me?" Tara asked.

"Because since this is not your game, I'll give you the time and space to decide if you wanna holla, okay?"

"Aight, I'll see what I feel," she answered and walked away.

Cheetah and Naj drove home in a good mood. Cheetah couldn't stop talking about Tara. Naj was pressed for time; it was already three in the afternoon. She had to pick Ja'nise up from work at four, and get the kids from Naj's cousin's house. The bedroom set was being delivered at 6 pm. Naj had promised Ja'nise and the kids' dinner and a movie. They had to meet up with the boys at nine for dinner at Mickey D's and she had three hours to take care of business.

They dropped Mrs. Johnson's things off and drove back to the house. Cheetah was beginning to feel the pain in her broken ribs. She wanted to rest before the meeting. The doctor had prescribed her some Tylenol 3 tablets with codeine. She popped two of them, drank some hot tea, and quickly fell asleep.

Naj woke Cheetah up a little after six that evening. The movers hadn't come with the bedroom set yet. She was on her way to the movies. Naj assured her she'd be back in time to pick her up for the meeting. Cheetah told her, "Aight", and rolled back over.

The pills made her drowsy and groggy. She hated taking pills. When she was a little girl she would scream and yell when her mom tried to give her medicine. Her mother and sister, Dana, would hold her down and force it in her mouth. Now that she was older, she only took it when necessary.

She lay there a little longer before getting up and taking a shower. The bedroom set was delivered not long after she got out of the shower. She didn't allow them to assemble it because she wanted to go out and get some gank before Naj got back. She threw on a pair of PePe Jeans and a white T-shirt. She put on a pair of her Air Forces and a dark blue flight jacket. She walked up the block, got the gank, and went back to the house. She knew better than to smoke in the house anymore so she went downstairs, got the blunt, and went and sat on the back porch.

The entire process took her two minutes.

She leaned back on the steps and lit up. She inhaled the smoke deeply, holding it in. It didn't take long for her to smoke the whole blunt. She flicked the roach over the fence and closed her eyes. She was high as a mothafucka!

She opened her eyes and sat up. She tried to stand up but she couldn't move. Nothing in her brain was registering. She lay back again and looked up at the sky and swore she saw heaven. She saw the pearly gates, the golden roads, castles, and angels. It was beautiful. She reached out and felt the clouds. She pulled one down to her and laid her head on it. It was so soft. She thought this would make a great pillow. She balled it up and put it in her pocket. She was going to put it in her pillowcase.

She sat up again, trying to stand again. This time her legs moved. It took her five minutes to get up the five steps because the steps kept moving. Every time she tried to climb the steps they would slide from under her foot. Diligently, she made it into the house. She went straight to the refrigerator and got the milk. She drank straight out the carton. She sat at the table and her cell rang. She didn't answer. She went downstairs, took off her jacket and shoes and lay down on her new mattress. Her cell rang again and it was the same number. She answered.

"Yeah, what's up? Who dis?"

"Hey, Cheetah," said a voice she didn't recognize.

"Who dis?" she asked again.

"It's me, Tara."

She instantly perked up when she heard her name.

"Oh, yo, what's good? You sound different on the phone," she said warming up to the voice.

"Nothing much," Tara said. "I was just calling to holla at you.

"Oh, so I see you made the right decision, huh?" Cheetah asked laughing.

"Whatever! What you doing?" Tara asked.

"Nothing, just lying here thinking about you." Cheetah was trying to lay her mack down.

"Yeah, right! I just called and didn't get no answer."

"Oh, I was on the toilet taking a dump," Cheetah said making a straining noise.

Tara laughed. "Eww, that's just too much information."

They talked for close to an hour. Cheetah found out she was originally from Somerset, New Jersey, but she now lived in North Newark with her two older brothers. She was twenty-one years old, and didn't have any kids. She was taking courses at Essex County College, majoring in journalism. They made a date for the following weekend and hung up.

Cheetah looked at her watch. It was eight-thirty. She knew Naj would be pulling up any minute. She was still high but the tripping part was over. She went to the closet and got the drugs and the gun. From now on, whenever she went out she was going to be strapped. She tucked the gun in her waist band and put the bricks of heroin in her Nike backpack. Each brick consisted of fifty bags of heroin. They were separated in bundles of ten bags, kept together by a rubber band. Five bundles were then wrapped up in magazine paper to make a brick.

She went upstairs to make sure the back door was locked, and then sat down on the porch. Naj pulled up a few minutes later. Cheetah got in the backseat and sat between Malik and

Malikah. They were one year apart, but could pass for twins. Cheetah enjoyed being around them. Sometimes she would bring Esh's oldest son, Ozzy, over to take them all to places like Zany Brainy or Jump & Jacks. They were good, well behaved kids.

"What's up, Ja'nise?" Cheetah asked as she sat back.

"I'm good, Cheetah. How you feeling today?"

"You know me, I'm a soldier. Can't nothin' hold me back too long."

"I hear that. Just be careful, okay. We need you around, not in the ground. Feel me?"

"Shit, I ain't going nowhere. The only way I'm going out is blazing. Ain't no punk ass beat down gon' take me out."

Naj threw a piece of paper at her. "Yeah, alright Pac," She joked.

"You see my kids back there. Watch your mouth. And you wonder why Ozzy be acting like he do."

Cheetah covered her mouth with both hands and looked at Malik and Malikah. She made her eyes go crossed and they both fell out laughing.

Naj spotted Ra'dee sitting at his usual booth in the corner of McDonalds. This was Ra'dee's office. He gave orders to the fifteen little niggas under him. He was only twenty-two and a better hustler than niggas ten, even twenty years his senior. Cheetah noticed that her second in command, Chill, was not there. Ra'dee had brought four of the dudes with him.

"What's the deal, my nigga?" Cheetah asked, sliding on the bench next to Ra'dee.

Over the years, Cheetah had built a solid team. Everybody acknowledged her in their own way. Some gave her pounds, a few gave her hugs. They all had mad respect for Cheetah. In the beginning, she had a few beefs. Some tried to test her because she was a female. When they saw how fierce her gangsta was, they grew to respect her. She took care of her workers. If they wanted to branch off and do their own thing, she didn't have a problem with it. If they got cased up with the po-po, she was at the precinct bailing them out. If they had to go do a bid she kept the commissary stacked and accepted their calls. She took care of the baby mamas and in return they were loyal to her.

Ra'dee was the first one to speak up. "So what's so important that we had to have this meeting?"

"Hold up. As soon as Naj gets over here I'll explain it all to y'all, okay?" she said looking around the table.

Naj ordered some burgers and fries, and joined them at the table. By the time she put her food down, their attention was directed to the door. Five of their soldiers walked in. The twins, Kareem and Raheem, were the first to speak.

"What's up, playboy?" Naj greeted them.

"Shit, ya know. Just came from battling some clowns on the Ave."

Cheetah perked up because they should have been had a record deal. Their flow was sick.

"Spit something, my niggas," Cheetah encouraged.

"Nigga, my nine so close you know when I blast it/it'll flip you back like you was doing gymnastics," Raheem spit.

"That weak ass shit, nigga, ain't no way you can do me/i'll slice you up quick, turn your hoodie into a Coogie," Kareem retorted.

Naj listened for awhile and enjoyed the freestyle. They were nice wit it! Naj sat the food down on the table. No sooner had it left her hands they were digging in. Typical, greedy ass hoodlums.

Cheetah was ready to get down to business. She didn't mind the workers being there. They were a team.

"Before I get into today's business, I just need to put a bug in y'all ear. The streets is talkin' and they saying it was the 52 boys who robbed me. I'm a put that shit on ice for a minute. Them niggas is too deep for us right now."

"Man, fuck them niggas. It ain't like they can't get touched," Raheem spat, stuffing another nugget in his mouth.

"Word the fuck up. They ain't pumping no fear over here," Kareem said, joining in with his twin.

"I'm ready to body one of those cats right the fuck now, ya dig?" Boogie stated, lifting up his shirt to reveal the .38 he had tucked in his waist.

"Nigga, cover that shit up. We already up in here deep as hell. Don't start acting crazy and shit," Cheetah stated.

Boogie was one of them wild ass young niggas who just didn't give a fuck about the repercussions of his actions. The only real reason Cheetah kept him around was because the boy was 'bout his money, and had no fear.

"Won't be no bodying nobody today. We 'bout to get our money right, and all that other shit will be handled real soon," Naj said. "But first, let's handle this shit right here." She then turned her attention to Cheetah.

"Right, fuck them niggas. It's time to get this bread…here," Cheetah handed Ra'dee a back pack. "Hand them out."

Ra'dee slipped the bag over his shoulder.

"Ra'dee," Cheetah continued, focusing her attention on him. "Make sure everyone here tonight gets two bricks a piece. I want three hundred fifty off of each brick. I need all my money, y'all. If y'all wanna keep caking I need my money," she said with emphasis. "When you see Chill, tell him to call me ASAP, okay? Whoever else is not here, tell 'em I'll get them on the next run. I don't want anyone bringing me anything. Ra'dee will collect the money and I'll hit y'all with more as soon as I get paid, okay?"

Cheetah planned on hitting the streets early. She knew it would be more suckas out. She aimed to catch them with their guard down.

MISSY JACKSON

CHAPTER 4

Let's Chill For A Day

When they got home, Cheetah was ready to smoke another blunt but decided against it. She had a long day and was tired. She and Naj assembled the frame and put the bed set up. Cheetah got fresh sheets and made the bed. She put all her clothes in the dresser and sat her cosmetics in the chest. She took a shower, changed into her pajamas and called Tara.

Cheetah was tempted to ask Tara if she could come and pick her up, but she didn't want to seem too forward. Instead, she started spitting slick shit out of her mouth.

"So, Tara, I know you gotta be feeling me. Why else would you be answering my calls and giving me some time?"

"Cheetah, you cool as hell, for real. I never entertained an aggressive female before. You're not the first one who tried to holla, but it's somethin' different about you that's making me want to know you a little more."

"Oh yeah? What about me?"

"Oh my God. What you want me to do, sit here and feed your ego?"

"Why not? It ain't been fed in a minute."

Tara laughed. "Listen, I'ma just say this. You intrigue me.

Your eyes hold a mystery I want to unfold. You spit all that hot shit, but I can tell you ain't nothin' more than a cream puff. Who knows, if nothing else, we could just become real close friends."

Now it was time for Cheetah to laugh. "Girl, you know we gonna be a lot more than just friends. You practically mine already."

"Yeah, aight, I'm glad you got all that confidence. That's a plus."

They bugged out on the phone for hours until they both were too tired to talk anymore. After they hung up, Cheetah laid there awhile and thought back to when she was eighteen and the first time she had sex.

Cheetah and Naj had been on the block hustling all day. With the dope sales slowing down, they decided to call it a night. Cheetah was not ready to go in the house. Naj suggested they hit up a club.

Murphy's was a gay and lesbian club located in the downtown section of Newark. It was a well-known jump-off spot for those in the life. Cheetah and Naj hopped in a cab and shot down there.

The crowd was mixed—guys dressed like women, women dressed like guys. Then there were the fags that had on the tightest jeans and tight polo shirts.

Stepping into the club, Cheetah got a jolt of the jitters, but nothing major. Although it was her first time at Murphy's, it wasn't Naj's.

"Aye, yo, look at all these jawns up in this spot, son. We about to get it in!"

"You about to get ya ass fucked up if Ja'nise see you getting it in," Cheetah replied.

"Nah, my dude. I'm not jumping in none of this ass in here. But I'm damn sure gon' have fun with the coupla hours I'ma be here," Naj said as she scanned the mixture of women in the club.

Cheetah was in awe, looking at all the fine females. Although she knew she had an attraction towards women, she had never acted upon it. Back in grammar school, the girls on her basketball team claimed to be gay. Cheetah always looked, but never touched.

Kids at school began to taunt her, but she was cool with being a lesbian. Once she graduated high school she hung at a few of the places other lesbian women hung out at.

"Come on, Cheetah. Let's get our drink on, son," Naj said, making her way over to the bar.

They ordered two glasses of Remy XO and two Coronas. After guzzling down the Remy, Naj hit the dance floor, Corona in hand, while Cheetah observed close by. With her blue and white Yankee fitted pulled down to the side and leaning up against a wall, Cheetah noticed a sexy red bone eyeing her. She tipped her beer bottle up and beckoned shorty over.

As shorty came closer, Cheetah checked her swag. Ole girl was killing the tight True Religion jeans she had on, and strutted in three-inch stilettos. The color of her skin was as close to copper as you could get. Long blondish-brown hair hung in soft curls around her angelic face.

Shorty walked right up on Cheetah and said, "What's up, cutie?"

"You," Cheetah said, maintaining her cool.

"Oh, really?" ole girl asked with a sideways smile, and Cheetah caught a glimpse of a set of pearly white teeth.

"Uh-huh," Cheetah murmured taking a sip of her beer. She swallowed and licked her lips a little slower than usual.

"So what's ya name, Ma?"

"I'm De'Shea and you?"

"I'm Cheetah."

"Cheetah? Like the cat or cheetah like the rat?" De'Shea asked with a soft chuckle.

"Oh, so you got jokes. You a comedian or somethin'?" Cheetah asked, loosening up to the conversation.

"Nah, I'm not no comedian. I'm just a sexy bitch who likes what she sees."

"Oh, I like that in you. You damn right, you sexy as hell," Cheetah replied, looking De'Shea up and down.

De'Shea was small built with the right amount of ass and tits. She was slightly bowlegged and had a flat stomach.

"So what's up, Cheetah? You dance?"

"I gotta little two-step in me."

"Well, let's see what ya working wit'."

Cheetah placed her beer on the table next to her and they headed over to the dance floor. Naj caught sight of 'em and winked at Cheetah,

"Aight!"

Cheetah was feeling De'Shea from the way she backed that ass up and her slick ass mouth. By the time the DJ called last call, they both were nice and buzzed.

"What's up? I want you to come home with me," De'Shea whispered in her ear.

"You inviting?" Cheetah asked. Although her insides were shaking like Jell-O, she remained as cool as Chester Cheetos.

"What ya think?"

"Aight, that's what it is. Let me holla at my peoples real quick."

Cheetah found Naj and told her what the deal was.

"Okay, player," Naj said. *"It's about time ya ass got that cherry popped."*

"Aye, yo, this shit got me kind of nervous, my dude. What I'm supposed to do?" Cheetah asked with a serious expression.

Naj noticed how tense Cheetah was.

"Listen, man, go in there and relax. Just follow suit. I know De'Shea from around the way. She ain't new to this, so I'm sure she gonna break that ass off just right. Just don't punk out. Feel me?"

"Aight, I got you. I'm straight. I'll holla at you tomorrow."

"No doubt."

De'Shea was a little more than tipsy so she gave Cheetah the keys to her Lexus jeep. They drove up to Barclay Street and parked in front of building fourteen. Cheetah noticed that De'Shea pressed two buttons, A6 and A2, on the keypad at the entrance of the building to open the door.

"What up? You don't have keys to this door?" Cheetah asked.

"Yeah, I got keys, but it's quick and easier to press these two buttons," De'Shea replied.

Cheetah made a mental note of that as they proceeded up six flights of stairs to her apartment.

Stepping inside the apartment, De'Shea kicked off her shoes and started undressing.

"I'ma go hop in the shower real quick. Make yourself comfortable," she said to Cheetah as she peeled her jeans off.

Cheetah watched as De'Shea bent over to pick her clothes up off the living room floor. Cheetah didn't know how big her ass was.

Damn, *she thought.* What the fuck I'ma do with all of that?

"Come on, let me show you to the bedroom," De'Shea said. She grabbed Cheetah's hand and pulled her down the hallway. "Here's the TV and stereo remote. I'll be right back."

As De'Shea handed the two remotes to Cheetah, she grabbed her housecoat off the back of the bedroom door, blew Cheetah a kiss, and sauntered out the room.

Cheetah, feeling buzzed from the Remy and Corona, lay back on the bed and flicked on the TV. Flipping through channels and not finding anything interesting, she decided to turn it off. Before she knew it, she found herself dozing off.

Moments later, De'Shea entered the room wrapped in her house-coat. She smelled like she had just taken a shower in a rose garden. She sat next to Cheetah, leaned over, and kissed her on the lips.

Cheetah stirred and opened her eyes, but didn't reject the kiss. De'Shea kissed her again, this time sticking her tongue in Cheetah's mouth. Cheetah's body tensed.

"What's the matter, baby?" De'Shea asked as she stopped kissing her.

"I think we need to talk, aight?" Cheetah replied as she stood up, rubbing her hand across her face.

De'Shea sat back on the bed. "Aight, what's good?"

"Look, I don't really know how to say this, so I'll just keep it gully. I'm a virgin. I never sexed or kissed anyone in my life. I know what I want to do, just never had the chance to do it," Cheetah said in one big breath.

De'Shea looked at Cheetah as if she had ten heads. "You got to be fucking kidding me? I didn't think there were any virgins left in Newark."

Although she felt embarrassed, Cheetah kept her game face on. "No, I'm not fuckin' kidding, so you gone turn me out or what?"

De'Shea was disappointed. She really wanted to cut into something with Cheetah, but she didn't want to force her. She stood up off the bed and held her hands up as if she was surrendering.

"Okay, cool. I understand. I'll back off."

Cheetah jumped up, grabbing her by the shoulders. "Nah, I don't want you to back off. I want you to teach me." She had the look of an eager child. "I'll pay you if you want. Just please don't stop." She was horny and wanted De'Shea and her phat ass to be her first.

"Pay me? Are you crazy? Shit, you fine as hell and I'm feeling your swagger. Come here!" De'Shea said, holding her arms wide open. "I'll teach you what you need to know."

Cheetah walked into her arms and as De'Shea closed her in a tight embrace, Cheetah whispered in her ear, "Aight, give me the full mafuckin' treatment."

De'Shea walked over to the dresser and lit a blunt she had from earlier. After hitting it twice, she handed it to Cheetah. She put on Zhane's CD. Grabbing Cheetah's hand, she led her to the bed and laid her down. Slowly, she began to undress Cheetah. She peeled her clothes off piece by piece until Cheetah laid there in her sports bra and boxers.

De'Shea climbed on top of Cheetah and straddled her body and gently kissed her face, starting at the forehead, kissing over her eyes, nose, and placing small pecks down to her mouth. She licked Cheetah's lips passionately before sticking her tongue between them.

De'Shea ran her tongue across Cheetah's top and bottom lip. Not knowing or caring if she was doing it right, Cheetah started kissing back. De'Shea put her leg between Cheetahs and spread her legs apart. Cheetah grabbed the side of the towel and pulled it off of De'Shea.

De'Shea laid her naked body across Cheetah's as she licked her breast. Cheetah's body quivered the moment the tip of De'Shea's tongue touched her flesh.

She slid Cheetah's boxers off of her and pulled her sports bra over her head. She grabbed Cheetah's nipple and lightly pinched it. Cheetah moaned out with pleasure.

Damn, this feels good, Cheetah thought as De'Shea continued to play with her nipples.

She moved her mouth to Cheetah's breast and sucked them like a straw. Cheetah's pussy got instantly wet. De'Shea's mouth felt hot on her nipple. She was sucking on them like a baby getting breast fed. Cheetah's moans grew louder as De'Shea licked between her breasts and slid her tongue down to her stomach. She circled her navel with the tip of her tongue, making her way to the pussy. Wet and pulsating, Cheetah was so hot you could feel the heat.

De'Shea opened the lips with her thumb and forefinger 'till she saw her clit pop out. She licked it with the tip of her tongue. Teasing her.

"What the fuck," Cheetah whispered as she rose up off the bed. The feeling was so intense, she began to move back.

De'Shea eased up off the clit and licked around the lips. Cheetah continued to squirm, forcing De'Shea to grab her under her ass, pulling her closer to her face. Once Cheetah relaxed, De'Shea stuck her tongue in her hole and blew softly. She brought Cheetah to an orgasm.

Cheetah came so hard, the juices squirted out like a water fountain and ran down the crack of her ass. Her body shook like a jack hammer.

De'Shea climbed up on top of her and slowly started body rocking her, grinding Cheetah's pussy with hers. Within minutes, Cheetah climaxed again. The shaking in her body increased. De'Shea grabbed her around the neck and held her tight until she calmed down. She kissed her again, rolled over, and lay down beside Cheetah. De'Shea layed her back to Cheetah's front and pushed as close as possible. Cheetah wrapped one arm around her waist, grinding on her ass. De'Shea rocked her ass from side to side, feeling the wetness of Cheetah's pussy. Cheetah turned De'Shea around and looked her in the eyes.

"Let me do you."

De'Shea didn't respond with words. She kissed Cheetah and guided her up on top of her. Cheetah positioned herself so that her clit and De'Shea's clit were touching. She then began to grind. De'Shea threw her legs up and clamped them around Cheetah's waist. She sucked on Cheetah's breast as Cheetah continued to body rock her, and felt her body responding to Cheetah's rhythm.

"Yeah Cheetah get this pussy."

Cheetah slowed down and began teasing De'Shea's body with her tongue. She licked her like she was a melting ice cream cone. Cheetah made her way down to De'Shea's pussy, and suddenly stopped.

"What's good Cheetah? Why you stop?" De'Shea asked. She sat up a little, and looked down at her.

"Nothing. I'm just looking at this pretty ass shit," Cheetah said.

"Well, you need to listen to it, because she's purring for you right now," De'Shea said, pushing Cheetah's head down. Cheetah dove in with all she had. She repeated on De'Shea what was done to her. De'Shea held on to Cheetah's dreads and grinded into her face. Her back arched and a spew of cum slid down her ass.

"Oh shit. Yes, yes, yes," she hissed as she fucked Cheetah's face to the last drop. She pulled Cheetah up, kissed her, and Cheetah lay back down.

Cheetah laid there in awe at what she just experienced. Not knowing what to say, Cheetah turned towards De'Shea and said, "Thanks," then turned back the other way, and she broke into a big cheesy grin.

Yeah, *she thought,* I definitely like me some women. Every mafuckin' thing about 'em!

Exhausted, they both fell into a deep sleep. Completely spent.

Early the next morning, Cheetah was up and dressed in her stickup gear and ready to ruin some hustler's day. She avoided the area she had hit up the day before. Hitting corner after corner, she cruised up Jeliff Avenue. Right when she was going to turn, she spotted Bolo.

Bolo was a pretty boy. He and Cheetah used to run together a few years back. Cheetah couldn't get with the gator shoes and Versace shirts he wore to hustle in. She always told him he looked more like a pimp then a hustler.

Cheetah used to run with him back in the day when she first started. She knew he drove around with his product in his car in a secret compartment. She had to play him quick. He was such a scary nigga that he was always looking around.

She pulled the car into the parking lot of the mini mart across the street. She got out and dashed back to the building. Bolo was parked behind in the little brick projects. He was still sitting in his car. Cheetah hid behind a tree a few feet away from the car. He opened the door, and as soon as she saw his black alligator shoe hit the asphalt, she dashed up to him, threw the door all the way open and pointed the gun right at his forehead.

"Nigga, be easy, open the compartment and let me get that!" she said in a deep, disguised voice.

Bolo opened the latch to a compartment under the dashboard and handed her the bag. She tucked it in her pants and hit him three times on the side of his head. After unclasping the Rolex watch, sliding off the pinky ring, and snatching the Platinum chain off his neck, she pulled his pants down. He had on some boxers with smily faces.

"Nigga, you gon' be cryin' when you wake up." She laughed. She looked down the alley to make sure the coast was clear. Running back to the parking lot, she got in and sped off. A few blocks down, she slowed down, trying to relax.

Cheetah went straight home and rolled up a blunt of gank. She put the bag on the bed and went out to the backyard and smoked. Her heart was pounding a mile a minute. She knew Bolo was a good sting. The nigga stayed caking.

She smoked half the blunt and went back to the basement. She stripped down to her boxers and sports bra. She was hot. Extremely hot. She turned on the fan and sat under it for a minute.

Once she cooled down, she started counting the money. The pocket money totaled eight hundred. When she emptied the bag on the bed she could not believe what she saw. It was three bricks of heroin and four bundles of money held together with rubber bands. She counted one of the stacks and it was five thousand. After a quick count of the other three she realized all four of them were five thousand stacks.

Damn, nigga, I feel yo pain. Must have been about to re-up, she thought.

Cheetah got up and turned on the TV. She had to check on the weather. She was going to celebrate today.

As she was waiting on the forecast, Naj came down carrying a bundle of clothes.

"I thought I heard you up," she said turning the washing machine on.

"Yeah, man. I've been up and out already. Come here and look at this!" Cheetah said excitedly.

Naj put the clothes in the washer and walked over to the bed. When she saw all the money she asked, "Where the fuck you get all of that from, man?"

"Yo, I went out again this morning and I ripped that nigga Bolo on Jelliff. Man, he had $20,000 in a bag with three bricks."

"Say word," Naj said.

"Word to my mother, man!"

Naj picked up a stack of money and held it. Now if they could hit a cat for this much all the time, then this stick up thing just might work, but Naj knew this was just a lucky sting. Naj wanted to get down with Cheetah but she wanted to go after the Big Ballers. Cheetah was amped up. She had no intentions on stopping. She was enjoying it too much. Naj saw the look in her eyes. She was in too deep.

"Cheetah, this shit is cool man, for real, but you can't keep hitting these niggas around here. They gonna get hip to the stickups and start preparing for it. Just take it easy for awhile. We can build back up off of this, all right?" Naj said, trying to see where Cheetah's head was at.

The money was enough to get them back on board, but Cheetah had a personal beef with the stickup thang. Those niggas not only stripped her of her goods. They also stripped her of her dignity and pride. She just couldn't see herself stopping right now. She didn't know who got her, so until she could get to those two niggas she was going to stay on her grind.

"Yeah, Naj, I hear you," Cheetah said after a minute. "But this shit is personal. I'm not going to do it everyday, but I'm not going to stop either. You my dawg, so whether you get down or not I'm still going to split everything with you. When you find a connect to hit some sucka off for some keys then we'll get 'em. Until then, I'm going to snake these punks every chance I get. Ya heard?"

Naj saw that she couldn't reason with Cheetah right now so she just kept quiet. She heard movement upstairs and knew Ja'nise was up getting the kids ready for church. She put the bundle of money on the bed, got up, and started walking towards the steps.

"Naj," Cheetah called out.

Naj turned around and faced Cheetah.

"Yeah, what's up?"

"Here," Cheetah said, throwing her two bundles of money and the diamond studded earrings she took from Bolo. "Give the earrings to Ja'nise or something. I told you we went half no matter what, okay?"

"Good looking out. Thanks, man," Naj said.

Naj went upstairs and Cheetah called Tara. It was 7:30am and she was sure she would be waking her up.

"Hello?" Tara asked sleepily.

"Hey, gorgeous!" Cheetah said into the phone.

"Hey, Cheetah," Tara said recognizing her voice instantly. "What you doing up so early?"

"I was just dreaming about us. I dreamt we were at a carnival or something. It was such a vivid dream. I had to get up and call you, see what you were doing today" Cheetah said, hoping she wasn't sounding corny.

Tara smiled on the other end of the phone. "Oh, really?" she asked.

"Yeah, really!"

"So let's say my day was empty. What did you have in mind?" Tara played along with her.

"The carnival of course!" Cheetah stated matter of factly.

"What carnival Cheetah? Ain't no carnival in Newark right now."

"No, there isn't but Bowcraft on Route 22 is just like a carnival. Wanna go?" Cheetah asked.

"I thought we made a date for next weekend?"

"We did, but I want to see you Tara. Will you go please?" Cheetah was laying on the bed with her fingers crossed like she used to do when she was in grammar school. "Well?" she asked.

"Okay, Cheetah. What time will you come pick me up?"

"I'll be there at two!" Cheetah said happily.

She got the address and hung up. She put on her housecoat and slippers and went upstairs. Ja'nise was making breakfast.

Cheetah went to the stove and grabbed a sausage out of the pan. Ja'nise smacked her hand and laughed.

"Yo, Ja'nise, what time do you and the kids get out of church?" Cheetah asked through a mouthful of sausage.

"Around twelve, why?"

"Because I want to take them with me to Bowcraft. I met a new shorty at the mall and I'm taking her out at two. Can they come?"

"Let me find out what Naj had planned. Watch the pancakes!"

Ja'nise went to the bedroom to talk to Naj, and Cheetah took the pancakes out of the frying pan. She made herself a plate and sat at the table. The kids came in the kitchen and she fixed their plates also. They were all eating when Naj and Ja'nise walked back in the kitchen.

"Yes, they can go with you. Me and Naj need to spend some alone time together."

"Go where, Mommy?" Malik asked.

"Auntie Cheetah is going to take you and your sister to Bowcraft after church. You better behave!" Ja'nise told him sternly.

"Oh don't worry," Cheetah said, "that nigga knows I'll dig in his ass if he steps out of place!"

"Cheetah, watch your mouth and stop calling my son a nigga," Ja'nise said, throwing a napkin at Cheetah.

Cheetah ducked and threw a fake punch at Malik. They all loved Cheetah like she was a part of the family. The kids knew her as Auntie Cheetah and they never gave her any trouble. Ja'nise had watched her grow from a teenager to a grown woman. She admired her strength, even though she didn't approve of the way she got paid. She had to respect her gangsta! Cheetah had a heart of gold and would help anyone, but ever since she got robbed the softness that used to be in her eyes was gone. Now they were hard and vacant. They held pain and anger. Ja'nise hoped that she would be able to let go of that anger, but she doubted it. Cheetah washed the dishes while Naj took them to church. Ja'nise loved Cheetah for the way she had her girl's back. The kids naturally loved her because she had a habit of spoiling them. She went back downstairs and got in the bed. She needed a few more hours of sleep before she dealt with those kids all day.

Malikah came down and woke her up at 12:10. She was excited and was ready to go to the play place. Cheetah got up and got dressed. She put on a Roc-a-Wear jean suit with her construction Timberlands. She wore a white t-shirt under the suit and a Timberland fitted hat the color of her boots. She put on a brown belt and the Rolex watch. She let her hair hang down. She put five hundred in her pocket and tucked the gun in her waist. She wasn't going to bring it inside Bowcraft, but she wasn't leaving the house without it. She'd lock it in the trunk of the car once they got to where they were going.

She went upstairs to get the car keys. Malik and Malikah were waiting for her by the front door. They got in the car and went to get Tara.

It didn't take Cheetah long to get to her house. She knew every street in Newark like the back of her hand. If she ever wanted to get out of the game before she got rich, she could always be a taxi driver.

Tara lived on North 5th Street. When Cheetah got a block away, she called her and told her to come outside. She was standing on the porch when Cheetah pulled up, looking just as good as yesterday, if not better. She had on Parasuco jeans with a fitted shirt. She wore a pair of silver and black Nike socks that matched her shirt, and a black leather jacket. Her hair was pulled back in a ponytail and she didn't have on any makeup except for some clear lip gloss. As soon as she saw Cheetah, she smiled. When she got in the car, Cheetah thought she was going to have an orgasm, Tara smelled so damn good.

"Damn Tara, what you wearing?" Cheetah asked. "That shit smells good as hell!"

"It's Burberry Touch. You like it?"

"Like it? Your smell alone got me wet as hell!" Cheetah said licking her lips.

Tara smacked her on the thigh and told her to watch her mouth around the kids. Cheetah introduced the kids to Tara and headed to the highway.

They stayed at Bowcraft for three hours. They had mad fun! The outside rides didn't open until the summer time. The inside had bumper cars, arcade games and carnival booths. They played skeet ball and shot basketball for coupons. They played the arcade games until their fingers felt like they were going to fall off, and ate gigantic pretzels and sloppy hot dogs. Cheetah was really enjoying herself. She couldn't remember the last time she had so much fun. She wasn't high. She was with a bangin' ass chick. What more could she ask for?

Tara clung to Cheetah like they were already a couple. By the time they left, they were completely worn out. Cheetah had planned on going to Red Lobster to eat, but the kids wanted Burger King. Cheetah found a Burger King and went to the drive through window ordering two Whopper meals and two Whopper Jr. meals. They sat in the parking lot and ate.

"So Tara, did you have a good time?" Cheetah asked. "I know I did."

"I had fun Cheetah, thank you!" she replied.

"So when you wanna do this again?" Cheetah said looking at her.

"What? Another arcade?"

"No, dummy another date, when can I see you again?" Cheetah asked putting her arm around Tara's shoulder.

Tara laid her head on Cheetah's shoulder. "Cheetah, as much as I wish I could hang out with you everyday, I just can't. I'm busy with school. Let's just hook up this weekend like we originally planned, okay?"

"Yeah, okay that's cool," Cheetah said kissing her on the forehead.

Cheetah drove Tara home, and before she got out the car she kissed Cheetah lightly on the lips. "Thanks for a wonderful time, Cheetah." I can't wait until the weekend," she said.

"Me neither," Cheetah replied.

A Few Hours Earlier
"Wow, when was the last time we had a day to ourselves without the kids?" Ja'nise asked Naj.

"Damn, to be honest I can't remember, Ma," Naj replied.

"So what you want to do? Play cards? Watch videos? Listen to music?"

"Girl, don't play with me," Naj began. "You know we are not cutting into that square ass shit. Come on."

She grabbed Ja'nise, leading her to the bedroom. Ja'nise decorated the room in African motif, rich chocolates, blacks, and tans, and lots of zebra, leopard and tiger prints. The patterns were very busy, but it pulled in nicely. One large tropical plant that was as tall as a small tree sat in the far corner of the bedroom.

The furniture consisted of mahogany wood, a canopy bed armoire, and a cedar chest. Above the bed was a family portrait with Naj, Ja'nise, Malik and Malikah.

Ja'nise grabbed one of the many remotes and hit the power button. The plasma came on.

"Dang, Naj, which one of these damn things turn on the stereo?"

"Let me see."

Naj looked at the remotes that sat on the dresser. "The small one."

Ja'nise grabbed the correct remote and played "*Lovers and Friends*" by Lil' John and Usher.

"You spend too much money on this crap," Ja'nise said, referring to all the electronics that Naj had to have. She spent a lot of money at Brookstones.

"We have to keep up with technology," Naj smiled. "Come here," she said, kicking off her Jordans, hopping up on the bed.

"All I'm saying is that spending three and four thousand

dollars on a radio is not going to get us our dream home."

"Don't worry, give me one year. Have I ever let you down?" Naj kissed her hand.

"No, baby, but I'm worried about you. Since that shit happened to Cheetah, it's like you two have been real secretive. Cheetah looks like an entire different person. She's suddenly turned hard, Naj. I don't want you out there getting involved in no other shit. You know how I feel about the drug selling thing. You have been promising me for years that you were getting out of the game. Now y'all getting robbed and all that shit. I'm worried and I don't want nobody coming here with no bullshit, Naj. We got kids here!" Ja'nise said, her voice rising.

"Okay, calm down," Naj replied pulling her closer. "Baby, please just trust me. I'm okay, don't worry. One year, and I'm gonna put this all behind us."

Naj kissed Ja'nise on the neck and Ja'nise snuggled closer. Naj continued to kiss her until she felt the tension in Ja'nise's body begin to fade.

"Umm, that's good," Ja'nise said as Naj lowered her kisses to her chest area. "Ooh, that's really good."

"You like that?" Naj teased

"Yessss, give me more."

Naj laid Ja'nise back on the bed and placed her mouth on hers. Sticking her tongue in, the two played twister with their tongues. Naj found the buckle on Ja'nise's jeans and unbuckled it. Letting down the zipper in one swift movement, she had the jeans off of her and tossed on the floor. Even though Ja'nise hadn't danced in years, her body was still in dancer's shape. Her smooth thighs were flawless. Naj ran her hands between her legs until she got to the crotch of Ja'nise's underwear. Moving them to the side, Naj felt the moistness.

"Wet already, huh?" she whispered in Ja'nise's ear.

"Uh-huh, get it, baby. Touch me."

Naj opened her pussy lips with her thumb and forefinger, found the hole and stuck her middle finger all the way in. Ja'nise, feeling as hot as a furnace, grabbed Naj's arm and pushed it in deeper. Naj took her remaining two fingers and stuck them in also.

"Uh-huh, yes…yes," Ja'nise moaned. Ja'nise removed her underwear completely and rolled Naj over. With fingers still in position, Naj was now on the bottom and Ja'nise was straddling her waist. Like a gymnast, Ja'nise positioned her legs on each side to form a split. Using her hands as support, she placed them flat down on Naj's stomach and began to whine like she was Sasha in Sean Paul's "*Dutty Love*" video.

"You like that, baby?" she asked Naj. "You want more?" she asked, lowering her body down.

"Oh, shit." Naj said. "Ma, I'm all the way in. Hold up, you gonna break my other two fingers."

"No, I'm not. Put them in too. Put them all in!"

Naj inserted her thumb and forefinger and was now fist deep into Ja'nise's extremely wet pussy.

"Oh, my God! That's what the fuck I'm talking about! Yes!"

Naj felt her body begin to convulse. Knowing she was about to come, Naj stuck two fingers from her other hand in her mouth until they were good and wet. Finding Ja'nise's clit, Naj rubbed until it was rock hard. Ja'nise let out a sound that was almost inhuman as the juices of her love ran down Naj's forearm.

"Aagh…don't stop…wait…don't stop…"

After a few more seconds, Ja'nise collapsed and laid against Naj's body.

"Ummm, I love you, baby. I love you so much," Ja'nise said, nuzzling close in Naj's chest.

"I love you too," Naj replied. "You tired? We done?" she asked.

"Hell no, we ain't done. That was just the appetizer. Just give me a second to get out of these clothes."

"Okay, you do that while I put some music on. I want you to do something for me."

"Oh yeah? And what would that be?"

"Come on, don't play stupid. You know what I want. Just let me find our song."

Ja'nise laughed as she removed the rest of her clothes. She

knew Naj had a fetish for go-go dancers, and if she wanted her to dance then that's exactly what she would do to keep her woman happy. A few seconds passed then Mystikal's "*Shake It Fast*" filled the room.

Naj stepped out of her pants and took her T-shirt off. Walking to the bed again, she came out of her briefs and sports bra. Ja'nise had already rose up off the bed and walked over by the door. Naj positioned herself on the edge of the bed and cocked her legs apart.

Nodding her head in Ja'nise's direction, Ja'nise began her show. Winding her hips, she began an exotic dance so sensual that an impotent man would get hard if he was watching. Reaching for Naj, she turned her back to her and sat on her lap. Ja'nise popped it and dropped it so hard Naj swore she felt the floor shake. Naj felt her pussy throbbing and grabbed Ja'nises's waist as she continued the lap dance.

Once Naj was gushing wet, Ja'nise got up and bent over. With her ass cheeks right in Naj's face she made each cheek jump simultaneously. Then as if they were hands, she made them clap. Looking between her legs, she saw Naj with her hands in her own pussy masturbating. Ja'nise turned around and knelt down.

Taking hold of Naj's breast, one in each hand, she began sucking, licking, and teasing them. Naj moaned, letting Ja'nise know that's exactly what she wanted her to do. Ja'nise circled her tongue around Naj's nipples like they were a blow pop. Naj beat her clit until her body trembled. Feeling her increased breathing, Ja'nise found Naj's treasure with one of her hands and stuck two fingers in. It took one more minute of Naj's rubbing, and Ja'nise's licking and sucking on her breast to bring Naj to a climax. With the juices running down her leg, Naj pulled Ja'nise up, threw her on the bed and spread her legs.

Ja'nise opened her legs so wide she felt the muscles stretching. Naj dived between her legs as if she was skinny dipping. She covered Ja'nise's pussy with her mouth sticking her tongue all the way in her hole. Naj had a long tongue and knew how to work it.

Ja'nise pushed her ass down on Naj's face and bucked. Naj worked her tongue like magic, causing Ja'nise to cream all over her face. Ja'nise tried to pull away as the orgasm made her body spasm, but Naj held her firm and licked faster.

Ja'nise climaxed with a squeal so loud it could have shattered glass. She clamped her legs around Naj's neck and Naj slowed it down. Naj licked and sucked gently, bringing her to one last climax.

"Uhh...ohhh..." Ja'nise exhaled as her body went limp. "What the fuck? You trying to drain me?"

"Nah, I'm just trying to love you," Naj said as she lay next to Ja'nise, holding her in her arms.

Cheetah was driving up McCarter highway when she heard somebody calling her name. She was going to keep riding until she saw her sister, Dana flagging her down. She pulled over to the side and Dana jumped in.

"Hey, lil' sis, how are you?" Dana asked.

"I'm good. What's up with you? What you doing way down here?" Cheetah asked.

"I was coming from a friend's house and I didn't have any money to catch a cab."

"Well, I guess I'm right on time, huh?" Cheetah asked, pulling off.

Dana has always been a fiend. After she gave birth to Esh at the age of fifteen, she met a nigga named Ra'sul, who showed her how to party. Ra'sul was nineteen and a hustling addict. By the time Dana turned sixteen, she was completely strung out. Her mother took custody of Esh, and raised her right along with Cheetah, who was five years older than Esh. Her mother tried every method there was to get Dana off the drugs and away from that no good ass nigga, Ra'sul. Dana had been to rehab so many times it wasn't funny. Nothing worked. Dana was so gone. The only thing her mother could do for her was pray, and she did that constantly. Dana's life spun downward fast when she went from snorting to shooting. She shot dope with anybody; the furthest thing from her mind was making sure the needle was clean. Three years ago, she was hospitalized for the flu, and found out she was HIV positive. The once beautiful, light-skinned, thick in the right places, hazel-eyed girl was now a mere shell of herself. She had abcesses all over her body. To say that she was skinny would be an understatement, weighing only ninety pounds soaking wet. Her front teethwere gone and her hair was very thin. She looked a mess, and it didn't help that she continued to have sex with whoever, still shooting up. Now her HIV status went up to AIDS. For lack of medicine along with other things, her health was deteriorating fast.

Still, Cheetah loved her unconditionally. She always made sure she had everything she needed. She would buy her clothes, give her money and drugs. Even though she was enabling her to use, she didn't want her doing anything drastic to get high. It hurt Cheetah deeply every time she saw her. She begged Dana to come home with her but Dana was beyond reachable. Cheetah just gave her what she needed whenever she asked for it, which was always. Today was no different.

"So what's up?" Cheetah asked. "You aight?"

"Yeah, I'm good, I'm good."

"Mommy wants to see you. I told her we'll come Sunday for dinner."

"Aight," Dana said. "I'll be there."

Cheetah knew Dana was just talking to be talking but she gave her the benefit of the doubt.

"Call me and I'll come pick you up from wherever you are, okay?"

"Yeah, sure!" Dana said hurriedly. "Listen, do you have some dope on you? I'm not feeling too well."

Cheetah never drove around with drugs in the car and Dana knew this. This was her way of asking for money.

"Nah, I don't have any dope with me but I got a couple of

dollars for you. Where do you want me to drop you off?"

"Take me to Avon and 13th."

Cheetah took Dana where she wanted to go and gave her a hundred dollars. By the time she got to the house the kids were asleep. She woke them up, took them in the house, and got them ready for bed. Naj had a Do Not Disturb sign on her door. Once the kids were safely tucked in, Cheetah went downstairs, called Tara to say goodnight, and fell into a deep sleep.

MISSY JACKSON

CHAPTER 5

Bonding

Ever since the day at Bowcraft, Cheetah and Tara had been inseparable. They talked on the phone for hour's everyday and spent every weekend together. They hadn't made love yet, but came close on many occasions. Tara wasn't ready. She wasn't sure she could cross that boundary yet, even though she enjoyed every moment she spent with Cheetah. She just wasn't ready to have sex with a woman. Cheetah didn't pressure her. She liked Tara for many other reasons besides her body.

Cheetah loved the way she felt when they were together. She could be herself. When she was with Tara, it was like all the weight of the world was lifted off her shoulders. Tara was a breath of fresh air on a muggy day.

Next week they were going to New York to the Gay Pride Parade. They had plans on spending Friday to Sunday in New York and coming back after the festivities. This would be their first time spending the night together. Cheetah couldn't wait.

CHAPTER 6

Is Y'all Niggas Crazy?

Cheetah was in the shower when she heard her cell phone ringing. She didn't jump out to answer it. Whoever was calling would just have to leave a message. Before she could finish her shower, it rang four more times. She cut the shower off and got out to see what was up. It was the twins.

They'd left five messages saying to call back immediately. She wondered what the fuck was so important that they had to call so many damn times. She really didn't want to talk to those niggas right now. They had been fucking up on their packages and coming up short with the money. They claimed someone was hitting their stash. Cheetah hadn't heard from them in three days, and she hoped they weren't calling again about her money being fucked up.

She called them back while she got dressed.

"Yo, it's me. What's good?" Cheetah asked.

"Cheetah, come see us. We got something very important to show you," Raheem said.

"Yeah, aight. I'll be there as soon as I can."

"Nah, we need you to come right now, for real. We got some serious shit going on!" he sounded nervous.

"Aight I'm on my way," Cheetah said and hung up. She finished getting dressed and went upstairs to get Naj. They got in the car and headed up to Avon Avenue. When they got to 12th Street, she saw the twins flagging her down as they came out of the diner. The block was nearly empty except for a few cars riding by.

Cheetah and Naj got out. "Yo, what's up? What's so important Raheem?" Cheetah asked impatiently.

"Man, we caught the fiend who has been hitting our stash," Raheem said. "It's a bitch Cheetah! We got here early this morning. We put our stash in the drain pipe with a mouse trap on top of it. When she went to steal it her hand got snagged. She screamed and we caught her ass. We tied her up in the old auto body shop and we've been torturing her all day: fucking her, making her give us blow jobs, and I done nutted in her mouth ten times."

"We told her we'll let her go as soon as we check with our boss. I don't know though, Cheetah. We fucked her up pretty bad. We might have to get rid of her, nah mean?"

Cheetah wasn't in the mood for this type of shit today, but what had to be done had to be done. "Aight," she said. "Stop running your mouth and take me to her."

The inside of the old auto shop smelled like a train station bathroom. It was pissy as hell. It had empty heroin bags and crack bottles all over the place. The fiends used it as a gathering place to get high. It was dimly lit. In the corner were an old tattered mattress and a makeshift table.

The twins had three candles burning to provide extra light. From where Cheetah and Naj stood, you could barley see the person lying on the mattress. Kareem lit another candle and the view became a little clearer. The body was naked and completely still. The person was probably dead. As Cheetah stepped closer she got a funny feeling in her stomach. She sensed something was wrong but she couldn't figure out what it was.

Kareem bent down and turned the body over. Before she was fully rested on her back Cheetah let out a scream.

"What the fuck? What the hell y'all do to her, man?"

Kareem was puzzled by the panic in Cheetah's voice.

"Cheetah, I told you she was stealing our shit! We caught her and we had to fuck her up."

Cheetah was no longer paying him any attention. She was on her knees untying the ropes. She was crying, telling her sister she was going to be all right. She could not believe what they had done to Dana. She was barely breathing and had bruises all over her entire body. Both her eyes were swollen shut and blood was dried up under her nose.

"Dana! Dana! Please answer me. It's Cheetah. You gonna be all right. Just hold on. I'ma get you to the hospital."

Naj was standing behind the twins, looking at the crazy look in Cheetah's eyes. She knew that at any moment Cheetah was going to freak out and Naj was ready for whatever she wanted to do.

Once Cheetah untied Dana, she put her clothes back on her. She called Naj over and told her to take her to the hospital. Naj was skeptical about leaving her there alone with the twins, but Cheetah insisted. She wasn't in the mood for debating. Naj picked Dana up and Cheetah stood, pulling her gun out of her waist.

Naj hesitated and Cheetah screamed for her to go.

Kareem and Raheem were still trying to figure out what the hell was going on. They had not caught on to the fact that they had raped and beaten Cheetah's sister, and stood there dumbfounded. They hadn't uttered a word until they saw the gun in Cheetah's hand.

"Cheetah, what's the deal? Why the fuck you tripping?" Kareem asked.

Cheetah raised the gun and pointed it at Kareem. "Man, that was my mothafuckin' sister!"

Oh shit! Thought Kareem. Before he could say a word Cheetah pulled the trigger, sending a bullet into his stomach. He looked at her in shock, clutched his stomach and fell to the ground. He was screaming and yelling like a bitch. Cheetah turned the still smoking gun on Raheem.

"You said you fucked her, right? You fucked her and beat her unconscious, right? Right? Answer me mothafucka!"

"Yeah Cheetah, but we—"

"Shut the fuck up!" Cheetah yelled. She was so angry, foam was coming out the side of her mouth. "I'm about to do you a favor, Son. You see my sister is HIV positive. So by me killin' you, I'll be saving you from a slow death."

"Cheetah, please, please, don't..."

That was all he could say before she pulled the trigger. She shot him at point blank range in the head. He was dead before he hit the floor. She turned back to Kareem and shot him two more times.

Naj heard the first shot on her way back to the car. She was telling herself that Cheetah was just scaring them, but in her heart she knew the truth. She couldn't just leave her here. She had to go back. She put Dana in the backseat of the car, drove around to the back of the auto body shop, and Naj ran back inside the shop. Cheetah stood there, still and silent with the gun dangling from her hand. There was blood all over her clothes and face. One of the twins' face was distorted, as if he was in shock, and the other didn't even have a face left.

"Dang, let's roll. The po-po probably on their way," Naj said. Cheetah didn't move. "Cheetah come on!"

"They killed her, man. They killed Dana," Cheetah cried.

"Nah, she ain't dead but we got to get her to the hospital. Come on. We gotta go now."

Cheetah turned toward the bodies one last time and spat on both of them. They were born together, they died together. Naj yanked her by the arm.

"Let's go!"

She got in the backseat with Dana, laying her head in her lap.

"Sis, hold on. I'm a get you to the hospital," Cheetah sobbed.

Dana was struggling to breathe. Cheetah checked her pulse. It was faint.

"Squeeze my hand if you hear me," Dana's fingers moved slightly. "Naj, drive this mothafuckin' car faster! Help me!" Cheetah was losing it. She couldn't lose her only sister.

"Dawg, everything is going to be all right. Just chill! I'm driving as fast as I can without getting pulled over." Naj was thinking about the two bodies that they had just left back at the garage. So many thoughts ran through her mind. Did somebody hear the gunshots? Did somebody see them? Would they go to jail? Whatever was going to happen, she was ready to ride with her dawg. Cheetah continued to rock Dana's small, limp body.

Naj went to the house first. She took the gun from Cheetah and went inside to get a wet rag and a new t-shirt. Cheetah changed her shirt in the car and wiped herself down.

Naj took out her cell phone and called Ja'nise.

"Baby, it's me," Naj said as soon as she heard Ja'nise's voice. "I'm on my way over with Cheetah and Dana. Dana's hurt real bad. Please be waiting for us by the left emergency entrance. I'll be there in like five minutes."

Ja'nise was just about to make her rounds when she received the call.

"Oh, my God. Baby, what happened?"

"I'll explain it all when I get there," Naj said, and hung up the phone.

Once they got to the hospital, she threw the rag and t-shirt in the dumpster.

Ja'nise was making her rounds when they brought Dana in. She quickly got a gurney, and took her in the back. Cheetah tried to follow behind her, but security turned her away. She found a seat in the corner and sat. She was crying so loud people were turning their heads towards her. Naj sat next to her and held her while she sobbed. They stayed this way for a while. When the crying subsided, Naj spoke to her.

"Listen, man, I know this is some serious shit and you're hurt, but we got to get a story together. They are going to question this shit. I don't think anyone saw us, but we can't be sure, okay?"

81

Cheetah nodded without saying a word. She didn't think words would come out if she even tried to talk, so she just listened.

"Let me do the talking. When the police get here, I'm going to say that somebody rang the doorbell and when I opened the door, she was sprawled out on the front porch."

Naj laid Cheetah's head on her lap and they stayed that way until Ja'nise came back out. She walked over to them and told them that the doctors had Dana in the operating room. It would be a while before they had a prognosis. Naj explained to her what happened, but left out the murders. They would all discuss that later.

The doctor came out after three long hours to brief the family on Dana's condition. If you had to put it in street slang you could say it like this—she was fucked up! She'd suffered severe head trauma, a cracked pelvic bone, several broken ribs, and a fractured jaw. They were able to control the internal bleeding, but she was in a coma. It was now up to Dana to fight. She had been moved to the ICU. Due to her HIV status, it was important to make sure no infection set into her wounds. The next twenty-four hours would be touch and go.

Cheetah called Esh and her mom, and Naj went to pick them up. She called Tara and told her to come to the hospital. Tara started asking mad questions and Cheetah assured her that she was okay.

Once the doctor got Dana cleaned up, he allowed Cheetah in the ICU to be with her. Dana was hooked up to so many machines, tubes were everywhere. Cheetah took baby steps over to the side of the bed. Dana's face was black and blue.

"Damn, sis, them niggas fucked you up," Cheetah said, tears in her eyes.

The first thing she had noticed was all the tubes that she was hooked up to. Cheetah pulled a chair up to the bed and started to cry.

"Why didn't you just come to me? You know I would have given you anything you wanted. You didn't have to steal. Don't I always look out for you? Don't I make sure you're never sick?

Sis, just wake up! Please!"

Cheetah heard the door open and looked up to see her mom walk in. Mrs. Johnson was a strong woman, but when she saw Dana lying there, she broke down.

"Oh God, my baby," she cried. Cheetah wrapped her arms around her mother.

"It's gon' be okay, Ma."

Mrs. Johnson pulled away, composing herself.

"Baby, we got to pray. Only God can fix this."

They bowed their heads.

When Tara arrived, she couldn't come to the room because she wasn't immediate family. Cheetah went out to talk to her. Tara knew something was terribly wrong from the redness of Cheetah's eyes. Once they were close enough, Cheetah grabbed and held her, needing Tara's arms atround her. Tears fell on Tara's neck and shoulder. Tara led Cheetah to a seat and Cheetah told her everything. She started with the phone call, how she found Dana, and about the murders.

Tara knew Cheetah was in the streets. She figured that she did something illegal, but she'd never thought it was that deep. She had to make a decision right then whether she was going to ride with her or not. Secretly, she had already fallen in love with Cheetah. Out of all the guys she'd ever dated, she never felt the passion or intimacy she felt with Cheetah. There was no way she would leave her now.

She told Cheetah that no matter what happened she wasn't going anywhere. Tara called Esh and briefly explained the situation. She told her to get in a cab and come to the hospital. Cheetah planned on staying all night.

When Esh arrived, Tara left Cheetah alone to be with her family. Esh loved her mother dearly, despite her short comings. Cheetah took her up to the room and left. When Esh saw Dana she broke down.

"Ma, oh, my God, ma," she cried as she knelt next to the bed. "What the fuck happened to you?"

"Watch your mouth, Esh," Mrs. Johnson said.

"Grandma, I'm sorry, but look at her. Who would do something like this to her? Why?"

"I don't know why or who, but I do know who could help her right now," Mrs. Johnson said, walking to the other side of the bed. She placed one hand on Dana's forehead, and reached the other out to Esh.

"Lord, God, in the name of Jesus. I need you to grace your mercy over my first born, Lord. Bless her with your loving care and touch her. You said by your stripes we are healed. I'm praying to you now for my daughter...Amen."

Esh got up and left the room. The sight of her mother looking that way was too much for her to stomach. She met back up with Cheetah and Tara.

The police finally arrived, just like they always do when somebody calls 911, taking their slow ass time. They went about the standard questioning: Who? What? When? Where? And Why? Faking their concern, promising a full investigation, arrest, and justice, but they really didn't give a fuck. Naj handled all their questions, took their card, and sent them on their way.

Cheetah didn't give a fuck one way or the other. There was no way she could have lived with herself knowing that the nigga's responsible were still out there. She was glad she could send them straight to hell.

Naj and Tara left shortly after the police. Cheetah, Esh, and Mrs. Johnson stayed all night.

The next morning, Dana was still in a coma but she had pulled through the rough part. Cheetah took Esh and Mrs. Johnson down to the cafeteria for breakfast. She really didn't have an appetite, but she wanted to make sure that her mother and niece had something in their stomach.

Once they sat down, Mrs. Johnson broke down and cried.

Cheetah got up to comfort her mother. "Don't worry, Ma. She's gonna be all right."

Mrs. Johnson tried to pull herself together.

"I want to kill whoever did this," Esh said out loud, not really speaking to anyone in particular.

"Don't worry, I already did," Cheetah confessed.

Both of them gasped. Cheetah went on to explain what happened.

Cheetah felt the vibration of her cell phone on her hip. She looked at the number. It was Naj.

"What's up, Naj?" she asked.

"Yo, Cheetah, check out the newspaper, the *Star Ledger*. Go to page twenty-seven in the B section, and hit me back."

Cheetah went up to the counter and bought the newspaper. She found the article and sat down and read.

Twins Found Murdered: Last night twin brothers, Raheem & Kareem Brown, ages twenty-one, were found murdered. They had both been shot. They were found in an abandoned auto body shop off of Avon Avenue. One eye witness claims to have seen them walking towards Rays Auto Body Shop earlier in the evening with two other young men. The bodies were found in a back room. Investigators believe it was a drug deal gone bad. Both young men were local drug dealers.

Even though the description is sketchy, the young men they were last seen with looked to be in their early twenties. One was between five-eleven and six feet with corn rows to the back. The other was shorter, five-eight or five-nine with long reddish colored plaits. They both wore white T-shirts and blue jeans. If anyone has any other information please call the Newark Police Department at 555-2222 ext. 11.

Cheetah walked her mom and Esh back up to Dana's room and left.

Cheetah hurried home to see what Naj wanted to do about the paper. She walked in the door and Naj was sitting on the living room couch. She had cut all her hair off, now it was close to her head and curly.

"What's good Cheetah?" Naj asked. "How's Dana making out?"

"So far she's pulled through the rough part but she remains in a coma. What's up with the cut?"

"Just trying to be safe, man. We got to do something with yours too. Before you start bitching, I already know how you feel about your locks, so all we gonna do is dye them jet black and cut them up to your shoulders. They looking for two guys remember?"

"Yeah, aight man. Whateva you think is best."

Cheetah was exhausted. All she wanted to do was crawl into bed before she went back to the hospital. She wanted to get a couple of hours of sleep and get her head right.

After Naj finished with her hair, she took a shower, called the florist and had some flowers delivered to Dana's room. She called Tara and asked her to come over, then called Esh at the hospital. She told Esh and her mom to go home and get some rest. They could meet up with her later at the hospital.

Cheetah laid down with her eyes closed. She was dog tired, but with everything going on she couldn't sleep. She was so deep in thought she didn't hear Tara come in.

Tara didn't want to wake Cheetah so she took off her shoes and jacket before climbing into bed beside her. Cheetah stirred and Tara snuggled closer to her. Cheetah turned around and kissed her. She kissed her long and hard. She wanted her more at that moment then she ever had.

Tara put one leg over Cheetah and Cheetah pulled her as close as she possibly could. She gripped her ass and caressed it. Tara responded with a soft moan. Cheetah palmed both cheeks as if she was testing for a ripe melon. Tara moaned and started grinding her pussy against Cheetah's.

Cheetah felt Tara finally succumbing. She rolled over on top of her and rained kisses on her face. She remembered how she felt when De'shea did this to her and wanted to make Tara feel the same way. Tara closed her eyes, wrapping her arms around Cheetah's back.

Cheetah stopped and slowly undressed her. Under the first layer of clothes was a red Victoria's Secret lace thong set. Cheetah inched them off with her teeth.

Tara lay under her naked. Her body glistened from the glitter of her lotion. Cheetah admired her beauty, her flawless, smooth skin. Running her fingers over the sun tattoo around her navel, Cheetah gently licked her stomach.

"Turn over," she whispered.

Tara laid flat on her stomach. Her ass cheeks sat up like two basketballs: nice, round, and firm. Right at the crack of her ass was a strawberry tattoo dripping with the word Juicy under it.

Cheetah bit the strawberry slightly and sucked it until it got redder. She got up, and removed her own clothes. As she watched Tara turned seductively over onto her back. She lay back on top of her and started sucking her breast until her nipples puckered. She put one in her mouth and thumbed the other one. Tara bit down on her lip to hold back the scream of pleasure she wanted to release. Tara hugged her tighter. Cheetah put one leg between Tara's and spread her legs. She began to body rock her, bumping pussies until Tara was dripping wet. They were both hot and ready and you could smell the desire in the room.

Cheetah felt between Tara's legs. She stuck two fingers in her and wet them with the juices. She brought them to Tara's mouth, and she sucked them like a two year old. Cheetah finger fucked her into a frenzy. The juices dripped down her hand. She began kissing her again, working her way down. She kissed and licked every part of her breasts, chest and stomach.

Tara was on fire! All the fear she'd held onto before this day had disappeared. She was on the verge of an orgasm just from that feeling alone.

Cheetah put Tara's legs around her neck and licked her pussy lips. She opened the lips with one hand, waiting for her clit to come out of its hiding place. She put the tip of her tongue on it and started licking.

Tara bucked and called out, "Oh, my God, Cheetah, yes baby, yessss!"

Cheetah continued to lick the clit.

Tara started grinding her hips, grabbing the back of Cheetah's head and held it close. Cheetah made love to her like she never did anyone else. She slid her tongue in and out. She stuck two fingers in her and eased them all the way in.

Cheetah stopped and got up. She had bought a strap on dildo to take with them to New York. She got it out of the closet and to put it on. When Tara saw her with this nine and a half inch artificial dick on, she laughed out loud.

"Damn, Cheetah. Damn, baby. What you doing?"

"What's so funny?" Cheetah asked. "Let me see if you gonna laugh in a minute!" she teased, hopping back in the bed. She turned Tara over and positioned her doggy style. She found the pussy and stuck the dildo in. Tara clawed the sheets. Cheetah held her ass cheeks wide open. Tara threw her ass back and they rode to ecstasy. Tara was going nuts.

"What the…? Oh shit! Yess! Oh, damn! That feels so good! Oh, my god, Cheetah! Yessss! I love you! I love you! Don't. Stop. I'm. Coming!"

Cheetah did stop, long enough to flip her over and hit it from the front. Tara's orgasm was so intense, her body shook violently. Cheetah pulled out and stuck her face between Tara's thighs. She opened her pussy lips and licked the juices that dripped out. She circled Tara's clit with the tip of her tongue as Tara grabbed a handful of her dreads, pushing her closer. Cheetah ate her pussy 'till she came two more times.

Tara cried.

Cheetah held her and whispered in her ear, "What's the matter, Ma?"

"Nothing, Cheetah, I just feel so good baby. Did you hear what I told you?"

"What you talking about?" Cheetah asked, kissing her neck.

"You know what I'm talking; about stop playing," Tara said as she playfully pushed Cheetah away.

"I'm not playing, girl. What you say, huh? Tell me again, yo."

"I said I love you, Cheetah."

"Oh, yeah, you loving a nigga now that I hit that thing," Cheetah joked, grabbing one of her titties.

"Quit, girl. I'm serious. I love you."

Cheetah looked into her eyes and saw that Tara spoke the truth. She knew she was Tara's first as far as women went. She just hoped and prayed Tara didn't turn out to be one of those crazy females who couldn't deal with the lesbian emotions. It's much more sensitive and emotional when two women fall in love.

"I love you, too. You know what this means right?"

Tara looked like, *What?*

"This right here is all me," Cheetah said as she ran her hands down Tara's body.

"Yes, baby, I'm all yours."

They held each other through the night. When they woke up they went another round before Cheetah took Tara home.

Cheetah went back to the hospital. She stopped in the gift shop and bought some roses, a teddy bear, card, and a couple of balloons. When Cheetah got to Dana's room, her heart started beating fast. She did not like seeing her this way, but she had to be there with her. Dana looked exactly the same as the day before. Cheetah put the teddy bears on the end of the bed and let the balloons float to the ceiling. She got the chair and pulled it up to the bed.

"Dana, hey, it's me. Sis, you need to wake up, girl. You're laying there like you don't have anything to live for. Listen, I'll make a deal with you. If you wake up I'll take you to the Bahamas. Remember when I was five years old, and you used to always tell me you were going to take me to the Bahamas? Well, when you get your ass up I'm going take you. How about that? I promise. Also, I'll take you shopping and get your hair and nails done. I swear I will. But first you got to wake up. Please, just wake up!"

Cheetah had read somewhere that even though people were in a coma they could sometimes hear what's going on around them. She also heard about miracles.

"Dana, remember when we were little, and you use to always sing that song by Sister Sledge to me? I think it was called *We Are Family.* I would do anything to hear you sing that to me again. I really miss you, big sis. I know you've led a rough life but you can change that. We love you! We ain't even mad at you. We all just want you to get better. I'm going to be here everyday until you open your eyes."

Cheetah stayed at the hospital 'til 2am. When she got home she called Tara.

"Hello?" Tara answered sleepily.

"Hey, boo, I miss you."

"I miss you too, baby. You just getting in?"

"Yeah, I chilled at the hospital 'til about half an hour ago."

"How is she, baby?" Tara asked, concerned about Dana's well being.

"She the same, Ma, but she gon' pull through. That girl tough as hell."

"You all right, Cheetah?"

"Yeah, I'm good. Just so much shit going on right now. Nah mean? I need to get my head right. You wanna pick me up in the morning? I need to cop me a whip."

"Yeah, I'll be there around 9am. That's cool with you?"

"Yeah, I'll be ready. Love you."

Cheetah needed to go to the dealership quick. She had enough of asking other people for their car or waiting on the next mothafucka to come get her. The next morning, Tara sat outside waiting on Cheetah to come out. Cheetah checked her clock. It was nine-thirty. The only thing that was bitch about her is that she was slow as hell. She heard Tara's Mustang's horn, and walked outside, pulling a car hat hoodie over her head.

Cheetah kissed Tara softly on the lips. "Sorry it took so long, baby."

"Next time, I'll just be late and have you waiting," Tara said rolling her eyes.

Cheetah sucked her teeth, "Later for that. Shoot me up to the Buy Rite on Washington Street."

Cheetah had seen a dark blue Expedition that she was interested in. It was a 2000 model but it was in good condition. They were asking for twelve thousand. She talked him down to nine and paid for it in cash.

Cheetah drove the truck and Tara followed in her Mustang. They went to the car wash and got a full detail. Cheetah bought the original pine tree air fresheners and a leather steering wheel cover. She got some floor mats and then filled up the tank. Once they were done with the car they went back to the house and ate dinner. Tara left shortly after.

Cheetah was helping clean up the kitchen when her cell phone rang.

"Yeah, who dis?"

"Hey, Ma, it's me, Chill."

Cheetah hadn't heard from Chill since before the meeting at Mickey D's. Rumor was he had started getting high and had robbed some cat from Ellis Avenue. He was now staying in Harrison with his brother. Cheetah was surprised to get his call.

"Yo, what's good, Chill?" Cheetah asked, sitting at the kitchen table. "What rock you been hiding under?"

"I'm out in Harrison. Just had to get a few things straight."

"Straight, huh? Like you running from them niggas off Ellis and gettin' high? Yeah, I heard," Cheetah said, cutting straight to the chase.

"Fuck you mean? I wouldn't fuck with that shit if a nigga paid me to. Listen, I had to chill for a minute 'cause I hit up one of those Ellis niggas for fuckin' with my sister."

"Yeah, whatever, man. What can I do for you?"

"I'm tryna eat. I heard you and Naj still doin' y'all thing. Put a nigga on."

"Oh, just like that. It's been forever since I've seen yo' ass. Now out of the blue, 'Cheetah, give me some work'," Cheetah said, mimicking him.

"You know I pull my own weight. I ain't never needed a nigga to hold my hand to get out there. I goes hard for mine."

"I hear you talkin'. Let me make a call to Naj and I'm a get back at ya, ya dig?"

"No doubt. I'll be right at this number."

91

Cheetah didn't have a problem with giving Chill the bricks. He had always been a loyal worker. Now with the twins dead, she needed to put some more product out there with someone who could keep the weekly intake leveled. She had to consult with Naj though. They were fifty-fifty in this business.

Cheetah hit Naj up and she was cool with it.

Cheetah hit Chill back.

"Aight, yo, meet me Saturday at 9:30 in the morning at Penn Station. I got you."

CHAPTER 7

Thank You God

With everything going on, the week flew by. Cheetah stayed at the hospital, taking breaks to change clothes, get sleep, or see Tara. Naj held down the business end. She understood that Cheetah needed to be with family. Without the help of their third in command, Naj wouldn't have been able to do it. Ra'dee was that nigga fo' sho! He held down the entire Avon Avenue. He picked up the money and made all the drops. The best part was he never came up short. It couldn't get any better than that.

Friday afternoon, Cheetah met up with Papi at Eve's Restaurant on 6th St. and South Orange Ave. Papi was a short, Hispanic man with a five o'clock shadow. He had sleepy eyes, and deep, tan skin. He always chewed double mint gum. He dressed in the finest linen and wore his hair cropped close to his head. One look at him, and you knew he was about his money. Cheetah walked to the table in the back and Papi stood up.

"Cheetah. Que pasa mi amiga?"

"What it do Papi?"

"Same ole', same ole' my friend. New day brings new money, capice?"

"Capice, I understand. Can we sit?" Cheetah asked, nodding towards the chair.

"Yes. Yes, be my guest," Papi replied as he pulled the chair out for her. Cheetah sat and he seated himself in the chair next to her.

"So, what can I do for you today? Would you like to order while we're here, or will this be one of those quicky meetings you're so famous for?" Papi asked with a smirk on his face.

Cheetah knew that Papi didn't approve of her hit and run meetings, but that's just the way she got down. Time was money, and right now she didn't have any time to miss out on any money.

"Nah, no food today Papi. I got some things to take care of. Maybe next time, Aight?"

"Next time it is then, so let's get to business, shall we?"

"Word, that's what it is. Listen, I need to cop one-hundred bricks from you within the next twenty four hours, feel me? Need to get a new ticket on 'em to."

"A new ticket? What were you considering?"

"I was thinking one hundred fifty dollars per brick. This way I'll be able to pay my workers and double my own money."

Papi nodded, calculating the money in his head. Cheetah was a very dependable buyer. He had no problem dropping her ticket to one-fifty. He had been trying for years to get Cheetah to buy raw heroin, cut and bag her own product. She would be able to quadruple her money at the least.

"The ticket is no problem. I will honor you that. However, if you bought a half pound of raw from me, you will come out a lot better, my friend."

Cheetah shook her head. "No, that's way too much work for me Papi. I would still have to hire a chemist to cut it correctly, hire the baggers, buy the bags, and by that time I'll still be making only a penny more. I'll stick with the fifty bag bricks for now."

"Okay, have it your way. I'll have my driver meet you at Shop-Rite on Rt 22 at eight o'clock sharp tonight. Just look for the tan and white station wagon."

"For sure. I'll be there," With that said, Cheetah rose up out of her seat, tipped her fitted cap and left.

Friday night at exactly eight o'clock, Cheetah was delivered one hundred bricks by an eighty-year-old woman in a station wagon. She couldn't believe her eyes. The old lady handed her a duffle bag, and Cheetah gave her two Shop-Rite bags filled with money. The old lady left, and Cheetah hopped in her truck and drove off.

She called Ra'dee, telling him to come over and pick up his weekly supply from Naj. She took out twenty bricks for Chill and put them up, leaving the other eighty with Naj before driving to the hospital.

She sat with Dana the rest of the night.

Cheetah was up and out early the next day. She hit the block, straight from the hospital. Cheetah hated to disappoint Tara, but their trip to New York would have to wait because she wanted to stay close just in case Dana came out of the coma.

She scooped Tara up and they sat out in front of Penn Station waiting for Chill. When she saw Chill she had to do a double take. Chill's chubby build was now small. His clothes hung off of him and his face was covered with hair. He looked bad.

"Damn, man! What happened to you?" Cheetah asked, staring at Chill from the front seat.

"I told you times were hard. I got to build my money back up so I can get my shit right. Who's the shorty?" Chill asked, raising a chin towards Tara.

"None of your business, nigga. All you need to know is that she's off limits. Here, there's twenty bricks in here. Call me when you done and I'll meet you."

"Yo, that's what's up!" Chill said snatching the bag out of Cheetah's hand.

Cheetah thought she saw that fiend flicker through his eyes, but she couldn't be sure. For some reason she felt like she was doing the wrong thing. Chill got out the car without saying anything further. Cheetah just shrugged her shoulders and drove to the parking deck.

Cheetah and Tara caught the Path train to 34th Street. They were going shopping for some outfits to wear to the parade. They went to Century 21, Cheetah wound up spending two Gs. They bought matching Coogi outfits. Cheetah got the short set and Tara got the sundress.

When they got back to Jersey, Cheetah drove straight to the hospital. All the nurses were familiar with her face so they paid no mind when she walked in with Tara. This was Tara's first time seeing Dana since she'd been hospitalized. It brought tears to her eyes. She had only met Dana once before when Cheetah brought her some money. Dana usually looked like the average heroin addict Tara saw everyday, but lying in this hospital bed she looked like a monster. Her face was still swollen and bruised. She was bandaged all over her body.

Cheetah sat beside her and did what she did every time she came to see her. She talked to her and told her how much she loved and missed her and was waiting for her to get better. They stayed close to an hour before leaving.

Tara stayed the night with Cheetah. They made love again. Tara wanted to reciprocate the pleasure Cheetah had given her but she didn't know what to do or where to begin. They kissed, caressed, and fondled. Tara kissed Cheetah's breast and put hickies on her chest. She wanted to eat her pussy but was worried she'd do it wrong. Cheetah felt her hesitate and told her it was okay. She didn't have to do it. Cheetah could nut just by making love to Tara. That wasn't enough for Tara though. She wanted to bring Cheetah to ecstasy.

Sensing that her breast was her hot spot, Tara went back to them. Taking one into her mouth, she sucked on each nipple while using her free hand to play with her clit. She played with Cheetah's clit the way she did herself when she masturbated. In a few seconds Cheetah's pussy was soaking wet. She could feel Cheetah's pussy throbbing. She did this until Cheetah had an orgasm and called out her name.

"Damn Ma, that shit felt good as hell," Cheetah said as she pulled Tara up to her face. Tara stared into Cheetah's eyes.

"I wanna make love to you, baby," Tara said as she placed a small kiss on Cheetah's forehead.

"You just did, baby."

"No, baby, I want to taste you."

"Tara, I told you, I'm good. That shit ain't mandatory."

"I know it ain't, but I want to do it, so what's up? You gonna let me, or do I have to take it?" Tara asked with a devilish grin on her face.

"Shit, you don't have to take this, it's yours," Cheetah said as she grabbed her crotch like a dude. "You sure you can handle all this?"

"Girl bye with, that little ass thing you better hope I can find it," Tara joked as she slid down to Cheetah's pussy.

"Open it for me, baby."

Cheetah opened her pussy lips, and her clit popped out like a Jack-in-a-box. Tara bent foward and touched it with the tip of her tongue. Cheetah's body jerked a little. Tara held her by her thighs, and began licking her. Cheetah removed her hands, and grabbed Tara's face, guiding her to the spot.

"Right there, baby."

Tara focused on that spot as she sucked and licked. Cheetah held on to her tight, bucking her hips up and down.

"Do that shit, Ma. Right there, Tara."

Tara continued to make love to her. Cheetah's body began to shake as her orgasm neared.

"Oh shit, don't move…stay right…there." Cheetah clamped her legs and came all over Tara's face. Tara crawled up next to her in bed.

"Did I do it right baby?"

"You did your thing, baby…I loved it," Cheetah said as she pulled her closer. Tara laid her head on Cheetah's chest.

"I love you, too."

Cheetah couldn't believe that she had snagged Tara. She told herself at that moment that she would never let her go. She was going to shower her with so much love that Tara wouldn't want anyone else but her. They would base their relationship on trust, honesty, and commitment. It wouldn't be hard as long as they both remained loyal. Cheetah knew that Tara had only dealt with men prior to her so she told Tara that if she ever felt like falling back, to just let her know, instead of cheating. Cheetah was in love for the first time in her life and she felt great!

The four of them got up early the next morning. They dressed and caught the Path train to Washington Square Park in New York. Naj and Ja'nise had on matching colors. Naj had on a dark green Lacoste t-shirt with some dark denim Capri pants.

They got to New York at ten o'clock and the blocks were already packed. People walked around in their rainbow attire. Vendors lined the streets selling flags, bracelets and other rainbow accessories. All ages and colors came out to celebrate Gay Pride Day. Love was in the air.

Once the parade began, flower, balloon and confetti adorned floats crept the streets. Chics, one hundred deep, came by on motorcycles wearing only bikinis. Drag queens marched with feathers attached sparsely around their bodies. One float came by covered in rainbow colored flowers in the shape of a rainbow. Sylvester's "*You Are My Friend*" pumped out of the speakers. Six body buffed guys wearing nine strings vogued to the song. Cheetah loved to see the fags dance. She did her own little imitation of the Vogue by throwing both her hands in the air, waving them side to side, and walking on her tippy toes.

"Okay, Ms. Thing," Naj said, snapping her fingers in a zee patern. Ja'nise and Tara fell out laughing.

Once the parade ended, they found a spot under a tree in the park. Festivities continued all around them—musicians, male impersonators, magicians, and break dancers entertained the crowd.

As they lay on a blanket they'd brought with them two women approached.

"Is it okay if we squat right here?" the masculine looking one asked, pointing to the empty space beside them.

Naj looked towards Cheetah, and she shrugged her shoulders.

"Yeah, sure," Naj said.

The boyish one laid a blanket out and the more feminine one sat across it. She held a satchel style coach bag on her arm. She removed it and took out some sandwiches and bottled water. "Y'all thirsty? I got an extra bottle of Hypnotic in here and some Henny," the chick asked, holding up the bottles.

Tara reached for the bottles. "Thank you," she said. "Oh, by the way, I'm Tara. This is my wife Cheetah, and our best friends Naj and Ja'nise."

"I'm Nissan," said the feminine one. "And this is my love, Qua," touching Qua's shoulder.

"What up?" Qua said giving them all a head nod. Qua was medium built, stood at five-eight, and had a head full of waves. Nissan was drop dead gorgeous with a small petite frame, long silky hair, and very light skin.

"So y'all from New York?" Qua asked.

"Nah, we from Jersey," Naj answered.

"Real talk? So are we! I live in Montclair and Nissan lives in New Brunswick."

"Oh, that's what's up. We rest in Newark."

Cheetah opened the picnic basket Tara had packed and pulled out macaroni salad, fried chicken and assorted cheese. They all ate and talked until the sun began to set. Qua exchanged numbers with Cheetah and Naj before they went their separate way.

They had a good time and didn't make it home until the wee hours of the morning. Cheetah slept a few hours before leaving to see Dana. She felt bad because she didn't stop to see her yesterday before the parade. She brought some fresh flowers and went up to the ICU.

When she got to Dana's room, it was empty. No machines, no balloons, no flowers, and... NO DANA! Cheetah's heart dropped to her toes. She ran out the room to the nurses' station.

"Excuse me, could you tell me where Dana Johnson is? She was in Room 521."

The nurse looked through some of the files she had. "Yes, here she is. She was moved to the 3rd floor, room 331."

"Thank you," Cheetah said and found the nearest elevator.

When Cheetah got to the room and opened the door she almost jumped out of her skin! Dana was propped up in the bed sipping water out of a straw. Cheetah was so happy she ran to her and hugged her hard.

Dana winced.

"Ouch! You know I'm sore. I feel like I've been hit by a Mack truck."

Cheetah released her and kissed her on the cheek. She was so overjoyed that she didn't notice her mom and Esh in the room. Cheetah walked over to them and they told her that Dana had come out of the coma last night calling Cheetah's name.

Cheetah called Naj and told her to come to the hospital. She wanted to surprise her when she got there. Cheetah waited for her at the entrance, but she didn't let on that Dana was awake. She just led Naj to the room.

When they walked in, Dana looked at Naj and attempted what looked like a smile. This was the first time Cheetah saw Naj cry. She hugged Dana but not as hard as Cheetah had. They stayed with her until visiting hours were over. Cheetah promised Dana that she would be back in the morning.

Dana looked at her and said, "You also promised to take me to the Bahamas."

Cheetah stared at her, shocked! Had she really heard her?

"Yeah, I heard you!" Dana said. "And I want my shopping spree and hair and nails done! Lord knows I'm gonna need it. And, sis, one more thing before you leave, thanks for being here for me. I love you."

There were so many things Cheetah wanted to say to her sister but she was too choked up. She just blew her a kiss and left.

CHAPTER 8

Okay Let's Do This

Dana had been out of the hospital for a few weeks. She was in a rehabilation center learning how to walk again and strengthen her muscles. Once she recovered physically, she had to sign herself into a drug rehabilitation clinic. She now was taking it one day at a time.

Cheetah and Tara was an official couple. They spent as much time together as they could. Tara pretty much lived with Cheetah. When her brothers found out that she was fucking with a woman, they were mad as hell. Tara had walked in the door one day from school and both of her brothers were sitting in the living room waiting on her. Her oldest brother, Tyrique, owned a barber shop. The youngest of the two, Sakyi, was in his second year at law school. Tara walked into the living room, threw her pocketbook on her couch, and plopped down next to Sakyi.

"What up, bro?" She asked as she took the clip out of her ponytail and shook her hair loose.

"You tell us," Sakyi said, looking her in the eye. Tara could tell that something was on their minds by the looks on their faces.

"Uh, nothing much. Why? Should something be up?"

"That depends," Tyrique said as he rose up off the couch, "You wanna tell us about this girl you fucking with?"

Oh shit, how they know? Tara thought, but instead of saying that out loud, she responded, "What girl?"

"Oh, so now you wanna play dumb. Carla saw you kissin' some girl with dreads while you were at campus." Carla was Sakyi's girlfriend. She went to the same college as Tara.

"Carla needs to mind her mothafucking business," Tara spat as she got up off the couch. "Yeah, I'm with a girl and I love her. What's the problem?"

"What's the problem? I know fucking well you not asking me what the fucking problem is! All of a sudden you a lesbian, Tara?" Tyrique yelled. It was clear to see that he and Sakyi didn't approve.

It was too late though. Tara had fallen in love with Cheetah and wasn't about to stop seeing her to appease her brothers.

"Ty, you just upset because I don't wanna be with none of your cornball ass friends. And Kyi, I don't know what's wrong with you, as much as you hang around Ra'fio and his gay ass."

"That's different, Tara. Me and Ra'fio grew up together. He's my dude regardless of his sexual preference, but you sleeping with another chick! What you think mom and dad would have to say about this?" Sakyi asked.

Tara blew out a long puff of air to release some of the anger that was building up inside of her. She looked at both of her brothers standing there trying to act like their father. She couldn't help but let out a soft chuckle.

"Look y'all, I'm good. I love her, and I'm not leaving her. It is what it is, and if that's going to be a problem, let me know and I'll bounce."

"Well, she can't come up in here," Tyrique responded.

"No problem. I'll go to her," Tara said as she walked to her bedroom and began to pack her clothes.

They tried to talk her out of it but Tara wasn't having it. She went and stayed with Cheetah for two weeks before her brothers accepted the fact that she was serious.

Cheetah and Naj's clientele was up! Business was booming.

They were caking all over town. They not only had Avon Avenue, they had Spruce Street under their wing too. Their empire was spreading. Cheetah smoked gank every once in a while, but only on days she knew she wasn't going to see Tara. She went out on an occasional stick up. She didn't hit the niggas in Newark though. She went to East Orange and Irvington, and caught a couple of suckas sleeping, and now had a whole shoebox full of jewelry. She bought a brand new .44 because she had to bury the gun she used to kill the twins in a vacant lot a couple of blocks away.

Qua and Nissan had somehow slid their way into Cheetah's circle. They would meet up at the Club Armory on Saturdays when it was all women's night. They went out to eat together every other Friday night and even spent a weekend on Fire Island, the gay and lesbian beach in Sayville, Long Island.

Cheetah enjoyed Qua and Nissan's company. They made a good couple, because they both were such head turners, but Nissan's life had gone from sugar to shit. Her mother's bills were backed up. Her brother was off the hook, one felony away from doing life in prison. She needed money and she needed it fast.

Nissan was determined to give her mother a better life and protect her brother from falling victim to the streets. Cheetah knew the situation all too well. The only way Cheetah knew to help Nissan make a lot of money fast was the streets. Nissan was leery at first. Being in direct contact with drugs turned her stomach.

What Cheetah didn't know was that Nissan used to be hooked on drugs bad. It was a time when all that mattered to her was where she was going to get her next hit. She'd stay up for days getting high, neglecting her mom, and paying absolutely no attention to her brother. If it wasn't for Qua she would probably still be running the streets using.

She met Qua at a Seton Hall University versus Rutgers University basketball game. At the time, she'd been enrolled at Rutgers, trying to get a degree in sociology. Qua was attending Seton Hall, studying for an accountant degree.

Nissan had just broken up with her boyfriend Sky. He was the one who introduced her to the heroin. He dealt it and fed it to her everyday. When he caught a three and a half year bid, Nissan was lost. She stayed in school as long as she could. Once the drugs took control, she dropped out, but not before meeting Qua, who helped her get clean.

Right now she was in need, so she had to overcome her past and get on her grind.

Nissan took the drugs to New Brunswick and got a few of the boys she went to school with to hustle for her. She gave her younger brother the job of collecting the money and paid him weekly. She would not allow him to sell. She told him if she caught him hustling she wasn't going to do nothing else for him.

It wasn't long before Nissan's name was ringing bells in town. She didn't sell ten or twenty dollar bags. She only sold by weight. An ounce or more was the only way her boys dealt with people. In less than a month, she was able to move herself, mom, and brother into a three-bedroom, ranch-style house in Hillside.

Qua stayed with her occasionally. She still had her garage apartment behind her parent's house. She was usually too busy with schoolwork, so the weekends were the only time Qua and Nissan really had to relax with each other. They made the most of it.

Qua disagreed at first with Nissan getting involved in the drug game but times were hard. The money her parent's gave her and the money Nissan made at her job barely got the bills paid. In nine months, she would be graduating and then she would be able to get out of the ghetto.

One day, Cheetah and her girls were sitting in 17th Street Park watching the kids on the playground when Scabs walked up to them. He looked a mess! His nose was running and he was dirty. He told Naj and Cheetah he needed to speak to them for a minute. When they walked away from the others, Scab started running his mouth.

"Listen, Naj, remember what you asked me a few months back? About the robbery? Well, I got wind of who it was. Three niggas from Stratford Avenue were bragging about it. I was out hustling with them the other night, and one of them had on a real nice pinkie ring. I asked him where he got it from, and he was so high that he started running his mouth. He told me how he and his boys had jacked this bitch for one hundred bricks and took her jewelry. They had to be talking about you, Cheetah."

"Yo, what's the cat's name?" Naj asked.

"Well, the one with the ring is Slick. The other two are Fats and Jo-Jo. They hustle on Stratford everyday."

"They down with the 52 Boys?" Cheetah asked.

"Nah, Slick's older brother is though. His name is JT but he lives out in Irvington."

"Aight, yo. Let me check this out," Naj told Scabs. "I'll get back at you. Here take my cell number and call me in three days okay?"

Naj gave Scabs the number and twenty dollars. She and Cheetah walked back to the others.

"Baby, who was that?" Tara asked Cheetah.

Cheetah explained the whole situation to them. She told them the names of the dudes and Qua said she knew who Slick was.

"That's my cousin Sha-Sha's baby daddy. She can't stand that nigga. He grimey as hell and used to beat on her. Don't do shit for their son at all."

"Word?" Cheetah asked. "You think she could find out about this for me?"

"Yeah, I'll call her right now and see what she says."

Qua called her cousin and Sha-Sha told her to give her two days and she'd have all the information she needed.

The next two days, that was all Cheetah could think about. She couldn't rest until she knew for sho if these were the niggas or not. She got the call from Qua early on the third morning.

"Yo, Cheetah, that's them niggas. My cousin told the same story that fiend told you. Whatever you want to do just let me know and I'm with you, aight?"

"Aight, Qua. Thanks, dawg!"

Cheetah and Naj met Scabs back at the park. Staying true to her word, Naj hit Scabs off with a thousand dollars for the information he gave them. Scabs told them he would be their personal eyes and ears. He promised that if he heard anything else he would holla at them.

That night, the four of them met at Nissan's house. Cheetah wanted revenge!

They all sat down together trying to figure out a way to get at these niggas. Qua told them that she knew her cousin used to make pickups for Slick all the time. The nigga was making a few dollars. He never copped under a kilo of cocaine. Qua thought that maybe she could get Sha-Sha to find out who was picking up their drugs for them.

Qua called Sha-Sha again and she said she'll do anything to bring that dude down. She needed a few weeks to get her shit together.

Sha-Sha was 'bout it and more than willing to make Slick feel it. She told that nigga that she would get some get back sooner or later for beating her and abandoning her and their four-year-old son. She met Slick at her best friend, Sa'mone's house.

Sa'mone was throwing a barbeque and Slick, Jo-Jo, and Fats had rolled through on some baller type shit. Slick was not a pretty nigga, but his money was long, so whatever he lacked in the looks department his *gwap* made up for it. Sha-Sha smelled his money as soon as he stepped in the backyard. His platinum and diamond chain gleamed like stars at night.

Sha-Sha knew before the night was over that she was going to fuck him and dry his pockets out. What had started out as a one night stand had turned into a rocky two-year relationship. Sha-Sha eventually got pregnant and Slick denied their son.

Sha-Sha loved to fuck and Slick knew it. He was not about to claim the boy and he wasn't going to take a DNA test. Sha-Sha knew her son belonged to Slick. She started stealing from him, and he whooped her ass. The last fight landed her in the hospital with six stitches in her lip, two black eyes, and a three-inch gash in her head. Sha-Sha vowed she would eventually get him back, and now was time. *Payback is a Mutha!* Just like the saying goes, "Revenge is the sweetest thing next to getting pussy."

Dana was finally coming home after a ninety-day stint in rehab. Cheetah couldn't wait to see her. She was in a rehab in Princeton so Cheetah and Tara rode down the night before. They rented a hotel room, watched a movie and ordered pizza. Exhausted, they fell asleep before the previews finished.

Dana was up and ready by the time Cheetah got there. She had gained forty pounds in the first six weeks she'd been there. She was clean, sober, and healthy. Cheetah had paid for her to get false teeth implants, her hair had grown down to her shoulders, and the marks on her arms were barely visible. Dana walked out of the rehab looking and feeling like a new woman. Cheetah was so happy to see her sister that she ran and picked her up, swinging her around.

Cheetah took Tara and Dana to the mall and let them do their thing. They got mani's and pedi's, hit up a few stores and had lunch. By the time they were finished, Cheetah was out of seven stacks. Tara had bought three pairs of Coach Shoes and a matching bag. Dana bought four outfits from Macy's, two from DKNY, and two from BeBe. She went to Foot Locker and brought three pairs of sneakers, and two pairs of shoes out of Wild Pair. They both bought earrings. Dana also nabbed a bracelet with dolphins and a matching necklace. The whole time they were at the mall, Esh was blowing Cheetah's phone up.

"Dana, your daughter keeps calling me. Let me get you over there before she loses her damn mind."

Dana was ready to see her grandkids. She hadn't seen the youngest one since she was born. Esh lived with three small kids on the East Side in a small, two-bedroom apartment. Her oldest was only four. The state had agreed to pay up to twelve hundred a month for a house for her and the kids, but Esh was too trifling to get up and go look for a new place.

Cheetah had offered to move her out on many occasions. She hated going over there. Toys, clothes, and dirty dishes were all over the apartment. The kitchen cabinets were falling off the hinges, the sink leaked, and there were roaches, but the way Esh and her kids dressed, they didn't look broke.

She kept them dressed in the latest hood apparel, thanks to her ex-sugar daddy, who she had tricked into thinking her middle son Nu-Nu was his. Every time he acted like he wasn't going to give her any money, she threatened to tell his wife, and expose him. His fear of losing his wife was enough that he gave Esh something everytime he got paid. He took them shopping, filled up the refrigerator, and gave her a couple of dollars.

When they pulled up to the apartment, Esh and the kids were waiting outside. They all piled up in the truck and Cheetah took them to TGI Friday's. Dana was overwhelmed when she saw her grandkids. All of them had changed practically over-night. She didn't know them, and they barely knew her. When they got back to Esh's house Dana decided to stay with her.

"Cheetah, I'm gonna stay here with Esh and help her out. I'll come out there tomorrow and meet you at Mommy's house, okay?"

"Aight, sis. You know I love you right?" Cheetah said, giving her a hug. "We all love you. Just remember, one day at a time. If you even feel like you want to use, just call me and I'll come get you. I got faith in you."

Cheetah kissed the kids, gave Esh and Dana some money and left.

Once they got into Newark, they stopped at White Castle to get some chicken rings and fries. Tara wanted to go through the drive-thru, but Cheetah liked to go inside to watch them put her food together. She hated onions, and she wanted to make sure they wiped the excess onions off the grill before putting her burgers on it. When they walked in, she spotted Ra'dee and his baby's mother, Michelle, in the other line. She walked up behind him.

"Damn, you can always find a greedy nigga like you in the fast food joints, huh?"

Ra'dee turned around and smiled.

"Oh, yo, what's up, boss lady?" he asked.

"Nothing much, just got the crave, feel me?"

"Yeah, I know what you mean. I'm gonna eat about fifteen of the double cheeseburgers and shit the rest of the damn night!"

They both laughed. After they finished ordering and got their tickets, they walked over by the tables to wait for their food. While Ra'dee and Cheetah spoke in a hushed tone, Tara and Michelle sat at the table. Two rowdy ass young boys walked in, obviously drunk. They ordered and went to sit in the booth next to the girls. Both Tara and Michelle got up and walked over to Cheetah and Ra'dee. Tara put her arms around Cheetah, and the bigger one of the two boys said something.

"Damn, Ma, you doing it likes that?"

Tara ignored him and held Cheetah tighter.

"Why don't you come back over here next to a real man and stop fronting," he said.

"Yeah, let us teach you how to stunt," said the other one.

Cheetah was about to say something when Ra'dee noticed what was going on. He spoke up.

"You talking to us, partner?"

"Nah, not you brotha, just those pussy eating hoes".

"Well, if you talking to the two young ladies right here, then you're talking to me."

The bigger of the two boys stood up and started walking towards Ra'dee. Michelle tried to pull Ra'dee the other way but he jerked his arm away from her. The boy was only three steps away when Ra'dee pulled out his .38 special. The other boy stood up and Cheetah pulled out her gun. They held them down by their sides not pointing towards anyone. A couple of other customers noticed what was going on and started leaving the fast food place.

Cheetah told Tara to go to the car, but she wouldn't budge.

Both boys stopped in their tracks. Ra'dee stared at one and Cheetah locked eyes with the other one.

"So, like I said before, you're talking to us?" Ra'dee asked.

Neither one of the boys moved. They were mad that they and let this nigga and bitch hoe them, but they weren't strapped and didn't want to see if Ra'dee was 'bout it. They backed slowly out the door and left.

Cheetah thanked Ra'dee for having her back.

"You know it's whatever, whenever, and whoever can get it!"
Cheetah gave Ra'dee dap. "Fo' sho. I love you, dawg."

"One."

Cheetah lost her appetite. When she and Tara got to the
house they went straight to her room.

"Tara, you think you can go out of town for a couple of
weeks?" asked Cheetah.

As if knowing the surprise, Tara started to grin, "Yeah, why?"

Cheetah tried to down play the mood, "Oh, 'cause I was
thinking about taking you to the Bahamas."

"What!" Tara screamed, jumping up and down. She had
always wanted to go to the island, but never had enough money
for it. Cheetah kissed Tara's face.

"Oh, Cheetah, baby, do you mean it? Are we going?
When?"

"Yo, slow down. You asking me a million questions at one
time," Cheetah said, grabbing her by the waist. "I want to leave
this coming weekend. Can you get out of school?"

"Yes, baby! I can get out of school."

"Okay, then do that and we good. Tomorrow, we'll go make
all the necessary arrangements."

"I love you, Cheetah," Tara said as she kissed her forehead.

"I love you too, baby girl."

The next day, Cheetah and Tara woke up early and went out to
breakfast at a local diner that was close to a travel agency. Cheetah
wanted to take her entire family on the trip. She asked Tara how she
felt about the idea. Tara was cool with it. They went to the agency
and purchased a family package for seventy-five hundred. They
would spend seven days and six nights in the Bahamas.

Afterwards they went to Esh's house to tell her and Dana.
When Cheetah told them she was taking them to the Bahamas
they jumped all around the room yelling and dancing, doing
everything from the running man to the cabbage patch. They
could be so silly at times.

Cheetah felt good. Her family was tight and she was in love. If only she was stable enough to get out of the game, shit would be great, but she wasn't yet. She still had mad paper she wanted to stack. She has been on the streets for years and should have been out by now but fate was against her. Cheetah wanted to hit a mil' and then she could get out of the game.

Next, she went to her mother's house. It wasn't easy convincing her mom to go on the trip. It took a lot of talking on Cheetah's end. Mrs. Johnson complained about being too old and missing church. Cheetah assured her that she was still a young lady and that they had churches all over the world. Besides, God would probably want her to get out of the ghetto, even if it was only for a week.

After a few minutes of debating, Mrs. Johnson finally gave in. It was a good damn thing too because Cheetah wasn't going to take no for an answer.

The next day, Cheetah took them all shopping. She took the kids to Foot Locker and grabbed them three pairs of shoes. Dana, Tara, and Esh tore the avenue up, getting all kinds of swimsuits, outfits and bags. Tara and Esh both brought five pairs of sandals. Tara also bought ten swimsuits alone!

"Where your clothes at?" Cheetah asked.

"I don't need any for when I'm not on the beach," she flirted.

After shopping for hours, they headed back to Newark. Cheetah dropped Dana and Esh off on the way, and took her mom and Tara home. When she hit Brick City she called Qua.

"Yo, what's shitting?" Cheetah asked.

"I'm good, where you at?" Qua replied.

"I'm coming up Central Ave. I'm going to stop at Coopers and get me a sandwich. Meet me?"

"Yeah, I'll be there in twenty."

"Aight, one."

Cheetah hung up and pulled up in Coopers' parking lot. Cooper's was the local sandwich shop. They sold the biggest mothafuckin sandwiches you could get. If you were low on ends,

111

all you had to do was buy a loaf of bread and a Coopers' sandwich and could feed a family of six.

Cheetah ordered a turkey and roast beef sandwich with Swiss cheese on a wheat roll and a V8 drink, and then sat in her truck to wait on Qua.

Qua had been leaving messages with Cheetah to get at her. It sounded serious. Cheetah had no idea what she wanted to talk about and she wasn't going to beat herself in the head trying to figure it out. She'd find out soon enough. She picked up her sandwich, took a bite, and then turned the radio to 98.7 KISS FM.

Qua pulled into the lot a couple of minutes later. She drove a white Lexus jeep. Her parents had dough and spoiled the hell out of her. All she had to do was stay in school and get that degree and she was set, but she had thug running in her blood. She was smart as a nerd, but she thrived off of the street life. Just looking at her you wouldn't believe that she was raised in corny ass Montclair. She had ghetto thug written all over her face.

She parked next to Cheetah's truck and got out. She had on a white velour Sean John sweat suit and some Nike ACG boots. She had a fresh haircut with a shape up so tight it looked like somebody drew it on with a ruler. When she got in the truck, Cheetah could smell Kenneth Cole's Black cologne on her.

Out of the three of them, Qua looked the most masculine. She kept a close cut and she was built like a body builder. One time they all had gone out to eat, and when Qua got up to go to the bathroom, the manager pointed her towards the men's room. After reading the signs on the door she went in the lady's room, and two old ladies washing their hands at the sink had looked at her in disgust. They left the bathroom and got the manager.

When Qua came out the manager was waiting on her. They had words until Qua lifted her shirt to show him her breasts concealed in a Polo sports bra. The manager was both angry and embarrassed. He apologized profusely and hurried away.

"What up dawg?" Qua said holding her fist out for a pound.

"Product prices and skirts, dawg," Cheetah replied tapping her fist on Qua's.

"Sho' you right."

"So," Cheetah said seriously, "what's the sitcho? Why you in such a frenzy to holla at me?"

"Yo, man, I just got back from upstate New York, Westchester County. I got some family up there in a small town called Mamaroneck. My cousin hustles out there. And yo, and its mad money out there! But it ain't no Big Ballers there, feel me? Everybody goes to the city to cop a few ounces to flip." Qua stopped and stared at Cheetah.

"Okay, aaaaaand?" Cheetah asked, waiting on the rest.

"And, I wanna get in. Let me put some product out there, son. They charge twenty dollars for what's a five dollar bottle of base out here. Man, that's the melting pot right there. Let me get in."

"How you figure on doing this Qua?" Cheetah asked seriously. "You got school work to worry about and you live out here. So how you gonna manage that?"

"Man, I'm not gonna do the hand to hand combat. I'm gonna put my cousin down with the weight. Let him supply these busters. He got the clientele already. I'll pay him and he'll help me get paid. I just need you to put me on, that's all."

"You sure, Qua? Come on, all you gotta do is this last year and you basically got found money. Shit, you gonna be an accountant, man. You can go over there to Wall Street and get at least fifty an hour! You wanna risk that?"

Qua knew Cheetah was going to try to talk her out of the plan, but she was dead set on getting paid like the rest of them. Shit, even Nissan was caking. Why the fuck shouldn't she get a piece of the pie? Wasn't no money like drug money.

"Yeah, I'm sure. I want to do it. Man, if I could get enough dough before I graduate, then I won't have to put in the footwork on a nine to five gig. I could just open up my own firm and shit. So what's good? You gonna hook a nigga up or what?"

Cheetah had the cheddar to put Qua on board. She just didn't want her getting caught up in the game. She already had her life mapped out. Qua was grown and that was her dawg. So if she wanted to get down, of course Cheetah would help her.

"Yeah, I got you. I'm going away in a couple of days. I'll get you a key of raw coke from my connect, and you just give me back what I put out. That should be enough to get it popping out there. Just do me a favor, okay? Promise me you won't make any sales yourself, okay? No matter what the price! That way the DEA won't be able to get at you if anything went down. Keep where you're from low key. Besides your family, don't nobody else have to know all right? You my dawg and I wanna see you get that paper. I'm talking about that degree, all right?"

"Yeah, son, I got you. Thanks, man."

"You don't gotta thank me. You my peeps. You know what they say, birds of a feather-"

"Flock together!" Qua finished. "I'm out man. I gotta hook up with Nissan. Be easy. Love is love."

"Fo' sho."

Cheetah went home from there and called Papi. She needed a couple of them thangs. She had to make sure Nissan was also straight before she bounced to the Bahamas.

Papi was that nigga! He was multi supplied. He had every drug and type of gun you would want or need. He was always coming out with some new type of firearm. He had taken a strong liking to Cheetah. He admired her drive and thugness. She was consistent in her purchases and never came at him with any sob ass stories, trying to get something on consignment.

When he heard about her getting jacked, he'd been willing to put her back on her feet. She never called him though. When he did hear from her she was ready to spend like she never took a loss. Yeah, she was a true baller.

Cheetah put in an order for two keys. She thought about getting some bricks, but she wanted to collect that money from Chill first. She hadn't heard from him yet, but she wasn't pressed though. Once he got his hustle on, she was sure he would call. If he got done while she was away, then Naj could handle the re-up. He was her partner in crime.

Cheetah would much rather get her own hands dirty. Naj had a family to take care of. Those kids looked up to Naj as a father figure, even though she was a woman. She took care of home like the 'man' of the house. She sometimes even referred to herself as a grown ass man.

MISSY JACKSON

CHAPTER 9

Ain't This Some Shit!

hill was having the time of his life. He was out in Harrison selling more than a little heroin. He bought some new clothes and got a fresh haircut. He sent his girl in Newark some money, for his son. He knew he couldn't go back to Newark unless the cat he robbed got locked up or killed. He had actually shanked a few other niggas from Bradley Court for their shit, so he was a marked man. Even in Harrison, he was paranoid as hell. He setup a house connection with this white chick that was shooting up dope. He paid her a bundle of dope and fifty dollars a day to hustle out of her basement. The arrangement was sweet.

The bitch had a shit load of friends that shot the shit. All of 'em white and all of 'em rich as shit. They came to buy dope, then would go in one of the spare rooms upstairs and shoot up.

Chill couldn't stand to see anyone put a needle in their arm. Something about that shit made his stomach queasy as hell. When he came to the house to hustle he stayed in the basement until he was ready to leave.

This particular night Chill was sitting in the basement looking at some pictures on the Internet. They had this website called *rotten.com* that had the craziest shit on it. You saw everything from someone shitting in someone else's mouth, to self-inflicted gunshot wounds, to people getting ran over by trains. The shit was nasty! But Chill was hooked. Everyday they showed a rotten of the day photo.

Today's photo was of a black man who weighed six hundred pounds. He died in his house in Florida. It was over 110 degrees inside the room he was in, and no one found his body for two weeks. He had swelled to double his size and was actually cooking like a fucking ball park frank!

Shirley, the white chick who owned the house, snuck up on him. She put her hand on Chill's shoulder. He jumped and pulled out his .38. He had it pointed straight at the bitch's head.

"Fuck you doin' walking up on me like that?"

"Damn, Chill. I just thought you might be lonely down here. I came to keep you company."

Shirley was one of those spoiled, rich bitches. Her father owned a Lexus dealership on Route 1&9. The bitch didn't work or go to school. She just sat in the house all day shooting dope. As far as a white bitch goes, she was aight. She had long blonde hair and greenish-blue eyes. She was about five-three and weighed no more than 120 pounds. She had white even teeth and full lips. Angelina Jolie type lips. When she shot that dope, the bitch got as horny as a dog. Chill had tricked off with her on many occasions. She sucked a mean dick. From the look in her eyes, Chill could tell she was in the mood for a *fudgecicle* to suck on.

"Damn, Shirley. You almost got your ass shot the fuck up. Why you keep sneaking up on me like that?"

"I'm sorry if I scared you, Daddy. I didn't mean to," she said seductively.

"Aight, what's good? What you need?"

"Nothing, just wanted to make sure you're alright," she replied, sliding her hand down Chill's stomach resting on his crotch. She stroked his crotch, and his dick began to grow.

"I'm good," Chill said. "But a nigga could always be doing better, nah mean?"

"Yes, Chill baby. I know what you mean."

Shirley undid Chill's belt buckle and unzipped his pants. She pulled them down to his hips and unleashed his dick. Chill was no big, muscular nigga. He was physically small, as far as a man was concerned, but what he lacked in body size, he made up for with his dick. His dick was unnatural: eleven inches long and fat like a polish sausage. And he had the nerve to love getting head. He tricked off with any bitch that was willing to let him ram that pipe in her mouth. Not too many could deep throat the nigga without gagging. He has been known to cause a few bitches to throw up. The only bitch who was able to handle him was his baby mamma. She had a hole the size of the Grand Canyon.

Shirley was a pro when it came to sucking dick. Something she did with those lips made Chill come in a matter of minutes. He never fucked her though. He had a thing about IV users. He was paranoid of catching AIDS. So the furthest they got was some dick in the mouth. Shirley was getting into position when Chill stopped her.

"Hold up, Ma, you know how I like to be when you do this shit. Let me get right."

Chill reached over on the table where he had a couple of bundles of dope sitting. He took a bag opened it and Scar Faced it, sniffing it all at one time. He held his head back and let the heroin go down his nose. Sticking his fingers in a cup of water on the table, he let the water drip off his fingers and into his nose. When he tasted the heroin going down his throat he got out his Newport and lit it up. His dick was now rock hard and throbbing. He stayed with his head leaned back and motioned for Shirley to continue.

When he felt the warmth of her mouth on his dick, he grabbed her hair in a bunch at the back of her neck and shoved her head down further. Without hesitation, she opened her mouth wider and sucked him down whole. Not once did she gag or scrape her teeth on his shit.

She sucked his dick until it felt like the skin was coming off. Chill held the lit cigarette in one hand and still had the other on Shirley's head. He felt the stirring of a nut coming on. He put the cigarette in the ashtray and used both hands to hold Shirley. He pushed his dick in and out of her mouth as if he was in the pussy. Shirley held onto his ass and when he began to shake and twitch she tightened her lips on the tip of his dick and swallowed every last bit of cum he shot out.

Chill pulled his dick out of her mouth and wiped it on her shirt. He pulled up his pants and handed her two bags off the table. Just as quietly as she approached, she left.

Chill sat back in the chair and lit another cigarette. For a moment he thought his playa days were over. Fucking around with those hoes, he felt his gangsta slipping. One bitch he met at the strip club introduced him to the feeling of a blow job while being high off of heroin. He enjoyed the high so much it didn't take but a few weeks for him to get strung out. Before he knew it, his bankroll was gone.

He started stealing stashes or whatever else he could get his hands on to support his habit. When he stuck up the cat on Ellis Avenue, he knew he had to get out of town. They knew he was from Montgomery Street and they were not the type to let shit ride. It wasn't until one day he was in the diner with the twins trying to get some credit that he got his opportunity of a lifetime. He saw the twins lead Cheetah to the Auto Body Shop. He saw Naj leave out with her sister, and he heard the shots. It didn't lake a genius to put together what went down.

Fuck that dyke ass bitch Cheetah, he thought.

He wasn't giving her shit off of these twenty bricks. Once he got finished he was going to go to New York and re-up on his own. Now that he had a steady place to hustle out of and he was supplying these rich ass crackers he thought he would be able to come up quick.

Chill had just clicked back onto the website when he heard a familiar pounding coming from upstairs. He knew someone was trying to get in the front door and no one pounded on the door like that except the narcos.

He gathered all his belongings and ran for the window. When he saw the bars on the window he almost pissed on himself. That was the only way out of the basement. He still had four bricks of dope on him and close to seven thousand in cash.

He was headed to the water boiler to throw the dope in it when two officers rushed him. They threw him to the floor and handcuffed him. Upstairs, Shirley and three of her friends were also handcuffed and being led out of the house. Chill couldn't believe this shit. Just when he was about to come up.

This shit! What the fuck!?

MISSY JACKSON

CHAPTER 10

Bahamas Up!

The day before they were scheduled to catch the plane, Cheetah called and made reservations for the airport transportation to pick them up at eight in the morning. She picked everyone up with their belongings and they all went to stay at her mom's house. Mrs. Johnson cooked fried chicken, corn on the cob, baked macaroni and cheese, and cornbread. They all sat down and ate together. After the meal was over, Dana, Esh and Tara went into the living room and watched a video with the children.

Cheetah stayed behind in the kitchen to help her mom clean up. Underneath the thug exterior, she was a crème puff. She was such a good girl. Mrs. Johnson didn't know where she went wrong in raising her. She was so much like her father that it sickened Mrs. Johnson at times.

Their father, Julius Johnson, had been a notorious man when he was alive. He sold drugs most of his life. Anything there was to be done in the streets to get money, he did it. He sold clothes, drugs, gambled and did hits. He was a good family man though. He always brought the money home and not one time in the entire fifteen years they were together, did he stay out all night. He came home every night for dinner, and if he went back out to handle his business, he was back home by twelve am.

One night he didn't show up for dinner and Mrs. Johnson instantly began to worry. After making sure Dana was safely in bed, Mrs. Johnson went out to look for him. When she drove up to Prince Street Projects, she saw the crime scene tape and knew that her husband was dead. He had been stabbed to death by a guy he was playing dice with. He died over a fifty dollar roll. Mrs. Johnson was six months pregnant with Cheetah. Looking at Cheetah, she saw her husband all over again.

"Stink, baby, I admire the way you take care of us but how long you think you're going to last in those streets? You're lucky you haven't gotten locked up or killed by now. I pray every night that you'll give up that gangsta life. Do you wanna end up like your daddy? Look how close to death your sister came. Please, think about what I'm saying to you, Stink. I'd rather die first than see any of y'all go before me."

Cheetah knew what her mom was saying was the truth. She did have a long stretch in those streets, but she couldn't pull out now. She just wasn't where she needed to be financially. She wanted to buy a house for herself, her mom and her sister and niece. She wanted to open a Laundromat and put some college funds up for the kids. She figured in six months she could give it all up. Yeah, six months and she should be straight.

"Mom," Cheetah said, "I got a plan. I won't be out there too much longer. A few more months and we'll all be straight. I'm gonna buy you a house."

"No, no you won't be buying me a house. I can't serve the Lord living in a house that the devil's money bought. I'm fine just where I'm at. Its bad enough I take the money you give to me, but Lord knows if I didn't need it, I wouldn't. I'm definitely not going to sign my name on Satan's lease."

Cheetah kind of figured her mother would react like that. She knew she couldn't change her mind so she just hugged her and said, "Soon. I'm going to give it all up real soon."

The trip to the Bahamas went smoothly. They made it on time for their flight and nobody hijacked the plane. Cheetah was paranoid as hell about terrorists. You couldn't get on a plane with an Arab and not think about 9/11. She had been shopping in New York the day before the attacks. She couldn't believe it when she saw the news the next morning. The sight of the towers collapsing was something Cheetah would never be able to forget.

During the flight she had a few drinks and watched a movie. Everyone else had fallen asleep. She woke them up just before the plane landed. She wanted them to see the view. It was beautiful.

After exiting from the plane, they claimed their baggage. From there they checked into the Atlantis, a beautiful resort, and immediately hit the island. Cheetah had never seen anyplace as beautiful as this. The brochures did no justice to the actual island. The beaches had white sand and crystal clear water that allowed you to see the tropical fish as if you were looking in an aquarium.

They rented motor scooters and drove around while Mrs. Johnson and the kids played on the beach. Cheetah was as happy as a fag in prison. She left no part of the island unexplored. That first night, they hit the clubs. The music was different from home, mostly techno club, but nonetheless, they partied like it was 1999!

That whole week was wonderful. They went sightseeing, boating, gambling in the casinos where Tara hit for seven thousand. Tara took Cheetah out to a romantic dinner in the hotel's five star restaurant. The table sat near a window that overlooked the beach. One candle sat in the middle of the table as a soft jazz saxophone soloist played near the paino. Cheetah ordered a bottle of the house wine along with filet mignon and shrimp. Tara ordered a porterhouse steak and a baked potatoe. The waiter brought the wine in a bucket of ice and hot steaming breadsticks covered with butter and garlic sauce. Cheetah popped the cork on the wine and filled their glasses.

"Let's toast," Cheetah said, raising her glass.

"Toast? What your ghetto ass know about toasting?" Tara asked as she raised her glass to meet Cheetah's.

"There's a lot I know. Shit, I may be able to teach your proper ass something."

"Oh yeah, well whenever you're ready, I'm ready," Tara said seductively. They touched glasses together, and sipped their wine. Cheetah placed her glass on the table and covered Tara's hand with hers.

"Baby, you know I love you, right?"

"Yes Cheetah, I know."

"Ma, listen…this lifestyle I'm leading in the drug game ain't gonna last too much longer. I'm just trying to stack my chips and fall back. I'm almost where I need to be. A few more months, maybe a little more and I'm done. We gon' take another vacation, just you and me, come back, and settle the fuck down. Maybe we'll fuck around and adopt some kids and shit. Whatever happens, I want it to happen with you in my life, baby."

Tara squeezed Cheetah's hand. "Boo, I'm not going anywhere. I'm wit' you till the end. Just promise me you won't get greedy and forget about all you just said to me."

"I won't, baby, I promise." Cheetah leaned over the table and kissed her. Tara wrapped her arms around her neck, and they enjoyed a long, wet, luscious kiss. The waiter arrived with their food, and had to clear his throat to be noticed. They separated and enjoyed their meal.

Cheetah sent everyone back home postcards. She filled her digital camera with photos from all over the island. Mrs. Johnson mainly stayed on the beachand she enjoyed herself immensely. She had a glow on her face that only fresh air and relaxation can give. In no time at all the week was over. As they packed to leave, Cheetah promised them all another trip next year.

CHAPTER 11

Everyday I'm Hustling

Qua didn't waste no time getting the product out on the streets. She called her cousin, Jimmy and let him know she was straight. That same night, Cheetah gave her the kilo and she drove upstate. Jimmy was waiting on her with a couple of his closest comrades. They spent the next twelve hours bagging the key up.

Jimmy had a glass coffee table in his living room. On it was three scales, a box of razors and ten boxes of Glad sandwich bags. He had gotten a black tarp and covered the entire living room floor.

They bagged up twenty, fifty, and hundred dollar bags of raw cocaine. Mike-Mike, the chemist, cooked up a quarter of the key and they bagged up nickels, dimes, and twenties of base. The rest of the key was bagged up. It would be sold as weight only.

Qua took two days off of school just to stay around and see how the product would sell. Besides helping with the bagging up she didn't touch the product anymore. The only reason she did that was to have an idea of how much product went into bagging up. Jimmy distributed packages amongst his homeboys and between the four of them, they got the cheddar flowing.

They gave out samples to the first twenty people that came to cop. It didn't take long before everyone was lined up to buy the new shit on the block. When it came to hustling, Jimmy was very efficient and business minded. He took no shorts and no shit.

For the next two days, Qua watched everything, from how the money was divided, to how much traffic was on the block. The fiends came with anything they could get their hands on to exchange for drugs. They would have sold their soul if they could.

Qua had never been this involved or close up to the game. Besides going to cop a couple of bags of hydro for the white boys at school she had never even touched drugs. She watched Jimmy over the years whenever she would go upstate to visit but she never joined in the hustle. She was both surprised and astounded at the hold crack had on a fiend. They came all hours of the night for a fix. Even after shop was closed, they would attempt to knock on the door or throw rocks at the window to get one more hit to quiet the beast inside of them.

Qua felt sorry for the numerous young women and men she saw fall victim to crack. She knew that in this game you couldn't be sensitive to the next man. It was about getting paid and getting out, that's it. She was definitely getting paid. The money was flowing like piss. In those two days, they had pulled in close to twenty thousand and they still had seventy five percent of the product left. At this rate, she could clear eighty thousand off of each key. Now that's what the fuck she was talking about! Drug money was the mothafuckin' found money!

Qua was satisfied in the way things were being handled. She had to get back to school. Two days was enough for her. She and Jimmy agreed on a seventy/thirty split. He would get 30 percent off of whatever was made.

For the first week, twenty thousand was good to him. It was more than enough to pay workers. Qua figured that once she hit Cheetah off for the work, she would still be looking at forty thousand. If she could continue to make eighty thousand a week, she wouldn't have to wait for Wall Street to get rich.

CHAPTER 12

This Shouldn't Be Hard At All

As soon as Cheetah touched down in Newark she called Naj. She had to let her know she made it back safely and she would be home soon. She dropped everyone off at their respective homes except for Tara. Before dropping her off, she drove to Weequahic Park and parked in the back of the park.

Cheetah looked over at Tara and her heart skipped a beat. She was so beautiful. Being on the island had caused her to tan perfectly. Her hair hung down in loose waves and her eyes sparkled like the sands on the beach. Cheetah leaned over and kissed her. Tara responded by sticking her tongue in Cheetah's mouth. They shared a deep, love filled kiss that left them both breathless.

Cheetah looked Tara in the eyes and said, "You know I'm in love with you right, Ma?"

"Yes, I know, Cheetah, and I love you just as much."

"Fo' sho you do. I just want you to promise me something, Ma."

"What is it, baby?" Tara asked, running her fingers through Cheetah's hair.

"Don't shit on me with none of these crab ass niggas, Tara. I don't know how I would deal with that. I don't want to share you,

Ma. I want you all to myself."

"Cheetah," Tara said, grabbing her by the chin and turning her head slightly, so that their eyes met. "I love you with everything I got. You're all I want and need. I would never hurt you. You got my heart on lock. I don't know how it happened, but it did, and I don't want it to ever stop. I'm in this for the long run, baby. Don't worry, you got this."

"That's what's up," Cheetah said, kissing her one more time. Cheetah reached into her pocket and pulled out a tiny, suede bag. She opened it up and shook something into her hand. She looked over at Tara.

"Ma, this right here is a token of my love for you. Just a lil' something to show you I'm serious about you." Cheetah opened her hand and Tara saw one of the most gorgeous rings she ever laid eyes on. It was platinum with a 2 karat pearl-shaped diamond. Tara's eyes opened wide and filled up with tears as Cheetah slid it on her finger.

"Ooh Cheetah, I love it!"

"Baby, this is just the beginning. One day soon, I'm gon' marry you, and the rock that will replace this one will make this look like a chip."

Cheetah kissed her again, and then pulled away.

She dropped Tara off and headed home. Riding up Irvine Turner Boulevard stirred something deep inside of Cheetah. She knew that somewhere, somehow, there was a better life waiting for her. She knew sooner or later the streets were going to catch up to her and just like her mother said, she was going to end up either locked up or dead. Something was telling her to slow down but she pushed the feeling away. She had things to do and money to make. There was no way she could pull out now.

As soon as Cheetah walked through the door, Naj was waiting for her with some news that helped snap her back to reality.

"Qua's cousin got back to us. She knows when that cat, Slick is going to make his next move. Listen to this shit. Them jokers are planning on copping five keys, man."

Cheetah couldn't believe her ears. Five keys was an easy hundred thousand. If they could hit this lick, it would definitely put Cheetah's stash in a good spot. Either way, the money or the cash, it would be a good ass hit. Even though Cheetah wasn't into the cocaine game, Nissan and Qua could handle it.

Cheetah would rather flip heroin versus coke. Heroin money was definite money. Those junkies had to have their fix and as long as she kept the good shit, she didn't have a problem with making money in that department. There was too much flim-flam involved with cocaine. They wanted shorts; always had funny money and crackheads would wild out when they couldn't get that next hit. She didn't have time for that bullshit and she didn't want her runners going through that either.

"So, Naj," Cheetah said excitedly, "what's good with that? We gonna meet her or what? When is this shit going down? How we gonna do it?" Cheetah was slinging question after question.

"Yo, slow down, man, let me tell you what the deal is. Sha-Sha hangs out with this chick named Sa'mone. Sa'mone is going to do the next pickup in three days. She told Sha-Sha that Slick and his boys are paying her ten thousand. Sa'mone and Sha-Sha have been friends since grade school, so are tight as hell. They don't keep any secrets from each other.

"Now dig, Sha-Sha done put her work in, man, so if we pull this shit off we got to hit her pockets with somethin'. She's coming by tonight to talk to all of us, okay?"

"Yo, that's what's up? You call Nissan and Qua to let them know?"

"Yeah, they'll be here."

Sha-Sha pulled up at exacty 9PM, in a candy-apple red Benz coupe. She was a very pretty girl. She had an ass like J-Lo and resembled Jada Pinkett. She wore long, micro braids pulled back in two ponytails. She was dressed in fitted jeans. She had on a short leather jacket with a low cut shirt underneath. Shorty was looking good for sho'. When Cheetah saw Sha-Sha her, first thought was, *If I didn't already have Tara.*

131

Ja'nise was working the night shift, which was a good thing. Naj didn't want her to know what was going on. She never kept secrets from her, but she knew that Ja'nise would not approve of this stickup thing. This had to be done. She had been waiting on this day every since she found out about Cheetah getting jacked. This shit was personal.

As soon as Sha-Sha called her, she hooked up with Papi for some hardware. Cheetah already had a new .9. She bought a .380 for Nissan, a .25 snub nose for Qua, and a nickel plated .45 for herself. She went out to Party City and got the four of them face masks, the kind the crazy white boys wore in the movie *Scream*. She also stopped at another store and brought them all black coveralls and gloves. She was ready for this shit.

With Malik and Malikah safely tucked away in the bed, Naj and the girls went down to the basement. Qua was the first to speak.

"Everybody, this is my cousin Sha-Sha. Sha-Sha this is everybody."

"Hey, y'all," she said removing her jacket and sat down next to Cheetah. Cheetah noticed a tattoo on her wrist that said ryde or die bitch. She was wearing Love Spell perfume from Victoria Secret and that tantalizing scent quickly filled the room.

"Damn, you smell good as hell," Cheetah said, inhaling deeply. "Yo, shorty, you lucky as hell I'm with somebody or else I'd scoop you up, fo' sho."

"Yeah, whateva," Naj said. "We ain't here to play no fucking matchmaking game, so shut your Don Juan ass up."

"I was just complimenting her, man. Shorty looks good as hell!"

Sha-Sha just sat there smiling. She had never cut into the lesbian thing but Cheetah was sexy as hell. She had heard about Cheetah from the chicks up on Avon. They always were talking about how much money she's getting and how cute she was. Now that she was finally able to meet her she made a mental note to holla at her later.

Nissan was sitting back watching the whole scene. She saw the flirtatious look that passed between Sha-Sha and Cheetah and shook her head. She was the first to speak up about the business at hand.

"So, Sha-Sha, what's the situation? When ole girl gonna make her move?"

"Okay, look," Sha-Sha started, "I'ma put y'all up on this for two reasons. Number one, I can't stand that no good ass nigga, Slick, so I'll do anything to bring his ass down. And number two, I love the dough. My girl can't get hurt. Do you hear me? We go way back and I sort of feel bad for putting her in this position. Y'all cannot hurt her. She will give it up without the violence, okay?"

"Ain't nobody gonna get hurt, Ma," Cheetah said, "but we need to know if she's going to be alone and how she's getting around."

"Okay, this is the deal," Sha-Sha said. "She's leaving Wednesday afternoon. She told me she was going to pick up some pocketbooks in New York to smuggle the keys back in. She doesn't have a car so she's going to catch a cab to Penn Station.

"Slick will probably drop the money off to her the night before. That's how he used to do me. Sa'mone has two kids that go to school, so I'm figuring the latest she'll be pulling out is ten in the morning. She can get back by four to pick up her kids."

"How we gonna know exactly what time she's leaving?" Naj asked.

"The best thing I can tell you is to be parked on Irvine Turner Boulevard by 8:30am. As soon as she gets in the cab, I'll hit y'all on the cell, and give you the color and number of the cab. Since Stratford is a one way that leads to Avon Avenue, which is also one way, she'll be turning down Irvine Turner going east, so you guys should park in front of the senior citizen's building. You can get a clear view of every car coming off Avon Avenue. You shouldn't miss her. Here, she just gave me this picture last week." She pulled out a 5x7 photo of Sa'mone and handed it to Naj. "She looks exactly the same. I don't care what happens, but y'all cannot hurt my girl."

Naj passed the photo to Cheetah, and Cheetah passed it to Nissan and Qua. The entire time Sha-Sha was talking, Naj was planning the stickup.

Naj got the photo back and looked at Sa'mone again. She was a dark-skinned, petite girl.

This shouldn't be hard at all, Naj thought.

Sha-Sha was getting up to leave, but Naj had one more thing to say.

"Okay, Sha-Sha," she began, "we can take it from here. Listen, we gonna give you twenty percent of whatever we get. That way the money can be split evenly between the five of us. As soon as we get safely back, we'll call you and arrange a time to meet so you can get your money. Don't, for any reason whatsoever, tell anyone else about this, okay, Ma?"

"Yeah, I got you," Sha-Sha said grabbing her purse. "I won't tell anyone. I know this is some serious shit you guys is getting into, and I ain't gonna be stupid and run my mouth. My cousin is involved, and I got love for my fam'."

"Aight, cool," Naj said.

"Well I'm out. I'll holla at y'all in a couple of days. Be careful."

"Yeah, we'll do that," Qua said. "Thanks, cuz."

"Anytime."

Cheetah got up and walked Sha-Sha to the door. Before Sha-Sha went out the door she turned around and looked at Cheetah.

"Whenever your girl acts up holla at me, aight? Maybe we can do a little somethin'."

Cheetah was tempted to say, "Let's bounce now," but she held it in.

"Yeah, I'll keep that in mind," she said instead.

She watched Sha-Sha walk to her car, picturing all the freaky positions she could have her in. She had an ass on her with the sexiest gap between her legs. She got in her car, licked her lips seductively, and winked as she drove off.

By the time Cheetah got back to the basement, Naj had already given everyone their guns. When Naj saw that Cheetah was back, she motioned for everyone to come over to the bed.

"Listen, y'all," she began. "This shouldn't be hard at all. It's not like we going up against some niggas. I got this shit already planned. Yo, I just read some shit in the newspaper and I know just how we gonna pull this off. We just got to get a car to handle this."

"Cheetah, I'ma let you handle that part. You know how to jimmie a lock so go out of town and get us something reliable. We're gonna wait exactly where Sha-Sha told us to wait. I'm gonna drive, and Cheetah, you'll be in the front with me. We already know she's going to Penn Station, so we'll just follow the cab. Once it makes a turn on one of those sides streets, I'll ram into the back of it hard enough to make the driver stop. When he gets out of the car to see what's up, we'll jump out.

"Cheetah, I want you to jump in the front seat of the cab while Qua holds her gun on the driver. You unlock the back door and Nissan, you go to the opposite side of Sa'mone's door and I'll go to her side. When the lock comes up, both me and Nissan will jump in and I'll get the money from Sa'mone. Nissan will keep her quiet with her gat.

"Cheetah, once you see us in the back seat, you go back to the car and get in the driver's seat. Qua, when you see me and Nissan heading back to the car, give the driver one good hit with your gun to send him down. This should take no more than two to three minutes at the most. Everybody will put their masks on as soon as I give you the signal. *Do not* take them off for nothing!"

Everybody agreed. The plan was foolproof as long as everyone held their position.

"Oh, yeah, one more thing," Naj said. "Ja'nise is not to know anything about this, okay? Qua, I need you to call me Wednesday morning and make up some kind of excuse why you need to see me."

"Aight, I got you," Qua replied.

135

They talked a little while longer before Nissan and Qua left.

It was Sunday night and Cheetah probably wouldn't get to see Tara again until the weekend. She thought about giving Sha-Sha a call but she didn't want to seem thirsty. It was only ten and she was far from being tired. She put her jacket on and went out to get a bag of gank.

It had been awhile since she smoked and she felt like getting faded. She rode up the block but didn't see the kid she usually copped it from. Some other kid was out there but he didn't have bags of gank. He had a bottle of liquid PCP. He was selling "dip." It was still gank, but it was made differently. Instead of already being mixed up with the weed, they dipped a cigarette into the liquid and didn't pull the cigarette out until it was completely soaked, then set out to dry. It cost twenty dollars for one cigarette. Cheetah had never smoked it like this before.

Shit, it was still gank so she thought, *What the fuck*, and bought one.

Pulling into the driveway, the thought of getting her own crib quickly came to mind since she couldn't smoke in the house. She turned off the engine and turned up the volume to Jay-Z's *"Blueprint"* album, listening to the music as she lit the cigarette.

She smoked half the cigarette and started feeling a funny sensation through her body. It started at her feet, which felt like they were on fire. The feeling then went up to her legs and quickly spread to her whole body. She took her shoes off and started patting at her clothes. The feeling didn't go away, so she started taking off her clothes.

She opened the door to the truck, got out, and stripped down to her boxers and sports bra. She was still burning. She looked back in the truck and thought she saw flames coming out of her seats. She picked her pants up and beat at the flames. The flames caught onto her jeans and they started burning. She threw them down and ran into the house to get some water.

Naj heard her and came into the kitchen to see what was up. When she saw Cheetah half-naked, she wondered what the fuck was going on.

"Naj!" Cheetah yelled. "My car is on fire. It got me. I'm burnt, come on and get some water. I gotta put the fire out."

Naj could almost see every part of Cheetah's body and she didn't look burnt to her. Cheetah finished filling up a pot of water and ran out the door.

Naj followed her.

When they got to the driveway, Naj could see that the car was not on fire. She smelled the acrid odor of the gank and knew that Cheetah was tripping. Cheetah threw the water in the front seat of the truck and was running back to get more water when Naj grabbed her.

"Fuck wrong with you? Look! Look at your truck! It's not on fire!"

"Fuck off of me, man," Cheetah said, yanking out of Naj's hold. "You can't see my truck burning? You don't see these burns and blisters on my skin? What's wrong with me? Fuck wrong with you, son?"

Cheetah was tripping hard. This was the worse Naj had seen yet. She knew she had to calm her down. She knew a few niggas from the hood who had tripped out so bad that they never got their shit right again.

She picked Cheetah up forcefully and brought her into the house. Cheetah struggled the entire time, but Naj kept her in a tight bear hug. Naj took her in the bathroom, put her in the tub, and turned on the cold water. Cheetah was screaming, struggling, and crying about her truck but Naj held her down.

"You gonna be all right," Naj told her over and over again. "Just calm down, man. Stay still and calm down!"

Cheetah sat down in the tub and let the water run over her. She had a wild look in her eyes, Naj was scared. After what seemed like forever, Cheetah began to relax. She laid back, closed her eyes, and let her head rest against the wall. Naj turned the shower water off and left.

Naj went out the driveway and got Cheetah's clothes. She went back in the house and got some towels to dry off the seats in the truck. She looked in the ashtray and saw the "dip" cigarette.

She grabbed it and went back in the house.

By the time Cheetah came out of the bathroom, Naj was sitting at the kitchen table with two cups of steaming coffee. Cheetah was wrapped up in Naj's bathrobe and had a towel around her head. She sat down across from Naj and sipped the coffee. After a few awkward minutes of silence, Naj spoke.

"Cheetah, man, you know I love you like blood. You're like a sister to me. You're the closest person to me besides Ja'nise and the kids. I'm worried about you, man. This gank shit is killing you softly. You already know what it does to people. You see all those young cats on the block that's fucked up from it. Why the fuck do you continue to smoke it?"

Cheetah didn't have any reason so she just didn't say anything. She didn't know why she smoked it. She knew the consequences involved but once she made it through the trip she was good. She loved the high.

"Yo, we about to get into some heavy shit," Naj continued. "I need you to have your head on straight! Cheetah, man, you got to promise me you're gonna stay away from this shit. Come on man, you wanna get caught slipping again? This ain't no fucking game we involved in. This shit is serious. You out here trippin' the fuck out, thinking your truck on fire and shit!?! Man, you need to get a grip. If you don't, I'm pulling the fuck out. I can't be fucking with you all fucked up off this shit. I need to know you got my back at all times, you feel me?"

"Yeah, man, I can do it. I'm not gonna smoke no more. That's it! I'm done."

Naj pulled out the other half of the dip and placed it on the table.

"So you won't be needing this then will you?"

"Nah, throw it away, I'm good."

"That's what's up," Naj said getting up and tossing the dip in the garbage. "Now go downstairs and get some rest, you crazy mothafucka."

Cheetah flashed her famous grin and headed towards the basement. When she got to her bed she called Tara. She hadn't spoken to her since she dropped her off. The sound of Tara's voice put Cheetah right where she needed to be, at ease. They talked for a few minutes since Tara had school in the morning, Cheetah didn't want to keep her up.

After they hung up Cheetah fell into a deep sleep. She dreamt that she was on the game show *Who Wants to be a Millionaire*. She had made it all the way to the million dollar question, which was, "What do the initials, PCP, stand for?"

She didn't have any life lines left and she didn't know the answer.

Cheetah woke up the next morning with a banging headache. The dipped cigarette was definitely different than the bags of gank. Flashes of the previous night came to her. She got up, dressed in a T-shirt, and a pair of basketball shorts. She then slipped on her house shoes and went out to her truck.

When she opened the door, the smell of the gank was still lingering. Her seats were wet and her cell phone was buzzing on the passenger seat. Cheetah picked it up and saw Nissan's name.

"What's up, Nissan?"

"Cheetah, I need to talk to you. You got a minute?"

"Yeah, what's good?" Cheetah asked, concerned.

"Well, remember I told you about my ex-boyfriend, Sky?"

"Yeah."

"Well, he should be getting out soon and I'm kind of scared. When I stopped writing him, he started sending me these threatening letters, saying how he was gonna get me for bailing out on him. I didn't pay too much attention to them, but just yesterday, I got a letter from him saying, *Times up!*"

"What? When that nigga coming home?"

"I don't know the exact date, but I know it's soon."

"You told Qua about this?" Cheetah asked.

"Nah, I don't want her to start acting all crazy and suspicious."

"Aight, listen, keep ya ears to the wind out there in New Brunswick. His release date should leak out and when you find out let me know, okay?"

"Aight, thanks," Nissan said, relieved.

"Cool, I'll holla at you later," Cheetah said as she hung up. She looked back at the wet seats and floor of her truck and couldn't help but laugh. She sure had tripped out last night. That was the end of the gank for her.

CHAPTER 13

Don't Test Me Son

Ra'dee was chilling on his porch with his baby's mother, Michelle. It was a nice day outside and mad heads were on the block. It had been over a week since Cheetah had given him the last package. All products were sold and the money was safely tucked away in an old tool box in Michelle's father's garage. As soon as he could get in contact with Cheetah, he'd give her the money and get the next package. He wasn't in any rush. The hustle game kept him away from home too much. He needed to spend some time with wifey and the baby.

His little girl was the sole reason he woke up every morning. She was the spitting image of Ra'dee, just a female version. She had her mother's nose and color but besides that she was daddy's little girl.

Most of the money Ra'dee made went into a savings account for his daughter's college education. Tuition was already sky high, so in the next sixteen years that shit would probably be through the roof. He also wanted to buy a house and present it to Michelle as a wedding gift when they made it official.

They'd been together for eight years, which was common law but that wasn't enough for him. When the hustle was done and over with, he wanted to have something to fall back on. He didn't spend his money on unnecessary bullshit. He got what was needed in the household, made sure the refrigerator stayed stacked, and kept his woman and daughter styling.

Himself? Well he was just a thug, so he wore the official thug gear every day of every week: a white t-shirt, jeans and Timberlands. When the winter months hit he pulled out the hoodies and long sleeved tees. His wardrobe was simple and satisfying to his taste. He didn't even own a car. Michelle had a hooptie that got her from here to there. Ra'dee wasn't sweating no ride. At least not at the moment.

When he was on his grind, you would most likely catch him on his Eddie Bauer mountain bike. This was the hood and he vowed that as long as he lived there, he would be no different from the next nigga. All that show boating wasn't called for. The three thousand those niggas spent on a platinum chain could get his daughter an extra semester.

Ra'dee gave all his praises to Cheetah. They went back like Lee jeans with sewed in stitches. When Ra'dee was running the streets, hustling for anyone who would give him some work, Cheetah put him on. After years of drama, they could finally see the fruits of their labor. Cheetah kept it gangsta and for that Ra'dee stayed loyal.

Cheetah was that bitch and Ra'dee loved her like a sister. There was nothing he wouldn't do for her. She proved her loyalty to him time and time again, and in return Ra'dee was indebted to her.

Ra'dee grew up on Avon Avenue. For years his parents tried to keep him from the streets. They enrolled him in PAL *Police Athletic League*, where he had learned how to box. The kid was nice with his hands, but Ra'dee turned a positive into a negative. He used his newly learned skills on any nigga in the hood who tried to get out of pocket. He eventually was given the nickname, Rowdy Ra'dee.

Sitting on the porch between Michelle's legs getting his hair braided, Ra'dee saw in his peripheral vision a strange cat walking up to the steps. He looked to be about Ra'dee's age, a little shorter, with two cornrows in his hair and a mouth full of gold teeth. He walked straight up to the steps and looked at Michelle.

"Yo, Chelle, how much you gonna charge me to hook my shit up?" he asked patting his head.

Ra'dee looked at him and couldn't believe the nigga had the nerve to walk up to them like that. It was Michelle's ex-boyfriend Fa'rad. The nigga had moved down south a few years back. Now his country ass was back and all that fresh crisp air must have fucked his mind up.

"Fuck you deaf or just ignorant? Bitch, I'm talking to you."

Ra'dee placed his hand on Michelle's leg, indicating to her that he wanted her to stop. She stopped braiding midway and let him up.

"Baby, go get Radiyah and go in the house, I'll be there in a second," he said.

Michelle left off the porch, got her daughter, and went into the house. Fa'rad was still posted up in front of the steps, oblivious to what he done got himself into.

"Nigga, you must've lost your mind coming up on my steps like this."

"Nah, my mind right here," he said, tapping his temple. "I just don't give a fuck about your soft ass, Rowdy Ra'dee."

He was obviously testing Ra'dee's gangsta. Naturally, Ra'dee responded by punching him in the nose so hard Fa'rad stumbled backwards down the steps. Ra'dee jumped down, grabbed Fa'rad's arm, and twisted it behind his back. He hit him with a jab to the spine and Fa'rad fell to his knees.

"Nigga, you must be fucking crazy testing me!" Ra'dee yelled.

Fa'rad tried to get back up.

Ra'dee kicked him in his mouth causing his gold teeth to turn a rusty red. Fa'rad tried to get up, but Ra'dee kicked him in his back. Fa'rad rolled over screaming like a sissy, and Ra'dee stomped him 'till blood seeped out of every hole in his face.

"Bitch ass nigga!" Ra'dee screamed. "Don't you ever come around here on no rah-rah shit."

Ra'dee was so absorbed in the beat down that he didn't notice the police cruiser pulling up. He didn't hear Michelle's screams or the police demands for him to stop. When he felt a hand grab his shoulder, he spun around with a closed fist and knocked out one of Newark's finest. The other officer pulled out his gun and told Ra'dee to get down on the ground.

Snapping out of his blackout, Ra'dee saw all the people that had gathered around him. He saw Michelle on the porch crying, but what made him comply with the officer's request was the sight of Radiyah standing in the doorway. He got down on the ground and allowed the officer to handcuff him.

After cuffing him, the officer brutally dragged him to the cruiser and secured him in the back seat. Michelle ran up to the window and he told her to call Cheetah.

CHAPTER 14

Niggas Got It Twisted

It was 7:30am and the phone was ringing. Ja'nise had only been home from work for a half-hour, and was fixing the kid's breakfast.

"Hello?"

"Hey, Ja'nise, it's me Qua. Is Naj woke?"

"No, she's in there snoring and farting. Why? What's up?"

"I got a flat and don't have a spare. I'm stuck in East Orange. Can you wake her for me?"

"Yeah, sure. Hold on!"

Ja'nise went in the room and shook Naj awake.

"Baby, Qua's on the phone. She got a flat and need you to bring her a spare. What you want me to tell her?"

"I got it. Let me see the phone."

Naj and Qua faked a conversation for about two minutes before Naj hung up. Naj went downstairs and woke Cheetah up and told her to get ready.

Cheetah was up and dressed in fifteen minutes. Naj went in the garage and got a tire, along with the guns and outfits.

They drove over to Loews movie theater on Bergen Street where Qua and Nissan were waiting. Cheetah had ridden down

145

to Trenton with Nissan the previous day and stole a '95 Honda Accord out of a supermarket parking lot. She parked it at the movie theater and let it sit over night. Most stolen cars ended up in the Newark area. The farther away from the city you go to steal a car, the more days you have to joyride.

Cheetah had purchased a temp tag, which she placed in the back window after throwing the original tags in a dumpster.

They all piled up in the Accord and rode to Mickey D's to grab something to eat. They parked exactly where Sha-Sha told them to. They ate in silence, each one caught up in their own thoughts. You could feel the excitement in the air.

Sha-Sha called them at 9:45am and said Sa'mone had just stepped into a yellow cab, number sixteen.

Seconds after the call, the cab pulled around the corner. Naj let him pass by and eased one car behind him. When he made his turn down Muhammad Ali Avenue, she was right on his tail. He drove down Quitman Street and swung a left. Naj told everyone to mask up. Cheetah put Naj's mask on her face for her, and then hid under her own. She turned and looked in the backseat at Nissan and Qua to make sure they were ready.

That's when Naj made her move. She pressed her foot hard on the gas pedal and crashed into the back of the cab. He swerved a little to the left and stopped. He opened his door and walked to the back of the cab and all hell broke loose.

Qua was the first one out. She ran up on the driver and put the snub nose in his neck. He made a move to turn around.

"I wouldn't advise that if I were you, mothafucka! Eyes straight, no noise," Qua told him through the mask.

Cheetah jumped in the car and unlocked the doors. Nissan and Naj hopped in the backseat. Sa'mone, realizing what the fuck was going on, began to yell. Naj put the tip of the .45 on her temple and she shut up immediately. She looked over to her left and Nissan had her .380 pointed at her chest. Sa'mone clutched the Louis Vuitton backpack she was carrying close to her chest.

"Listen, bitch, give me the bag and you live, try to be wonder woman and die, your choice," Nissan said, inching a little closer.

Sa'mone let go of the backpack and Naj grabbed it.

They ran back to the car where Cheetah was waiting behind the driver's seat. Qua saw that they had the money and she hit the taxi driver on the back of the head twice with the butt of the gun. He crumpled to the ground and she ran to the car with the others. Cheetah hit the gas and they sped off.

Cheetah drove up Quitman Street until she got to West Kinney. She drove fast and skillfully. She didn't want to get stopped for speeding, but she did want to get as far away as she possibly could in as little time as possible. She hit Springfield Avenue and parked in the New Community Projects Building. They hurriedly took off the masks, gloves, and jumpers. They stuffed all that along with the money in some Dr. Jays shopping bags they had stashed, and abandoned the car.

They walked a couple of blocks up to the movie theater, got in their own cars, and rode out to Nissan's house in Hillside.

"Yeah!" Naj screamed.

"Hell, yeah!" Nissan echoed.

"We did that shit!" Cheetah shouted with excitement.

"We did it!" Qua stated, joining in their celebration.

They were all gathered in Nissan's living room, screaming at the top of their lungs. Naj dumped the backback over onto the living room floor and bundles of money came spilling out. Each bundle held a hundred $100 bills. There were eleven bundles, so in total they'd scored $110,000!

Naj couldn't believe her eyes. She had never seen this much money in her life. Her adrenaline was pumping.

"Fuck me!" Naj yelled. "Do y'all see this shit?"

"Hell, yeah, we see that shit, son!" Nissan replied. She went into the kitchen and got a six pack of Corona. She passed everyone a beer and turned the radio on. Ironically, Junior Mafia was on singing *"Get Money!"*.

"Fucking right Lil' Kim," Cheetah yelled. "Get that money."

Naj called Sha-Sha and told her all was good and she would holla back at her when they finished counting.

147

Naj gave everyone three packs of money to count and grabbed the other two for her. She already knew what the total would come out to, but they still did the math. In the end, it was just as she thought, $110,000! Not one dollar short.

"Okay, y'all, you know we got to do this thing right. A five way split. So that should be what, Qua?" she asked looking Qua's way. "You the accountant, dawg. How much we get a piece?"

"Twenty-two thousand dollars."

"Okay, twenty-two thousand a piece for two minutes of work! I could get use to this shit right here."

They split the money and each took their share. Cheetah took Sha-Sha's cut and got up ready to leave. Naj had to get back before Ja'nise started to worry. They said their goodbyes and left.

Cheetah knew exactly what she wanted to do with her money. As much as she loved Naj and Ja'nise, she needed her own place. When she got home, she was going to call Tara and let her know they were going out house hunting the coming weekend. She didn't have enough money to pay in full, but she did have more than enough to put a down payment on one. Maybe she would get a condo or a townhouse.

She thought about looking for something on the outskirts of Newark but she knew she couldn't live anywhere else. This was home and she was staying. She couldn't leave even if she wanted to. This life was all she knew. Tara was always trying to talk her into leaving and getting out of the game and doing something positive with her life. Cheetah didn't want to hear that. Maybe one day she would get tired, but for right now, she didn't want to think that far ahead.

Cheetah and Naj had a security company install a huge safe in the back of the house. Each week they put the money in there from the block, separate from the money they made. At the end of the month, they would sit down and split the money two ways, taking enough out for them to re-up.

Cheetah put her share in her personal safe and called Tara. She wanted to share the story of the robbery with her but she couldn't. That was to be kept between the four of them and Sha-Sha. The crew's secret! She didn't like keeping secrets from her but her loyalty to the crew ran deep. Some things were better left unsaid. This was one of them. Maybe one day down the line, when they were safely out of the game, she could reveal all of her life to Tara. Cheetah told her about her plans on going house hunting instead. She told her how much she missed her and loved her and couldn't wait to see her. After hanging up Cheetah fell asleep.

Cheetah met up with Sha-Sha the next day at a strip club in Elizabeth called Cinderella's. The plan was to just give her the money and bounce but Sha-Sha was all amped the fuck up. She wanted to have a few drinks and converse for awhile. Cheetah didn't really have anything else to do so they took a seat at the bar.

Sha-Sha was looking even better than the first time Cheetah saw her. She was dressed in a black leather dress that left nothing to the imagination, paired with some black knee boots. Her hair hung down her back in a long straight weave, and her lip gloss matched the undertone of her skin. The way she moved her head, the dimple on her left cheek gave her a sex appeal that Cheetah found very hard to overlook.

Again, she found herself thinking, *If only…*

Sha-Sha ordered a double shot of Henny for Cheetah and a Smirnoff Ice for herself. She got change for a hundred dollar bill, all five dollar bills, and motioned for one of the strippers to come over. Hustle was a short, darked skinned, well-built chick. She had an ass you could shoot c-low on and a perfect set of 38DD breasts.

R. Kelly's *"Thoia Thoing"* was playing and Hustle moved her ass cheeks to the bass as if the song was written just for her. She stood in front of Cheetah and gave her the lap dance of her life while Sha-Sha stuffed bills in her g-string.

Cheetah leaned back on the stool and enjoyed the dance she was being treated to. When the song ended, Sha-Sha gave Hustle a few more bills and she sashayed away.

"Oh, you think you slick, huh?" Cheetah said, smiling at Sha-Sha. "You probably had that shit set up before I got here."

"Nah, that's just my girl. You look like you needed some excitement in your life."

"Oh, yeah, and how do a nigga look when they need excitement?"

"Like you, boo," Sha-Sha said, laughing and getting up off of the stool. She grabbed Cheetah's hand and led her to a booth in the back. She slid in next to the wall and patted the cushion, telling Cheetah to slide next to her.

"Aight, yo, I'ma chill for a few secs, but I can't hang out too much longer."

"Damn, Boo, the missus got you a time schedule or a leash?" Sha-Sha questioned sarcastically.

"Neither, I'm my own woman. I just don't like to mix business and pleasure."

"Yeah, whateva. You must be sprung," Sha-Sha said, rolling her eyes.

"Call it what you like, I don't give a fuck. You don't even know me to be trying to pick my gangsta."

"Well, I'm trying to get to know you," Sha-Sha said seriously.

Sha-Sha was the type of chick you had to be careful around. She was intriguing and enticing. She gave you those looks that said, "Come fuck me." Cheetah was definitely attracted to her, but there was no way she could disrespect Tara.

"I'm good," Cheetah said after a few moments. "I love my girl, and I ain't about to fuck that up."

"Damn, why can't these niggas be like you. I'll respect that for now. If you ever get lonely, call me."

"Yeah, I feel you. I'll keep that in mind."

As Cheetah got up to leave, Sha-Sha said some slick shit about them hooking up soon. Cheetah wanted to tell her there was no chance of that ever happening, but something inside her told her that Sha-Sha knew what the fuck she was talking about.

Outside of the club Cheetah checked her cell to see if Tara had called. The message envelope was blinking in the corner. It was five messages from a number she didn't recognize. She hit the send button and listened to the phone ring. After three rings a girl picked up.

"Yeah, who called Cheetah?" she asked.

"Oh, hey Cheetah. It's me, Michelle, Ra'dee's girl."

"Oh, what's good Shell? You alright?"

"Nah, actually, I'm not, Cheetah. Ra'dee got knocked off for beating up this nigga I used to talk to. When the police came he was so gone that he stretched one when they tried to stop him. He's locked up at the County and he told me to holla at you."

"Okay Shell, I got you. I'm on it. Let me holla at a bondsman and I'll get back with you later. You gonna be at this number?"

"Yeah, I'll be right here waiting on your call."

"Give me an hour and I'll hit you back, okay?"

"Thanks, Cheetah."

"Nah, Ma, don't thank me. Ra'dee is my dawg and he could get that all day."

Cheetah hung up and called the bondsman. She gave him all the info on Ra'dee and he called the county on a three way to find out the bail amount. Ra'dee was charged with assault and assaulting an officer. He had a seventy-five thousand bail with a ten percent option. Cheetah could both pay the entire seventy-five thousand and get it back when he showed up for court, or give the bondsman seventy-five thousand and let him get Ra'dee out. She chose the bondsman because most cats from the hood never went back to court hearings. They'd rather let the law catch them than to willingly go to jail. She made a payment plan with the bondsman, promising him five thousand when they met up at the county and the other twenty-five thousand within a week.

She called Michelle back and told her everything was good and got the address to where she was. She drove home, took five thousand out of her personal safe and picked up Michelle.

Cheetah hated going anywhere near a jail. Each time she got close to one, she got claustrophobic and shit. She had never been to jail, and she never visited anyone in jail. She heard of visitors that had become prisoners so she avoided them. She knew that if she ever had to do a bid, it would mentally scar her for life.

151

Cheetah was like a wild animal. She needed open space, enough room to roam and do as she pleased. If she got locked up, she would lose her damn mind. She promised herself that she would not go to prison for shit. If and when something popped off that would send her down, she would hold court in the mothafuckin' streets first.

It took over three hours for the paperwork to go through and for Ra'dee to be released. Cheetah was just about to leave and give Michelle some cab fare when she saw Ra'dee walk through the gate. He was a pretty black nigga. He had a head full of thick jet black hair to match his dark skin. He had thick eyebrows and sexy big brown eyes. His teeth were as white as a Colgate commercial and evenly spaced. He was a pretty thug and Cheetah had mad love for him.

When Ra'dee saw Cheetah and Michelle, his face broke into a big smile. He kissed Michelle and hugged Cheetah.

"My mothafuckin' dawg!" Ra'dee exclaimed.

"No problem dawg. You my main man. You know I got you."

"Aight. Oh yeah, Cheetah, did you know that punk ass nigga, Chill is up in here?"

"Yeah, I read about that nigga in the papers. I ain't even gonna sweat that. That nigga flaked out on me with my money. I gave him twenty bricks and out in Harrision he was getting twenty dollars a bag. When he got locked up he only had seven thousand and four bricks left. That left five thousand unaccounted for. He didn't even give me my cut. So fuck 'em."

"Yeah, he in there popping some hot shit about needing to get at you and it's important. He's a sucka. Don't fuck with him Cheetah."

"He don't got shit to holla at me about unless it's my money, you heard?"

"I hear you, but he was over in B-Unit telling cats he knew something about you that would put you away for years. He said if you didn't holla at him soon, he was gonna drop a dime against you. I was on C-Unit and I couldn't get to him. He lucky too 'cause I would of split his shit to the white meat for disrespecting you."

"Don't worry about it, Ra'dee. That nigga got it twisted. He don't know shit about my moves. He just talking out the side of his neck 'cause he a coward and want me to bail him out. I'm cool."

Cheetah knew that Chill didn't know shit about her pick ups. Her and Naj were the only ones who handled that end of the business. Not even Qua and Nissan knew who the connect was. Nonetheless, Cheetah was curious about what the fuck Chill knew. She had to pay him a visit to see what was up.

"William Black, you got a visitor!" Chill got off of his bunk wondering who the fuck it was coming to see him. He wasn't expecting a visit. He'd been locked up a week and hadn't heard from anyone. He was dressed in the orange county jumpsuit with a pair of flimsy ass shower shoes on his feet. He grabbed his ID off the end of the bunk and headed to the visiting hall. It was crowded as hell and he didn't recognize any of the faces. He quickly scanned the room and spotted Cheetah in a seat by the wall. He walked over to her and sat down on the other side of the table.

"What's up Chill? You needed to see me?" Cheetah said impatiently.

"Damn, I don't get a hello? No dap? No love?" Chill replied holding out his arms.

"Don't fucking play with me nigga! Either start talking or I'm gonna spin off."

"Okay, aight. Listen Cheetah, I need you to get me out of here."

"Ha ha, very funny mothafucka. Fuck would I do that for when you shitted on me with my money?"

"Yo Cheetah, you know I wasn't shitting on you. I just ran into a few problems. I was going to get at you."

"When nigga? You already had seven bills. The only problem you had was putting that shit up your nose. I gave you a ten thousand dollar pack and didn't get back a fucking quarter! Nigga, you was making double in Harrison!"

Cheetah had heard about Chill's drug use but he had always been a good worker. She never thought he would dis' her the way he did. The money wasn't shit to her, it was the principle. The nigga did her grimey and she wasn't going to help him get out.

"Cheetah, you need to know I didn't want to do this but you leave me no choice. You need to think real hard about getting me out of here. I could ruin you if I wanted to. I got some shit on you the po-po would love to hear."

"Nigga, you don't know shit about me," Cheetah yelled standing up. "What you gonna tell 'em? That I was your boss, mothafucka? You can't even prove that shit. Fuck you! I'm out, nigga."

Cheetah turned to leave, but stopped dead in her tracks when she heard Chill's next words.

"Damn, I sure do miss the old crew, Cheetah, especially the twins. What about you? You miss 'em?"

Cheetah didn't know where he was going with this, so she just let him talk.

"It's fucked up how they got taken out. You wouldn't happen to know who did that, would you?" Chill asked her, a menacing grin stretched across his face.

Cheetah felt sick to her stomach. How the fuck could he know? She could tell by the look in his eyes that he knew she killed them. She sat back down.

"Now look, bitch," Chill said, feeling himself now. "We can do this easy or hard. I was in the diner with the twins when they called you. I saw y'all walk to the auto shop. I knew they had that bitch in there. I was gonna get my dick sucked too, but I had other shit to handle. I left right after y'all walked away."

"When I found out the next day that they were dead, I knew you did it. I don't know why you murked them, and I don't care. All I know is that you or that other bitch did it. That's why I took those twenty bricks. If I didn't get knocked, I was going to get more from you. Bitch, just 'cause you strap on that fake dick, you still bleed every month! I suggest you bail me the fuck out or I'm going to grab the mic and spit a few lyrics down here for the detectives."

Cheetah had no choice but to get Chill out. Even though his word wasn't law, she couldn't take the chance of him running his mouth.

Times like this and snitches like Chill, made Cheetah remember why she never licked dick and loved pussy.

"Tonight, hoe! I want out tonight."

Cheetah went back to the same bondsman and gave him the money to get Chill out. She didn't meet up at the jail the way she did for Ra'dee. She wasn't waiting on him to walkout. She didn't give a fuck about his movements once he got sprung. She knew that this was just the beginning of his blackmail game. She rode back home to let Naj know what was going on.

When Naj heard the news she freaked the fuck out! She wanted to kill Chill's ass that night, but Cheetah wanted to see what his next move would be. He was a shiesty nigga and she had to play him from a distance. He probably would go into hiding anyway. That bitch ass Chill called Cheetah later on that night.

"Yo, I need a few of those bricks to get back on my feet, aight?" Chill said with authority.

"Yeah, I'll meet you at the same spot, same time tomorrow morning."

"I'm dead broke Cheetah, dragging my ass, so make it enough for a nigga to get his status back, aight?"

"I got you," Cheetah said and hung up.

Cheetah called Ra'dee and told him to meet her in twenty minutes at the Chazz Bar on Avon Avenue. She went upstairs and told Naj she'd be back and jetted.

When she walked in the bar, Ra'dee was already there waiting on her. He sat on a stool, close to the jukebox. Cheetah walked over to him and took the stool next to his.

"Damn, Cheetah," Ra'dee said, looking in her eyes. "You look like you lost your best friend. What's really good?"

Cheetah told him the entire story from the beginning. She left nothing out. Ra'dee paid close attention to every word that came out of Cheetah's mouth, thinking, *I'm gonna kill this nigga.*

Cheetah asked him to put a contract out for her. She wanted Chill eliminated and would pay ten thousand to whoever deaded his ass.

"Yo, Ma," Ra'dee began, "you my peoples on some real shit. You don't have to put out no contract. I'ma handle this nigga myself. Wack ass bitch. Yo, I got 'em. Ya heard?"

"You sure Ra'dee?" Cheetah asked, placing her hand on his shoulder. "I don't want you getting cased up. I need you out here with me."

"Didn't I say I got you? That nigga is down to his last twenty-four and it's on the house. I'm so ready to do him, my dick's getting hard."

"Damn, Ra'dee, thanks! I got mad love for you, son!"

"And I you, baby girl."

Cheetah knew that Ra'dee wasn't joking. By this time tomorrow, Chill would be tagged and frozen.

"So look, should I bring him those things?"

"Yeah, yeah do that just as you planned. I'll take care of the rest. It's going to be a pleasure too. I can't stand that fag ass nigga."

CHAPTER 15

Money, Murder, Hoes

"Sa'mone, I'm going to ask your ass one more mothafuckin' time about my money," Slick said standing over her chair with the bicycle chain in his hand.

Sa'mone didn't know how long she'd been tied up in the basement, but what she did know was that it had been too long. As soon as the robbers had hopped back into their car she'd gotten on the phone and called Slick.

"Slick, it's me, Sa'mone," she said with a shaky voice.

"Yeah, what's up? Shouldn't you be on your way to handle that business?" Slick asked as he puffed on the blunt Jo-Jo just twisted up.

Even though it wasn't even noon yet, he'd already been through the blocks he had on lock and collected over sixteen thousand in dope money. He figured that by the time she got back, and they packed up the vials and wholesales, he would be ready to put more work out for the late night rush. Right now, he was headed to one of his hoes' houses to relax until she got back. Since Jo-Jo messed with the sister, he would most likely get his fuck on for a couple of hours, too.

"Yeah, that's what I need to talk to you about, Slick. Some crazy shit just went down. Some really crazy shit," Sa'mone said, hysterically.

Slick passed the blunt back to Jo-Jo and motioned for him to turn the radio down, even if Kem was belting out his new hit song "Love Calls". Feeling in his bones that something just was not right Slick's facial features screwed up.

"Some crazy shit? What the fuck you saying, Sa'mone? Stop babbling, bitch, and tell me what's going on with my money."

"I just got robbed!" Sa'mone screamed into the phone.

"Robbed!?" Slick's stomach did flip flops, and he was hoping he didn't hear her right. "Robbed?" he repeated. "What the fuck you talking about?"

"Slick, I'm standing down on Quitman Street. Could you come get me?" Sa'mone asked, knowing that all hell was about to break loose.

"Bitch, don't move. I'm three blocks away from you. Don't move one goddamn inch!" Slick said flipping his phone closed.

God only knows how many days had passed, but she was still in a dirty ass basement with Slick, Jo-Jo, and Fats trying her best to convince them that she didn't know who had robbed her, and that she didn't have anything to do with it.

"Slick, I already told you everything I know. Please, believe me. I don't know who it was."

Slick drew his arm back and swung the bicycle chain at Sa'mone's head. The tip of it connected with the side of her face, causing an immediate gash that leaked blood down her cheek. The chair she was bound to tipped over and fell to the ground.

"Pick her up, Jo-Jo. This bitch knows more than what she's saying and she's going to tell me before it's over with!" Slick yelled. He was so mad that foam was forming around the edges of his mouth. His sweat soaked shirt was so wet it clung to his body like he was in a wet T-shirt contest. He wrapped the end of the chain back tight around his fist, and when the chair was set back up he swung again.

"Where's my money, bitch!" he hollered as his fist connected with the top of her chest.

Sa'mone cried out in pain and tried helplessly to free herself from the binds.

"Keep still, bitch," Fats said. So far he had not participated in the torture, but he stood close by, waiting on Slick to give him the word. With the stun gun in hand, Fats was armed and ready to do some damage. Out of the three of them, he was the "handler." Big as a WWF wrestler, he didn't care who he inflicted pain upon. It actually got his dick hard when he put in work causing bodily harm.

Slick looked at the two of them with the eyes of a mad man. "What y'all think?" he asked the other two. "You think she's lying?"

"Hell yeah, she's lying," Jo-Jo said. He stood behind the chair holding up Sa'mone's head, so that she could look into Slick's eyes.

"Let me get at her, Slick," Fats said, holding up the stun gun. "No bitch could hold back after I hit them with the clit burner."

Slick didn't really want to do that to Sa'mone. He actually dug the chick, but it was a thin line when it came to his money. This was not some chump change. This was $110,000, and could not–would not–be overlooked.

Slick walked closer to Sa'mone and held her chin between his thumb and forefinger. Sa'mone averted her eyes away from his and he spit in her face.

"Bitch, you would want to look at me," he said. "I got your life in the palm of my hand."

Sa'mone looked at Slick and saw a maniacal look in his eyes that she only saw in horror flicks. Tears dropped automatically because not only did she see that look, she also saw what she believed was her demise.

"Look," Slick began, "this shit cannot be handled based on my emotions. If I reacted to them alone then I would probably let this shit slide. This shit right here is dealing with my business and with such a large amount of money missing, it forces me to figure out what happened to it. Right now, you are not cooperating and it's pissing me and my boys off. You see, us four in this room are the only ones who knew about that drop off, unless you set all this shit up, I'm not understanding how someone else knew about it. I want you to think long and hard about who you told about this, because if I don't get no answers, I'm going to have to let my man Fats loose on you. Do you understand?"

"Yes, I do," Sa'mone said.

"Good, now that we are on the same page, let's start at the beginning. Who got my money?"

Sa'mone didn't answer immediately. Instead, she just stared in Slicks eyes, hoping he could somehow see that she was telling the truth. She knew the only person she told was Sha-Sha, but she just knew that there was no way on earth Sha-Sha was the one who told on her. She also knew that if she mentioned Sha-Sha's name, that Slick would surely kill her. So instead of implementing anyone else, Sa'mone, sounding like a tape recorder, repeated the same words she had been saying for the past twenty-four hours.

"Slick, there's no more to it. I told you all that I know. Why would I set you up? You take care of me and my baby. I would never do that to you. Please, Slick, look at me! I'M TELLING YOU THE TRUTH! There were four people, but only one said something to me. The voice was deep and soft. They drove a black Honda and wore masks, but I didn't know them, and I didn't tell anyone. That's all I know. Please believe me," Sa'mone said with pleading eyes.

"So that's your story?" Slick asked as he stood up. "You sticking with that?"

Still holding Sa'mone's chin, still looking deep in her eyes, Slick was trying his hardest to search for the truth. He knew that even if she didn't set it up herself, she said something to somebody that caused all of this mess, and for that she had to pay.

"Is that your story?" he asked one more time with a seemingly new outlook towards the entire situation.

Sa'mone, taking his softer tone of voice as a sign of a possible breakdown, she nodded, hoping that he was beginning to believe her. Slick let go of her face and walked towards the door. Reaching for the door knob, he stopped and turned around. Looking towards Fats, he gave a slight nod and said, "just don't kill her."

Meanwhile on the other side of town.

Chill was having a good day. He set his shop up on Johnson Avenue and sales were coming back to back. He had just bought a DVD player from a fiend for a bag of dope. His baby's mother had just left with his son and he was on his way to hook up with some hoe he'd met earlier. As soon as he met up with Cheetah at the train station, he sniffed three bags of dope and went up on Johnson Avenue. He had been there all day slinging his package.

He had Cheetah in the palm of his hand. He wasn't even worried about flipping his money. When the product and dough ran out, he would just hit her up for some more. Simple as that. He was going to take full advantage of the stupid bitch.

Fuck she think she is? He thought. *Gonna just leave a nigga for dead in the county?*

If he didn't know what he knew on her, he would still be in that joint.

Yeah, crime really does pay, huh?

It was eight and the sun had long gone down. Chill had to meet up with shawty at nine. He was going to call it a day and pick back up in the morning. He stood there counting the last of his money, when a fiend came up to him. The nigga looked and smelled like shit. He had on some raggedy ass dirty jeans with holes in them. Some run over Nikes that looked like they were singing "*Lean on Me.*" He wore a hoodie pulled tight over his face with a skully over that.

"Yo, man, can I get two bags for fifteen?" the fiend asked.

Chill didn't usually take any shorts but since he was on his way in he decided to do it. He walked into the alley, and bent down behind a brick to pick up his stash. When he got back up the fiend had walked up on him.

"Yo, dawg, don't nobody come back here where the stash is, you understand?"

Ra'dee took the hoodie off his head and pulled out his .9mm fitted with a silencer.

"I ain't just nobody, you bitch ass nigga!"

Chill stared at the gun in disbelief.

"Yo, Ra'dee, what's the deal, man?"

"You ain't my mothafuckin', man," Ra'dee spat. "You a fucking coward. I got a message for you from Cheetah, son."

Ra'dee raised the gun, and Chill put his hands up as if he was Superman and could really catch a speeding bullet. Ra'dee squeezed the trigger and Chill's facial features disappeared. His head split open, leaving a bloody hole. Ra'dee stepped over him and picked up the stash. He emptied Chill's pockets and fled out of the alley through the other end. He walked a few blocks before he called Cheetah.

"Cheetah, the headache is all gone."

Cheetah sighed. All day she was waiting to exhale. She had no doubts he would come through.

"You safe?" she asked.

"Yeah, I'm walking up Clinton Avenue. Pick me up on the corner of Bergen."

"I'm on my way."

Cheetah didn't recognize Ra'dee at first because of the way he was dressed. She almost rode right past him until she noticed him flagging her down. Cheetah pulled over and Ra'dee jumped in. She looked over at him and bust out laughing.

"Oh, you see something funny?"

"Yeah, you, nigga! I didn't know who you were for a minute."

"That punk ass Chill didn't know who I was either," Ra'dee said, winking at Cheetah.

There was no need to ask for details. As long as he was dead, Cheetah could now breathe easy.

"Thanks, Ra'dee."

"No problem, Ma," he said, reaching into his pockets. "Here, I got something that belongs to you." He gave Cheetah the money and the drugs. "I took it off that nigga after I murked his ass. Take it."

Cheetah shook her head. "Nah, you keep it, man."

"Look, I told you I didn't want nothing. I'm good but if you insist on paying me something then let's ride to Popeye's and get some of those biscuits. I'm as hungry as an Iraqi hostage!"

Cheetah took the money and drugs, and tucked them in her pants. They rode to Popeye's and ordered through the drive up window. She dropped Ra'dee off at Michelle's house and drove to the car lot she got her truck from. It was close to nine, but they were still open. She had noticed a money-green Ford Explorer and thought it would be the perfect gift for Ra'dee.

Fuck what he said about not accepting anything. She had to do something for him. It was about time for him to put that damn bike in the backyard anyway.

It was a 2000 model and they only wanted nine thousand for it. She told the salesman to hold onto it until she got back the next day.

She went home and called Tara. Cheetah was missing the hell out of her, but she wouldn't see her until the weekend. She thought about riding over to her house and just chilling in the truck for a few, but she knew that Tara's brothers weren't all that fond of them dating. Cheetah didn't want to start any unnecessary shit.

After hanging up with Tara, she looked around the basement room. She was bored as hell. Naj had already taken it down for the night and she didn't feel like smoking any gank. Even the X-box couldn't entertain her tonight. She wanted some body heat, some comfort, some company. Cheetah got out her cell phone and called Sha-Sha.

"What's up? Who dis?" Sha-Sha answered with that sexy ass voice.

"It's me, Cheetah. What's good with you? What you doing?"

"Waiting on you to come over. How long before you get here?"

"You know I don't even fuck around on that end of town. How 'bout you meet me at the Exxon on Elizabeth Avenue in an hour?"

"Aight, I'll be there. Oh, damn, I knew I had something to tell you," Sha-Sha said before hanging up the phone.

"Oh, yeah, what is it?" Cheetah asked.

"Do you read the paper?" Sha-Sha questioned.

"Sometimes, why? Tell me what's up?"

"Well, they had Sa'mone in there today. They didn't mention her name, but as soon as I read the article I got a bad feeling. I went downstairs and everybody was talking about how they found her on Milford Place in the basement of an old abandoned house. She was beaten and burned all over with a stun gun. Whoever found her had to find ID to identify her instead of asking family. Damn, that's fucked up."

"You think ole boy did it?" Cheetah asked, not wanting to mention Slick's name.

"I don't think, I know!" Sha-Sha said matter of factly.

"Well is she alive or what?"

"Yeah, she's still alive. Word has it that her mother had her flown down to Georgia. I just tried to call her, but the answering machine is on. Do you think she brought my name up?" Sha-Sha quizzed.

"Nah, if so somebody would of got at you by now and she probably wouldn't be in the condition she's in. Don't freak out. Just lay low and stay calm. The main thing is not to panic. We got this shit under wraps. You good." Cheetah assured.

"Aight, you said an hour, right? I'll be there. See ya sooner than later."

Cheetah knew she was making a big mistake, but she couldn't get Sha-Sha out of her mind. The girl had her curious as hell! She only wanted to fuck that one time to satisfy her curiosity.

One time, she told herself and she wouldn't see her anymore.

Cheetah took a quick shower and got dressed in a pair of blue Nike sweats and a white T-shirt. She put on a pair of her Air Force Ones and a blue and white Nike jacket. She took five hundred out of her safe and got the dildo out of the closet. After tonight, she would have to throw it away. She couldn't use it with Tara after this.

Cheetah pulled in the gas station and saw Sha-Sha's car

parked by the pay phones. She pulled up next to her and blew the horn. Sha-Sha stepped out of the car and Cheetah noticed she had changed her hairstyle again. It hung loose over her shoulders and was dyed a burgundy color. She had on a long, black trench coat with a pair of hooker boots.

When she sat in the car, the scent of her Issey Miyake perfume filled Cheetah's nostrils. Cheetah had a fetish for good smelling women. She took notice of a lot of perfume scents. It was sort of like an aphrodisiac for her.

"Hey, Ma," Cheetah said as Sha-Sha closed the door.

"Hey, Cheetah. What you wanna get into?"

"You," Cheetah replied with a mischievous grin.

"All right, let's do this then."

Cheetah went to Hilton Garden Inn on Route 9. She gave Sha-Sha the money to get the room. They walked to the room holding hands like a couple. Cheetah opened the door and as soon as they walked in, Sha-Sha took her coat off and let it fall to the floor.

Cheetah's eyes got wide and her mouth fell open. Sha-Sha was totally naked! She didn't have a stitch of clothing on except for those hooker boots that went all the way up to her knees.

"Damn, Sha, you doing it like that?"

"Nah, I'm doing it like this," she said, and pushed Cheetah down on the bed.

She climbed on the bed and straddled her, giving Cheetah a show by herself. She leaned back a little and grabbed her breast. As she fondled her nipples until they stood at attention. She wet her fingers with saliva, playing with her pussy. She rubbed the clit until the juices started to flow, and put two of her fingers inside of her pussy sticking them all the way in. She played with herself, in and out.

"How you like that, baby?" she asked. "You hear how wet I am? You want some?" she teased, taking her fingers out and sticking them in her own mouth. "Ummm, damn, this shit is the bomb."

Cheetah laid back and let Sha-Sha do her thing. When she

had enough of the show to get her ready, she flipped Sha-Sha over. She stood up off the bed and took her clothes off, then strapped on the dildo. When Sha-Sha saw the fake dick, her eyes got wild with excitement.

"Sha, you talk all that shit but you still ain't showed me nothing!" Cheetah said as she lay on her back with the dildo standing straight up towards the ceiling.

Not being the one to be challenged, Sha went for what she knew. She climbed on the bed and slid between Cheetah's legs. She grabbed the dildo with one hand and began stroking it, making sure each time she pressed down she shifted it enough to cause friction to Cheetah's clit. Cheetah raised her hips slightly off the bed with each stroke.

Sha put the dildo in her mouth and sucked it as she stared in Cheetah's eyes. Cheetah became so aroused she flipped Sha over.

Cheetah climbed on top of Sha-Sha and spread her legs apart. Sha-Sha's shit was wet as a river. Cheetah didn't kiss her, touch her, or tease her. There wasn't any foreplay except for the self masturbation she did herself.

Cheetah stuck the plastic pleasure in and in one thrust she was all up in her. Sha-Sha let out a gasp and grabbed Cheetah around the neck. She wrapped her legs around Cheetah's waist and worked her hips in slow circles. Cheetah had to admit that as far as pussy went, Sha-Sha was that bitch. She knew just how to move, moan, and maneuver.

Cheetah was ramming into her so hard, she thought she would throw her back out. She fucked Sha-Sha from the back. She spread her cheeks open and hit her with long deep strokes.

Sha-Sha threw her ass back like a champ. Cheetah sped up as her own orgasm built up. She came a second before Sha did. Cheetah slowed the pace and continued to fuck Sha-Sha. Sha-Sha busted nut after nut. Cheetah fucked her in the ass.

Two hours and five orgasms later, Sha-Sha ate Cheetah's pussy. The bitch had a tongue that was out of this world. She got her lick game on, damn near driving Cheetah up the wall, literally! Cheetah came in her mouth as strong as a water hose, and

Sha-Sha swallowed, and then licked her dry.

Sha-Sha tried to climb up and sit on Cheetah's face, but Cheetah stopped her.

"Whoa, what you doing?" Cheetah asked.

"Oh, what? You not gonna let me see how good that head is?"

"Naw, I can't do that shorty."

"Why?" Sha-Sha asked, sucking her teeth.

"No disrespect to you, Sha-Sha, but I got a girl that I kiss damn near everyday. I can't be going down on other bitches. Now I'll give you a shot of trigger anytime," Cheetah said, referring to the dildo. "But this tongue ain't going on no ass but my boo's."

Sha-Sha was both hurt and disappointed, but she kept her game face on. They fucked the rest of the time and left. Cheetah dropped Sha-Sha back off at the gas station and handed her three hundred dollars?

"Here, this is for you."

Sha-Sha looked at the three hundred dollars like they were diseased. "Fuck is three hundred dollars," She spat angrily.

"I was just throwing you something."

Sha-Sha took the money and put it in her coat pocket. She really didn't want to take it, but what the fuck. She didn't turn down nothing but her collar. At least she didn't have to ask. Cheetah wasn't her bitch...yet! So she could pass off her money. Sha-Sha really enjoyed the night and hoped to see Cheetah again.

"So, when can I see you again?" Sha-Sha asked.

"I'll holla, soon."

"Aight, see ya."

Sha-Sha got out and Cheetah pulled off. She drove home in deep thought. She felt guilty as hell and couldn't believe she had cheated. All that shit she spoke to Tara about creeping off and here it was she had cheated. She felt like shit!

It was three when she got home. She had deliberately left her cell phone on her dresser. She checked her messages and there were ten calls from Tara. She got in the bed and called her.

"Hey, baby."

"Cheetah, where the fuck you been? I've been worried as hell."

"Yo, I had to go check on my niece. She needed some money and once I got there I fell asleep. I left my cell here by mistake. I'm sorry, baby I should have called you."

"Yeah, you should have. I'm just glad you're all right. I was worried."

"I'm okay, baby. I'll see you Friday, okay? I miss you so much, Tara."

"I miss you too, Cheetah, and I love you more than you'll ever know."

Cheetah felt a stabbing pain in her heart. She told Tara she loved her and hung up.

CHAPTER 16

Lord, Save 'Em

Specials! I got specials! Two bags for fifteen dollars all day!"

Ra'dee was back on the block. He wanted to pay Cheetah back for the money spent on his bail or at least pay the rest of it himself. He was back out on his grind. He bought his own wholesale and was going to run specials all week. That way he could hustle his own and still sling Cheetah's product as well.

Competition was no problem for him. He owned Avon Avenue now. All those who wanted to hustle had to go through him first. If they were not going to get down with him then they were paying twenty percent of their daily intake to him. Either way, he was making money.

Ra'dee did the advertising and sent the sales in the alley where his young soldiers were set up. He had people on every corner with walkie talkies keeping a lookout for the po-po. He actually didn't have to be out there, but hustling ran heavy through his blood. The streets were his home. He liked to be out there making sure shit went just the way it was supposed to go.

"Ra'dee!"

He heard someone call his name and turned around to see

the source. At first he didn't know who it was until she was two feet away.

"Oh, shit! De'shea, what's up girl? How you?"

"I'm good. How you been?" De'shea asked.

"I'm living. You know how it is in the jungle, ball or brawl! I'm doing both!"

"Yeah, I feel you. Dig, you got the specials, right?"

"Yeah, why what's up?"

"I got some people who need some of 'em, she lied. "Let me get a bundle for seventy-five dollars."

Ra'dee knew she was lying. You could tell just by looking at her that she was dipping in the shit. She had dark rings under her eyes and she was at least fifteen pounds lighter than the last time Ra'dee had seen her. He didn't want to sell to her but he knew she would get it else where. He would talk to Cheetah about it later.

"Yeah, you got that, Ma. Go over and see Slim by the diner, okay?"

"Alright, Ra'dee, I'll see you."

Ra'dee looked at her ass and noticed how small it had gotten. Damn! What a fucking waste. De'shea was one of the baddest bitches. He'd thought about running up in her on many occasions. If it wasn't for the fact that Cheetah had dealt with her before, he sure would have laid the wood down, lesbian or not! Shit, they actually had the tightest pussy hands down. They weren't getting it beat up on a regular.

Ra'dee ran into a lot of tight pussy lesbians. They talk that shit about not liking dick but money talks. Before long, he knew De'shea would give it up for the right price once that monkey got on her back. He made a mental note to talk to Cheetah about her. As if on cue, his cell phone rang and it was Cheetah.

"Yeah, what's up Ma? I was just thinking about you."

"Yo, I'm down at the Buy-Rite car lot. Meet me okay? I gotta holla at you."

"Aight, let me track down Michelle and I'll get her to drop me off."

"Yo, I need to see you ASAP. Hop in a cab ok?"

"Aight, I'll be there in a minute."

Ra'dee stepped out the cab, and saw Cheetah standing next to a green Ford Explorer. He walked over to her, planting a kiss on her cheek.

"What's up baby girl? You coppin' this?" Ra'dee said, running his hand over the hood.

"I already did. You like it?" Cheetah asked.

"Hell yeah, this shit is butta and it's my favorite color."

"Aight, then here," she said, handing him the keys. "It's yours!"

His eyes lit up. "Say word is bond?"

"On everything I love, it's yours!"

Ra'dee took the keys and opened the door. The inside was the same green as the outside. The leather was fresh and it had a CD player already hooked up in it. Ra'dee shut the door and locked Cheetah in a bear hug.

"Damn, Cheetah you know you the shit, right? Thanks, baby girl! I love you!"

"I love you too Ra'dee, for life!"

"To the mothafuckin' grave, boo!" Ra'dee yelled. They went to the office and handled the rest of the paperwork. Twenty minutes later, Ra'dee was driving off the lot in his new Explorer. Cheetah was right behind him. They went to the car wash and got a full service. Ra'dee just could not believe Cheetah had copped this truck for him.

"Yo, Cheetah, thanks a lot again for the truck. You didn't have to."

"Don't tell me what I didn't have to do. You didn't have to either, but you did. One good favor deserves another."

"Aight, I got you. Oh, yeah, I knew I had to holla at you about something," Ra'dee said with a serious look on his face. "Remember that chick, De'shea, you use to freak with back in the day?"

"Yeah, why? What's up?"

"She came to the spot today to cop some dope. She said she

was buying it for a friend but I knew it was for her. I could tell by the way she looks that she's dipping. I wasn't going to let the boys serve her, but I figured if she didn't get it from me she would get it else where, nah mean?"

"Yeah, I hear you. So she look bad, man, or what?"

"Nah, not real bad but she's on her way. I just thought I'd tell you. If you don't want me to sell to her anymore, let me know, okay?"

"Man, just like you said, she'll get elsewhere, so go ahead and sell to her. Listen, all the money she spends with you just put it to the side. At the end of the week when you turn in, give me hers separately, okay? I'll take care of it from there. Ra'dee, did she have her son with her man?"

"Nah, Cheetah, she was alone."

"Aight, just do like I asked you, okay?"

"I got you, baby girl."

Cheetah was down on Market Street, trying to find a parking spot. She was feeling guilty as hell about the Sha-Sha episode. She needed to see Tara so she was meeting her at the college.

Cheetah went into the Gold Coast jewelery shop and bought Tara a three karat diamond tennis bracelet. She had it gift wrapped and left. She made it to the college just as classes were being let out.

After a rush of students, Cheetah spotted Tara walking towards the corner. She pressed on the horn and called out to her. Tara waved and ran to the car. As soon as she got in, she was kissing all over Cheetah, telling her how much she loved and missed her.

Cheetah returned the gesture thinking, *I'm never going to cheat on her again.*

"Damn, Ma, what you trying to do suffocate me?" Cheetah asked after they parted lips. "You miss me, huh?"

"Yeah, you know I missed you. What you doing here?"

"I missed you too, baby, and I wanted to find out what you wanted to cut into this weekend?"

"Let's go get a room at the Loop, baby. I want to spend the entire weekend with you."

"Okay, it's done. Whateva you want."

"I love you, Cheetah."

"I love you too, Ma. Do me a favor and reach in my pocket and get that box out."

Tara stuck her hand in Cheetah's pocket and got the box out. When she opened it, she screamed.

"Oh, Cheetah, baby, is this for me?"

"Who else would it be for, hun? You my woman, right?"

"Yes, baby, yes. I'm all yours!"

"Well, let me put it on you, then."

Cheetah put the bracelet on her wrist and pulled her close for a kiss. Tara snuggled her head into Cheetah's chest savoring the moment. After a few minutes, Cheetah drove Tara to her car.

"I'll see you tomorrow night, okay baby?"

"I can't wait," Tara said as she got out.

Cheetah drove up Springfield Avenue with a smile. She couldn't change what went down with Sha-Sha but she knew it would never happen again. She was in love and she wasn't going to risk ruining her relationship over a quick piece of ass. As long as Tara never found out, she was good.

The sound of her cell phone snapped her out of her thoughts. She pushed the answer button on her Bluetooth and spoke.

"Yeah who dis?"

"Cheetah, oh my God, could you come over?" It was Esh and she was hysterical.

"Esh, calm the fuck down and tell me what's wrong?"

"Cheetah, Ozzy found a syringe in the bathroom. My mom must have left it in there. He just brought it to me."

"Where she at? Put her on the phone!" Cheetah yelled into the receiver.

"She's not here, Cheetah. She was gone when I woke up! She took $100 out of my pocketbook too!"

"Aight listen, did Ozzy poke himself with the needle?"

"No, I don't think so, it still got the top on it."

"Good, give me an hour and I'll be there. Just calm down and we'll find your mother."

Cheetah was crushed. She had spoken with Dana two days ago and she sounded like she was fine. She was working at a telemarketing job and had registered to go to night school. Cheetah had just given her a thousand last week. There had to be some type of explanation for this. Cheetah was trying to figure it out but deep inside she already knew what time it was. Dana had relapsed.

Cheetah went home and told Naj what was going on. Naj offered to ride with her but Cheetah wanted to be alone. She got in her truck and headed to Route 22.

Cheetah wasn't religious or anything, but she did have her own personal relationship with God. She had one gospel CD in her car by Smokie Norful. She heard a song by him one day when she was visiting her mother, and she bought the CD soon after. She played "I Need You Now", turning the volume all the way up.

"Ooh, not another second or another minute/not another hour or another day/Lord I'm here with my arms outstretched /I need you right away /I need you now."

Cheetah prayed right then and there.

"Lord, I know I don't pray to you like I should. I'm sorry about that but I know it's you that has had my back over the years. Good looking out. I need you to do me a favor, please look out for my sister. I love her so much. Can you just touch her in some way that will help her to see how much we love her? Can you do that for me? Please Lord, I need you now."

Cheetah felt the tears stinging before they fell from her eyes. She had put so much faith into Dana. She couldn't believe that she hadn't tried harder. She hoped she could get to her before it was too late. She pressed the repeat button and listened to the same song the whole ride.

Esh was on the porch waiting when Cheetah pulled up. Cheetah got out and helped strap the children in the car seats. They drove around all the drug areas in Plainfield. They hit

Liberty Projects and Second Street Projects but no one had seen Dana. They had some family on Fifth Street, so Cheetah swung by there but still no one saw her. Cheetah got the feeing that Dana wasn't even in Plainfield. This wasn't her stomping ground. She was probably back in Newark.

Cheetah dropped Esh and the kids off and gave her the hundred dollars that Dana had stolen from her and told her to call if Dana showed up.

Cheetah drove back to Newark and spent hours looking for Dana. She left her cell number with a couple of fiends and promised them fifty dollars if they could tell her where Dana was. Exhausted, Cheetah went home and called it a night. Tomorrow she would search some more.

CHAPTER 17

Shit Falling Apart

N issan was on the block collecting some money when she ran into Sky's sister Fatima.

"Hey, Nissan, I haven't seen you in awhile. How you?"

"I'm good, Fatima. How you?"

"I can't complain. Did you see Sky yet? You do know he's home, right?"

"Nah, Fatima," Nissan began, "I didn't know he was home. Do me a favor. When you see him, tell him to call me."

Nissan thought about giving Cheetah a call, but quickly changed her mind. She was going to arrange a meeting with Sky and get some closure. She knew he was a time bomb and so was Cheetah. To avoid anyone getting hurt, she was going to handle this one herself.

She gave Fatima her cell number and bounced.

"Hello."

"Hello. Who is this?" Nissan said into the phone.

"Oh, so you don't know my voice now?"

Damn, that nigga didn't waste any time getting at her.

"Oh, hey, Sky! What's good?"

"I wanna see you, Nissan. When can we meet?"

"When is good for you? I'm open."

"How about right now?"

"How 'bout not. It's too late. I'll be out in New Brunswick tomorrow night. I'll call you when I get there okay?"

"Yeah, aight. Don't stand me up!"

"I'll be there, Sky."

Nissan hoped that the three and a half years he spent in jail had matured his ass. She didn't feel like putting up with this unnecessary bullshit. She damn sure couldn't tell Qua she was going to meet Sky. She would have a monkey fit. She was too jealous and this is one thing Nissan would have to keep from her.

Nissan met Sky the next day in New Brunswick at the Somewhere Else bar on Remsen Avenue. The first thing she noticed was how big he had gotten.

Damn, he must have been pushing the weights from sun up to sundown. His arms were cut up. When he went away he looked like Ja'Rule. Now he had a body like 50 Cent. He still had the same close fade haircut he'd always worn, but now he had sideburns tapered into his goatee. He looked nothing like the nineteen-year-old boy he had been when he'd left. She was looking at a grown ass man.

She walked over to him and kissed him on the check.

"Hey, Sky!"

"Hey, to you. Damn, you look good as hell, Nissan."

Sky also noticed how much Nissan had matured. She was flossing! She had on tasteful diamond flooded jewelry, a pair of teal colored Steve Maddens, and a teal Baby Phat jumper.

Even though Nissan had on what she considered casual, she exuded femininity throughout the room. Sky had already heard she was clocking hard. He knew she supplied eighty five percent of the cocaine sold in New Brunswick. He also knew she had jumped to the other side of the fence and was a lesbian. That shit right there he was not feeling.

They sat in silence for a few minutes before Nissan broke the ice.

"So, what's up Sky? How you been?"

"Now, you would know all of that if you hadn't left me for dead in that prison, wouldn't you?" Sky said with a slight frown on his face.

"Listen, Sky, I didn't come here to argue with you."

"Then what did you come here for?" he asked, frowning even more.

"I just want to talk to you, let you know why I did what I did."

"Yeah, well run your mouth. I'm listening."

Ever since the phone call the night before, Nissan had been thinking about what she was going to say to him. Sky wasn't the average nigga. He was mental and if shit didn't go his way she knew he was bound to flip. She had to be careful not to bruise his ego.

"Okay, listen. When you got knocked off, you know I was fucked up in the game. I was strung out on that shit. I didn't have a job and had already dropped out of college. My life was raggedy as hell and you didn't even care, Sky.

"I loved you, I really did, but when you left I had to get myself together. It was hard as hell. I tried three or four times to kick my habit but I failed each time. I was struggling until I met Qua. I know you heard about her. She helped me get my life back on track. I love her, Sky, and I'm not leaving her just to go backwards."

Sky stared Nissan with hate in his eyes. He was boiling on the inside. He waited for this day for three and a half years. She had left him to rot, broke his heart and bruised his ego with this lesbian shit. Nah, the bitch wasn't going to get away with it. She had to pay.

"Okay, if that's how you feel, then it ain't no need for us to be having this discussion. Could you drop me off at my man's house?"

"Yeah, I'll take you."

They drove a few blocks before Sky pulled the gat out.

"Bitch, pull over and cut this mothafucka off."

179

Nissan saw the gun and quickly did what he asked. She pulled over to the side of the road and killed the engine. Sky grabbed her by her chin and turned her face to his.

"I know damn well you didn't think I was just gonna let you walk away, did you?" he smacked her across the face hard enough to draw blood.

"I made you, bitch! Now that you gettin' a little paper you ready to shit on a nigga? Nah, I can't let that happen."

Nissan was about to say something but he punched her in the mouth. Her tooth bit into her lip, splitting it and causing blood to flow into her mouth. He stuck the gat in her stomach and raised his voice a few notches.

"And another bitch? You fucking another bitch and thinking it's acceptable? Nah, Ma, Daddy is home! I think I need to remind you what a woman is put on this earth for."

He stuck the gun further in her stomach, and made her drive up to Feaster's Park. As soon as she parked in the lot he started hitting her with the butt of the gun. Nissan tried to fight back but she was no match for him. He was beating her like she was a punching bag. Nissan screamed at the top of her lungs.

"Help! Please, somebody help me! He's going to kill me."

"Bitch, shut the fuck up!" Sky stuck the gun into Nissan's mouth. "You say one more thing I'ma blow your wig back. Do what the fuck I say and I might spare your life. Bitch, take those mothafucking clothes off," he said as he unzipped his zipper. "Now I'ma take this gun out your mouth and replace it with something a lot meatier and tastier. I don't got to tell you what to do, do I? You do remember how to suck a dick, don't you?"

Sky pulled his dick out of his boxers and stroked it until it got hard. He removed the gun out of Nissan's mouth and stuck his dick in. Nissan's mouth was swollen and bloody from the beating but this didn't stop him from shoving his dick into it.

"Bitch, hold it! Don't make me fuck you up some more."

Nissan grabbed it with both hands and through the pain she managed to bring him to a climax. He pulled his dick out of her mouth, and shot his cum all over her face, turned her over on her stomach and roughly entered his dick into her asshole. The pain was excruciating. Nissan yelled out and he punched her in the back of the head.

"Didn't I say shut the fuck up?!"

He put his hand over her mouth and sodomized her until she lost consciousness. Over and over again he raped her. Each time she gained consciousness he knocked her out again. This went on for over an hour before he stopped and left her there.

A guy walking his dog found Nissan and called an ambulance. When she got to the hospital, one of her co-workers recognized who she was and called her mother. Her mother called Qua, and Qua called Naj and Cheetah, and told them she'd meet everyone at Robert Wood Johnson Hospital.

Qua got to the hospital first. She drove like a bat out of hell. She had no idea what happened. All she knew was that Mrs. Branch had called in hysterics saying Nissan was hurt and in the hospital. She couldn't get there fast enough. She found a parking spot and ran to the emergency room desk.

"Excuse me," she said, out of breath. "I'm here to find out about Niemah Branch."

"Give me a minute," the receptionist said. She paged the doctor and told Qua to have a seat.

In less than a minute an Indian doctor approached Qua. He knew Nissan from running into her in the hallways while at work. When he saw Nissan come in he attended to her personally. He walked over to Qua and extended his hand.

"Hello, I'm Dr. Sanj."

"Yeah, hey! How is she? What happened?" She had so many questions.

"Well, right now she's in the operating room. She was badly beaten and raped."

Qua's stomach did flip-flops after hearing this.

Raped! Fuck was she doing to get raped? Where was she at? And who the fuck did this to her? Qua wanted to blurt this out but knew the doctor did not hold those answers. Instead she asked, "How bad is she? Please tell me."

"Well," the doctor began, "she has a broken nose and her jaw is broken in three places. She's missing four teeth and was raped so many times that the lining of her uterus is torn, and her anus was torn. As we speak, she's getting her jaw set and stitched up. You'll be able to see her in a couple of hours. As bad as it may sound, it's nothing life threatening."

"Aww, man," Qua said, as tears escaped the corners of her eye. "I don't believe this shit. I don't fucking believe it!" she said as she broke down into long deep sobs.

The doctor patted her shoulder, showing a bit of sympathy. "I will let you know when you can see her," he said as he walked away.

When Ja'nise and Naj arrived, Qua told them everything the doctor had told her. She didn't know where or why it happened. She had spoken to Nissan earlier that morning. Nissan told her she had to go to New Brunswick to make a drop off. That's the last thing they had talked about.

Cheetah and Tara had just stepped out of the Jacuzzi when they got the call. They had rented the Jungle Room at the hotel. It was equipped with a heart shaped bed and a Jacuzzi. Its main attraction was a swimming pool you could reach by going up the spiral staircase built into the floor. The pool was decorated with a waterfall and fake trees. If you turned the switch, the water ran down the waterfall and jungle noises came out of the overhead speakers.

When the call came they didn't hesitate to get dressed and rush to the hospital. They got there not to long after Naj and Ja'nise. Together, the five of them sat in the waiting room, waiting on the doctor's okay to go up and see Nissan.

Sky knew he had to get out of town from the moment he'd first spoken to Nissan. He knew he was going to kick her ass if she acted stupid. He hadn't intended to rape her. Something inside of him just snapped when he heard her talking about that bitch she was with and how she was in love with her, and how she wasn't going to leave her to come back to him. After hearing all of this, he'd raged out of control. Now he had gotten himself into some serious shit.

Damn! He hadn't even been home a whole week. He couldn't let the police catch him. He wasn't going back to prison!

He ran to Fatima's house and banged on the door. When nobody answered, he kicked the door in. He found a toolbox, and grabbed a screwdriver. He ransacked the house looking for money but when he came up empty handed, he ran down the stairs and into the next door neighbor's yard. They had a blue Honda Civic in the driveway. It took him less than three minutes to get inside the car and start it up.

He drove down the block and looked around for someone to stickup. He had ten dollars in his pocket and that wouldn't get him far. Nobody was out except for the fiends looking for a hit. Robbing them would be useless. They most likely didn't have more than twenty dollars in their pocket and he would definitely have to kill someone to get that!

He should have killed the bitch Nissan! He thought about going back to the park and seeing if she was still there so he could take her out. That would be too risky. If he would have killed her, she wouldn't have been able to point him out.

He looked at the gas gauge and the damn thing was almost on empty. He drove to the gas station. Pulling up in the gas station, he checked the area. Realizing that he was the only customer, he got out and walked inside. There was an old dude behind the counter, straightening out the cigarette rack.

Sky pulled out his gun.

"Give me the money!"

The attendant gave him all the money out of his pockets and the register. Sky grabbed the money and fled the store without tying him up or anything. The attendant pulled a sawed off shot gun from under the counter and ran behind him. He reached the door just as Sky was getting back into the car.

KABOOM!

The first shot caught Sky in the shoulder. It spun him around

183

full circle and he let off a wild shot.

KABOOM!

The attendant's second shot found its mark tearing a hole in Sky's chest big enough to crawl through. Sky flew back and landed on the hood of the car where he laid dead. The attendant went back in the store and dialed 911.

Nissan was heavily medicated when the crew walked in the room. Qua walked over to her and began crying.

"Baby, what happened? Oh my God! What the hell happened?"

Nissan couldn't talk. She had to let them know it was Sky who did this to her. It took all the strength she had left to raise her arm and point out the window to the sky. Nobody knew what she was trying to insinuate. She kept her finger pointed at the sky until all the strength drained out of her and her arm dropped to her side.

Qua knew Nissan was trying to tell her something. But what?! What was out the window?

Qua walked over to the window and looked around. She didn't see anything unusual. When she looked up, it hit her in the pit of her stomach. Sky! She was pointing to the sky. Qua went to the bed and kneeled down close to Nissan's ear.

"Baby, did Sky do this to you? Were you with him? Is that what you were trying to say? Let me know. Wink your eye if I'm correct."

Nissan winked and the tears rolled down her cheeks.

Qua stood up and left the room.

Cheetah and Naj followed.

"Yo, Qua, what's up?" Naj asked.

"It was her ex-boyfriend, man. His name is Sky. That's why she was pointing out the window. I didn't even know this nigga was back out on the streets. He's been locked up since we met," Qua said, visibly angry.

Qua paced back and forth, tears streaming down her cheeks. Naj put her hand on her shoulder. Qua snatched it away from her. Naj put her hands up in surrender.

"Dawg chill," Naj told her. "I know you're upset. Fuck! What was she doin' wit the nigga?"

Qua's face twisted. "You think I'm on that shit right now? I'm ready to body this nigga, yo!"

Always ready for war, Cheetah spoke up first. "Fuck we standing around here for? I'm ready to fuck something up!"

"I'm ready, let's go find this nigga!" Naj said walking back to the room.

Naj told the girls that they would be right back. Ja'nise knew what was about to go down but Tara was confused. She ran into the hall.

"Cheetah, where you going? What's going on?" Tara asked, grabbing her shoulders.

"Look, Ma, we gotta handle something. I'll be back. I promise I will. Just wait here with Ja'nise," Cheetah said, removing Tara's hands off her shoulder.

"Please, Cheetah, let the police handle that. Please, baby! I don't want you getting hurt."

"Look, girl, we from the hood, the ghetto! We don't let the police handle nothing we can't handle ourselves. Now you go back in there and wait for me, okay? I'll be back." Cheetah kissed Tara on the cheek and they left.

The first stop was to Nissan's sister-in-law Yasmin's house. She was sitting on the porch when Qua walked up. Qua explained everything to her. Yasmin walked into the house, and got a picture of Nissan and Sky that Nissan's brother had given her. It was old but it was a clear shot. She told them where Sky's sister lived and they left.

When Qua pulled up in front of Fatima's house police were everywhere. People were crowded around, trying to find out what was going on. Qua parked and went up to one of the bystanders.

"Yo, what's going on here?" she asked.

"Well, the girl who lives here, her brother went crazy and broke in the house, stole the neighbor's car, robbed a gas station, and got killed in the process."

"Word? What's his name?"

"Ernest James, but we all call him Sky. You know him?" the bystander asked.

"Nah, nah, I don't know him," Qua said and walked away.

Qua climbed back in the car and relayed the news. She was mad that someone else did the work for her.

"Damn!" Naj yelled. "I wanted to murk that nigga myself!"

"Yeah, we all did," Cheetah replied.

They rode back to the hospital and Qua told Nissan what happened. Nissan felt a mixture of relief and pity. She didn't want Sky to die, but in a way, she was glad he was out of her life. Ja'nise told them the police had just left. Nissan was able to write down Sky's name on a piece of paper for them. When they saw his name they just took the paper and left. About an hour later everyone left, except Qua.

Cheetah and Tara went back to the hotel room. Cheetah was in an uproar. She couldn't stand nigga's that raped women.

"Punk ass bitches!" She yelled.

There was so much free pussy in the streets, she couldn't understand why niggas raped.

"Dirty dick dogs!" She yelled.

Cheetah was so heated, Tara could feel the warmth coming out of her body. It was no use to try to calm her down. Tara just let her vent.

Nissan was released after six days in the hospital. Qua was still trying to get a complete explanation as to why she had met Sky. Since Nissan's mouth was wired up, she had to write everything down. Over and over again she wrote the same thing, trying to get Qua to understand why she hadn't told her where she was going before she went. Qua was so jealous, she still thought Nissan was hiding something.

The rape and murder spread all over the news. The television made him into a monster. They brought up his entire criminal history leading back to when he was only eight years old. Qua was glad he was dead. The only regret was that she wasn't the one who did it.

The next couple of months went by quietly. Everyone was still making money in their spots. Naj had opened up a shop in North Newark and all together they were pulling in $250,000 a week.

Cheetah found a three bedroom condo on 19th street. The area was good. The condos sat on the corner across from an elementary school. No block boys were out selling dope. Kids were able to play in front of their homes without seeing drug deals go down. She gave the broker a down payment of forty-five thousand dollars. Tara was excited to take this step and finally get some privacy.

Naj and Ja'nise decided to move to Atlanta. For the past week, they had been down there checking out different cities. They decided on a new subdivision in Buckhead, a prominent area of Atlanta. The house had three and a half bedrooms, three baths, and a Jacuzzi in the master bedroom. The living room had a fireplace and ceiling to floor windows. Three inch carpet ran throughout the house. It had a two car garage, and sat on one acre of land. The house was under construction and would be ready in three weeks.

Nissan wasn't feeling well lately. She went to the doctor for her annual checkup and he told her that she was pregnant. It came as a shock, but not a surprise. Sky did rape her raw, without a condom. She thought about an abortion, but since he was dead and both her and Qua wanted a child, they decided to keep the baby. They wouldn't have to go through the "baby daddy drama," and they wouldn't have to pay for artificial insemination.

Qua continued to supply Jimmy with product upstate and Nissan was the "big dog" in New Brunswick. She quit her job after the rape and focused on the hustle. No one sold drugs in New Brunswick unless they copped it from her. She had someone working every area. For the sake of the baby, she fell back on hand to hand transactions. She now just sat back and supplied her posse. Each of them, Naj, Qua, Nissan, and Cheetah had their own posse of soldiers under their wing.

They had come a long way since Cheetah had gotten robbed all those months ago. Sitting with over a couple of mil', a new house, and fresh whips, they were ballin'. Cheetah shared her wealth with the hood. She loved the kids, paid for summer camp, new sneakers, and gave money away for good report cards.

Naj invested her money into L. *(Lady)* L. *(Lovers)* Camp Entertainment. She threw gay balls, parties at local clubs, and stayed on the scene at the hottest parties. She even picked up her old habit of hanging out at the strip clubs. Ja'nise didn't like it one bit.

Even with all this activity in their lives, Cheetah was still thirsty for the hype of another robbery. They had gotten away with Slick and his boys' money so easy, she craved to do it again.

Slick had put out a fifteen thousand dollar reward for any info about the robbery. Nobody had even the slightest idea that they were behind it. The only others who knew were Sha-Sha and Scabs. Cheetah kept Scabs straight with dope and money. She even allowed him to hustle from time to time. He was loyal so far. She had gotten him a room in a local rooming house and paid the rent for a year.

Sha-Sha had called her four times since the hotel incident. Each time Cheetah gave her an excuse as to why she couldn't see her.

"Cheetah, what the fuck you think I am, just a hoe you hit and throw some money at?"

"Nah, it ain't even like that. I'm just real busy, that's all."

"Well, I want to see you."

"Aight, as soon as I get some free time I'll holla."

"Yeah, do that, one way or the other you gonna see me!"

"Fuck, you threatening me?"

"Nah, baby, that's a promise."

Sha-Sha was sweating Cheetah hard. Cheetah wasn't beat. As soon as she paid up on her house, she was going to buy Tara an engagement ring and get out of the game. She was in love with

Tara and wasn't ever going to cheat again.

Ra'dee and Cheetah were counting the weekly intake when Ra'dee pulled out a separate knot.

"Here, this is what De'shea spent this week."

Cheetah took the rubberband off of the money and counted out $375. For the past month Ra'dee had been giving Cheetah all the money De'shea had spent.

"Okay, we done here, right?" Cheetah asked.

"Yeah, we good."

"Aight, take a ride with me."

They walked outside and got in Cheetah's truck. Cheetah rode down to Irvine Turner to the Pilgrim Village Apartment. She got out and walked to apartment 3C. She knocked on the door and De'shea's mother appeared.

"Hello, Ms. Dotson, how are you?"

"I'm fine. How are you?"

"I'm okay here. I just stopped by to bring you some money," Cheetah said, handing her the $375.

"Thank you, baby, but before I accept it this time, I want you to tell me why you really bring this money to me every week."

"It's like I told you, I met little Dishon at the Youth Center one day and I want to make sure he has something setup for college."

"As much as I want to believe that you are telling me the truth, I just can't. Something in my heart is telling me there's more to it. So would you like to tell me? 'Cause if not, you can just take the money and not come back anymore."

"Okay, I know your daughter. She was a close friend of mine a few years back. I know she's using drugs, but now fortunately she buys her drugs from a friend of mine. Now I know when a parent is using drugs that the child suffers. I met Dishon when he was two years old. Every kid deserves a chance, so I told my friend to give me all the money De'shea spends. The money I bring to you is the money she spends throughout the week. Would you please just accept it?"

Mrs. Dotson admired Cheetah's honesty. The money did help her with clothes and shoes for Dishon. She couldn't remember the last time De'shea had given her money for him.

"So," Cheetah said, "will you take the money or do I have to save it myself?"

"Yes, I'll take it, and I'll make sure it goes to good use."

"Thank you. I'll see you again next week."

Cheetah hopped back in the truck and Ra'dee asked, "Isn't that De'shea's mother's house?"

"Yeah, I bring her the money you give to me so she can use it for Dishon."

"Oh, word? That's some good shit right there, Cheetah. You gonna get your blessings for that."

"Man, I'm not worried about no blessings. I just want the little dude to have a chance in life, you feel me?"

"I'm feeling that. That's some real shit."

"Nah, you that nigga, dawg," Cheetah said, pulling off.

"Yeah, I am him," Ra'dee said, looking in the rearview mirror rubbing his thumb and forefinger across his top lip. They both broke out laughing as they rode up the block.

Cheetah's cell was ringing when she looked at the unavailable displayed across the screen. She usually didn't answer those, but it could have been something important.

"Yeah, who dis?"

"Hey, Cheetah, it's me Sha-Sha."

"Yo, what's up? Didn't we just speak?"

"That was over a week ago and you said you were gonna holla at me. Why you playing me out?"

"Ain't nobody playing you out, Sha-Sha. I just been mad busy, yo!"

"Yeah, so you say. When we gonna hook up? I miss you!"

"I'm about to go out of town for a month, but when I come back I'll holla, okay?"

"Why can't I see you before you leave, Cheetah? Damn, you acting like you trying to shit on me or something."

"It ain't even like that. I'm just tied up. I'll get at you as soon as I get back, aight?"

"Yeah, I guess. I don't have a choice, right? Just don't stand me up, Cheetah."

"I got you, Ma. I'll call you."

Cheetah hung up and Ra'dee looked at her and raised his eyebrows.

"Whoa, what was that?"

"Just some shorty sweating me."

"If she's just sweating you, why you lie to her? I didn't know you was leaving for a month."

"Man, it's a little deeper than that. I can handle it though."

"Aight."

Cheetah didn't have any intentions of ever calling Sha-Sha back. She knew that she was going to have to tell Tara what went down with her and Sha-Sha sooner or later, just in case the bitch tried to do it herself.

Dana was once again strung out. She had hooked back up with Ra'sul and was right back on the streets. She ran into him one day in Elizabeth while she was shopping. He managed to sweet talk her and it was a wrap. She went back home and the next day stole the hundred dollars out of Esh's pocketbook.

She met back up with Ra'sul at his cousin's house. Ra'sul was hustling to keep them high all day. Yesterday, he got locked up and today Dana was sick. She needed a fix and didn't have any money. She called Cheetah.

"Cheetah, it's me, Dana. I need to see you."

"Dana? Oh my God! You okay? Where you at?"

"I'm in Elizabeth, Cheetah, on Broad Street. I'm sick. Can you come get me?"

"I'll be there in twenty minutes."

Cheetah was so glad to hear Dana's voice. She had been looking for her everyday. Since Dana stole the money from Esh, she had heard she was back with that nigga Ra'sul but she couldn't find them. It was like she had disappeared into thin air.

Cheetah pulled up in front of the bus stop and saw Dana sitting there. She couldn't believe how bad she looked. She had a scarf on her head and slippers on her feet. She was dirty and once again skinny as a bean pole! The abscesses were back and her face had black spots all over from where she picked her skin raw.

Cheetah got out and walked over to her.

"Hey, sis, you all right?"

Dana shook her head and threw up all over Cheetah's boots. She was sweating and shaking. Cheetah picked her up and sat her in the back of the truck. Cheetah had brought a bundle of dope with her. She rode to Mickey D's and gave Dana the dope. Dana went in the bathroom while Cheetah ordered food.

When Dana came out she was no longer sweating. Her eyes weren't watery but had a glossy faraway look. She was clearly embarrassed by her appearance because she kept trying to fix the scarf on her head. She sat down and Cheetah dug into her.

"Dana, what's up? Why you ain't call me. I would have helped you!"

"You can't help me. I don't want no help."

"Yes you do. You was doing so good. I'm going to fuck that nigga, Ra'sul up. His ass is dead. If he really loved you, he wouldn't have you out there. Why didn't you get at me when you felt like using?"

Dana wiped her nose. "Cheetah, give up, sis. I'ma junkie and that is who I am."

"Naw, sis, you are so much more than that. What about Esh and the kids?" Cheetah tried to reason.

"Them damn kids don't know me, and I don't know them. Esh is used to this. I love 'em to death, but the drugs love me more. I'm going to die in these streets."

"Don't be fucking talking like that," Cheetah said, grabbing Dana's hand. "Come on, let me find you another rehab, sis. Let me help you, please!"

"Cheetah, are you listening to me? It's too late! It's too fucking late!" Dana yelled. "I'm in too deep and you wanna

192

know what the sad part is? I love being a junkie!"

Cheetah felt like a cinderblock had dropped on her head. All the years of helping her, praying for her, wishing that Dana would get clean and come home were gone. Cheetah was looking at a walking corpse. Dana had died a long time ago, she just didn't realize it. Cheetah suddenly felt tired and defeated.

"All right, if that's how you want it. Just call me. Don't be out here, man."

Tara was walking out of the mall where she had just brought some venetian blinds when a red Benz drove up to her. The girl behind the wheel asked if her name was Tara.

"Yeah, I'm Tara, do I know you?"

"Nah, not yet bitch, but you will soon!" Sha-Sha said, and sped off.

Tara was baffled by the altercation. She had never seen the girl before in her life. Maybe she had Tara mixed up with someone else.

Oh, well, she thought.

She had to meet Cheetah at their new home. They were finally moving in together. Tara loved Cheetah so much. Never in a million years did she think she could ever fall in love with another woman. You know what they say, "Never say never." Here she was, head over heels in love with a woman. No one could deter her feelings for Cheetah. She was willing to spend the rest of her life with her. They were going to get married and grow old together.

When Tara pulled up in front of the townhouse, Cheetah was outside with Ra'dee. They had just come from Circuit City where Cheetah picked up a 61-inch flat screen TV for the living room. She had also purchased a fully equipped entertainment center that would be delivered later on in the week.

Tara got out of the car and yelled over to them.

"Hey! You two, what y'all up to?"

"Nothing much, lil' sis," Ra'dee said.

"We just got that big ass TV up those steps. I'm getting ready to bounce and let you two christen this new place of yours."

"Okay, Ra'dee," Cheetah said. "I'll get at you later on in the week, okay?"

"Yeah, Ma, one!"

"One!"

Cheetah walked over to Tara and gave her a passionate kiss. She picked her up and carried her up the steps to the house. Even though it was empty, it was beautiful. It was hers! Just a couple more payments and she would own her own home.

Together they put the blinds up and ordered some pizza from Dominoes. Cheetah programmed the TV while Tara laid some comforters down on the floor. When the pizza arrived, they ate. They played cards and watched TV that night. It was a new show on cable called the L Word directed by Spike Lee. When that went off they made love until they ran out of energy.

Cheetah was holding Tara in her arms when Tara told her about the girl in the car. Cheetah knew it was that bitch Sha-Sha as soon as Tara described the car. She didn't want to ruin the first night in their new house, so she still didn't tell Tara. Instead, she told her just what Tara had thought earlier. That she probably got her mixed up with someone else. Tara said she had thought the same thing and they fell asleep in each others arms.

CHAPTER 18

House Warming

O zzy was playing in the living room when he heard the knock at the door. He pulled a stool to the door and unlocked the top lock. He got down and unlocked the bottom lock and opened the door.

"Hello young man," the social worker said. "Is your mommy here?"

"Yes, she is in the room sleeping."

"Well, could you wake her up for me?"

"Come on, I'll show you to her room."

Ozzy opened the door to the room and Mya, the baby girl, was on the floor covered with baby powder. The younger boy, Nu-Nu was standing over her slicked up with Vaseline from head to toe. Esh was lying on the bed wearing a wife beater and a thong. The nigga next to her only had on boxers.

Ozzy woke her up. When she saw the caseworker standing over her, she grabbed a robe to cover herself. She scowled at Ozzy and led the caseworker out to the kitchen.

"Hello, I'm Mrs. Harris from DYFS, Division of Youth and Family Services. Ms. Johnson, I don't believe you are handling your duties as a parent very well," the caseworker began. "Why is it that a four year old answered the door, as you slept, while the other three children were awake? That's not safe at all."

"Mrs....ummm?" Esh said, trying to remember the case-worker's name.

"Harris, my name is Mrs. Harris," she said sarcastically.

"Mrs. Harris, I take good care of my children. I got up with them this morning and cooked breakfast. We watched the movie Shrek and then I fixed lunch. I put them to bed at one for a nap and then I laid down. They must have waked up just before you came." Esh explained.

She was so upset at Ozzy for opening up the door. Now here she was trying to talk this lady out of taking her kids from her. She was going to whoop his ass later.

"Mrs. Harris, please don't take my children."

"Ms. Johnson, I'm not going to take your children but I am going to give you one month to find a better place to live in. One month! Or else I will have to place them elsewhere."

"Okay, I will do whatever I got to do. Thank you so much."

Needless to say, that was a month ago. She had slow rolled and Mrs. Harris called her this morning, asking her if she'd found a place yet. She lied and told her that she was going to look at an apartment that day. Mrs. Harris gave her a few days extension. Esh called Cheetah.

Cheetah wasn't going to allow the children to be taken away. She had three bedrooms and she and Tara only needed one. She told Esh she could move in with her but she couldn't bring that sorry ass nigga with her. She told her to pack their clothes and bring her valuables. That was it. She would get everything else they needed.

Cheetah and Tara shopped 'till they dropped. They bought a beige, leather living room set and got tan and mint green drapes. Cheetah bought four inch thick carpet and an all glass coffee table with matching end tables. They got a platform, king sized bed for their bedroom. The set was hand carved mahogany wood. The set had cost fifteen thousand alone.

Cheetah bought Esh a white ivory bedroom set and had Ikea come hook the kids room up. She bought a six chair dinette set with a matching hutch, a silver washer and dryer and refrigerator and ten different bathroom ensembles. In total, Cheetah spent forty thousand in one day on her home. She rented a U-Haul truck and went to pick Esh and the kids up.

When Esh saw the house she fell in love with it instantly. Once they settled in, Esh planned a house warming party for the upcoming weekend. The only people she invited were the L.L. Camp and their families.

Nissan brought her mother and brother. Mrs. Johnson was there and so were Naj and her family. Ra'dee came with Michelle and his daughter. Everyone was there except for Dana and Qua, who stayed home to study. She had her final exams coming up and did not want to fail. She sent Cheetah a vacuum cleaner as a gift and called to congratulate her.

The party went well. Mrs. Johnson did all the cooking. Cheetah and Tara loved the gifts. They received everything they needed for their new home. Mrs. Johnson took Tara to Pier 1, Macy's, and Target to register for their gifts. Thanks to Naj, they wouldn't have to finish off the list. Being the electronic junckie she is, Naj bought them a 42" plasma for their bedroom, complete with surround sound. After everyone left, Mrs. Johnson stayed to help with the clean up. She had to admit that Cheetah did well for herself, but she knew that for all the good things going on something bad was bound to happen. She just prayed that it didn't happen to Cheetah.

MISSY JACKSON

CHAPTER 19

Dumb Ass Bitches

Jimmy, what's good? The entire week and all we made was seven thousand?"

"Yeah, Qua, and I didn't even pay the workers yet! It's those Latin chicks. Ever since they moved into town, the money has been funny."

The Latin chicks were better known as the "Mamis." They bought a house and opened it up to the junkies and crack-heads. They allowed the junkies to buy drugs from one room and use in another room for a small fee. The house would stay open twenty-four hours and they sold specials, two for one, all day long. They were stepping on Qua's toes, and she wasn't feeling that at all.

"I'm saying we got to do something about them. You gonna let a bunch of girls come and take over the turf, Jimmy?" Qua asked angrily.

"It's not just that, cuz. They down with one of the biggest Puerto Rican cartels in the state of New York. Going up against them is like going up against a nuclear bomb. They got mad man power behind them. They not feeling the fact that you're from Jersey and you getting all the money up here, cuz."

"Aight, have you received any threats against you? How about the boys?"

"Nah, we had a few small beefs with them but nothing major. When they saw that we weren't shook, they opened the house and started slinging specials. I barely get any money now. A few of the old customers come, but most of them have stopped buying from me and are going to them."

"Aight, look, continue to get as much money as you can. I'ma take care of this problem. If any serious threats come your way, let me know, okay?"

"Aight, cuz. I got you."

When Qua introduced the problem to Cheetah and Naj, the first thing that came to Cheetah's mind was to jack the bitches. Cheetah wanted to kick the door in, beat them down, and take their shit. Naj had a better plan. She knew that Qua didn't want to lose that spot upstate. There was too much money flowing from it. Since they didn't know Naj and Cheetah all they needed was two white boys and a Crown Victoria car to complete the plan.

Rosa was the head of the Mamis. She was a short, thugged out Puerto Rican chick. She was twenty-three years old and had already done two prison bids. She had two teardrop tattoos on her face under her left eye. She wore a yellow bandana everyday, representing the Latin queens, with her hair hanging loose under it. The rest of the Mamis were all family members of some sort. In total, there were seven of them. The youngest just being seventeen years old.

They were wild girls. They smoked weed all day and gambled, shooting dice in the hallway of their house. Even though they were making lots of money they had no real idea on how to run a business. They didn't have any lookouts and sold to anyone who came to the door. They were too busy trying to get a foot in the game to take precautions. That was their one mistake, besides underestimating Qua.

Dan was dressed in jeans and a leather jacket. He had a five day old beard and wore an old pair of work boots. Phil wore clothes identical to Dan's and together they looked like two white fiends. Naj and Cheetah dressed more conservatively, in khaki pants, white button up shirts, and Clark shoes. Cheetah had her hair pulled back in a ponytail and Naj rocked the short curly look.

The four of them pulled up in the burgundy narcotics car unnoticed. Once Dan and Phil got out, Naj and Cheetah pulled around the corner. Phil walked up to the front door with Dan close behind.

He knocked and Rosa answered.

"Yeah, let me get two twenty-five dollar specials."

"Aight, come in."

They walked in the house and did a quick scan of the adjoining rooms. Rosa went in the kitchen and got the cocaine. She came back and exchanged the drugs for the money Phil was holding.

"For an extra five dollars you can go in the next room and do your thing," Rosa said.

Phil handed her five dollars and she led them to the back room.

The room had one big table in the middle of the floor with a wall lined up with milk crates. The crates were to serve as chairs. There were already four other people in there smoking pipes made out of everything from soda cans to asthma pumps. Dan and Phil grabbed a crate off the wall and found a spot at the table. They took off their jackets and were just about to sit down when Naj and Cheetah kicked the door in.

"Police! Everybody freeze!" Naj screamed with her .45 pulled out.

Dan and Phil pulled out their guns and made the same announcement.

When Rosa saw what was going on, she broke for the back door in a quick sprint. Cheetah ran after her. Rosa was right at the door when Cheetah tackled her. Rosa swung at Cheetah but she bobbed quickly to the side. Cheetah came back with a jab that crashed into the side of Rosa's face. Rosa struggled to get up, but Cheetah hit her again, this time breaking her nose.

Cheetah flipped Rosa over and put the plastic handcuffs on her. She dragged her back into the front room where Naj, Phil, and Dan had everyone else cuffed and lying on the floor.

They'd gotten fake IDs made and bought shoulder holsters for their guns. Phil had stolen the metal handcuffs from his brother who actually was one of Newark's finest. Qua had drafted a fake search warrant on the computer Cheetah was now pulling out. The Latin chicks were too scared to ask about the paperwork, which was a good damn thing because if they would have they would have seen the name "Jane Doe" written in the owner's spot.

Phil and Dan tore the house to pieces. They cut the furniture, emptied every cabinet, closet, and drawer. They found four guns and cases of bullets, eighty thousand in cash stuffed in a bag of dog food, over three kilos of cocaine in a suitcase in the bathroom linen closet, and a half pound of weed and thirty-five ecstasy pills.

They put everything in plastic shopping bags and let the dope fiends go. There were four Mamis in the house at the time of the raid, Naj and Cheetah roughly pulled them up off the floor and loaded them into the car. Phil and Dan squeezed in and they drove them to the train station.

"Listen, wait here. I'll be back in less than twenty minutes," Naj said, and drove off. She then drove to a deserted street and cut the car off. Naj put on her professional voice and turned toward the backseat.

"Listen," she began, "I know you are just a bunch of young, dumb broads who have no real clue about this drug game. I really don't want to arrest you, so I got a proposition for you. If you do me a favor, I'll do you a favor. We really want the chick from Jersey they call Qua.

"We know she's bringing lots of cocaine into the town and

for months she has been slipping through our fingers. We need your help to catch her. We found a lot of money and drugs in your house, enough to put the four of you away for years. Either you help me, or you go to jail. Let me know now."

Rosa, who was obviously in pain from the broken nose Cheetah had given her, spoke for the rest of them.

"Yeah, we'll do it. I can't go back to prison. I just got out and I'm still on paper. Tell me what we need to do."

"It's easy," Cheetah said. "You got to set her up. Get someone to make a deal with her for a couple of kilos of cocaine and let us know when she's going to deliver. Don't try to flake out because I already know who all of you are and I can bring charges against you anytime I choose.

"Once we seal the deal, I'm going to let you go. *Do not* go back to the house. I'm gonna tell my boss you got away so find somewhere else to lay your head, okay?"

From the back seat you heard a chorus of eager "*Yesses*".

Naj got out, walked to the back door to let them out and unlocked the handcuffs.

"Okay, here's a number to reach me at," she said, handing Rosa a piece of paper with an old cell phone number written on it. "I'm gonna give you a month to setup the deal. If I don't hear from you in a month, I'm gonna put an APB out on your ass. Don't even think about shitting on me."

"Nah, we ain't gonna do that," Rosa said. "I'll get the deal setup."

"Good, good. Now go to the hospital and get your nose taken care of."

Naj got back in the car and sped off. She went to the train station and picked up Phil and Dan, then hit the turnpike going down I95 south. They drove for twenty minutes in silence. When they passed the Yonkers exit leading into the Bronx, everyone broke out laughing.

"Did you see those dumb ass bitches?" Cheetah yelled. "They were scared as hell, Naj!"

"Yeah they were! They were stupid! When we dropped Phil and Dan off at the train station, they didn't even question that shit. Dumb bitches!"

"Damn, Phil, Dan, y'all tore that mothafucking house to pieces. That was some fun shit wasn't it?" Cheetah asked high fiving Dan.

"Hell, yeah, it was fun. I'll do that anytime!" Phil said, lighting a cigarette.

"Wait until Qua see how we came off. She's gonna shit in her pants," Cheetah yelled as she turned up the music.

The phone number Naj had given them was an old cell she never used. Anyone who called would automatically get the answering machine after two rings. The names were fake to. When they called, which she was sure they would, she would call them back and set up a meeting to make it look official. She had no plans on showing up. Qua could safely continue to sell her product. She never did hand to hand combat, so no one could ever say she sold them anything. Naj was sure the Mamis would go into hiding when they failed to hold up their end of the bargain. You had to admit this was a brilliant stick up!

CHAPTER 20

She Loves Me, She Loves Me Not

Sha-Sha was getting real tired of Cheetah brushing her off. She had now been chasing and sweating her for four months with no results. Cheetah was always coming at her with that busy shit.

Cheetah was blowing up too! Everybody in town was screaming her name and Sha-Sha wanted to be a part of her world. She couldn't even get Qua to get Cheetah to holla at her.

Sha-Sha wasn't use to rejection. She couldn't stand to be ignored. At first she just thought about Cheetah every now and again, but lately thoughts of Cheetah became an obsession. Each time Cheetah's name was mentioned, she got a funny feeling deep down in her soul, like she was in love. The bitch was a major figure in the game and Sha-Sha wanted to be the one up under her wing. Not that stuck up bitch, Tara. A month had passed and Cheetah didn't call her. Hell, nah! Now it was time to play dirty.

As time flew by, things got better for the L.L. Camp. They didn't pull anymore stickups because there was no need to. They were self-made millionaires. As soon as Qua graduated, they were all going to put their hustling shoes up and begin a legit life.

Cheetah paid off on her home and purchased an old laundromat on Central Avenue. She renovated it with fifty washers and dryers. All the washers were triple loaders and they cost $1.50 per wash. For 50¢ you could run the dryer until your clothes were dry.

Cheetah had to give something back to her people. She remembered when she was a little girl, how her mother would get on her hands and knees and scrub her and Dana's clothes. She always said she would open a laundromat in the hood and make it affordable for the low income people. One dream accomplished! Cheetah gave Ra'dee fifty percent partnership and let him and Michelle operate it.

Now, the last thing to do was to get Tara's ring and propose to her. Cheetah purchased a five karat, pear shaped diamond set in platinum. Tomorrow she would take Tara to Justin's in New York and propose to her. She was going to do it the old fashioned way, on bended knee. If Tara accepted, she would be the happiest person alive.

Cheetah, Ozzy, and Tara were coming out of the barbershop where Cheetah had gotten a shape up. They were planning on going to the bowling alley and were almost to the car when Sha-Sha pulled up on them.

"Cheetah, you no good ass bitch! So you think you cute, huh? You think you can just fuck me and then act like I don't exist."

Tara turned around and saw the same red Benz with the same chick behind the wheel that ran down on her when she was coming out of the mall.

"Who the fuck is that, Cheetah?" she asked, trying to get a better look.

"Nobody, baby, just keep walking. I'll explain it to you later," Cheetah said, pushing her towards the car.

"Bitch," Sha-Sha continued, "fuck you think you are? I'm not just one of your hoes you can fuck and leave. I got feelings, Cheetah."

Tara pulled away from Cheetah and walked up to Sha-Sha's car.

"Excuse me. Are you talking to one of us?"

"Yes, I am," Sha-Sha replied getting out of the car. "Me and your bitch have been fucking for months. Every time she wasn't with you, she was slobbing all over my ass. She ain't never tell you about me? I'm Qua's cousin, Sha-Sha. I'm the mistress."

Tara looked back at Cheetah who stood behind her with a stupid face. The look not only confirmed that what this bitch was saying was true, it also let Tara know that Cheetah was not to be trusted.

Tara turned back around and Sha-Sha stood there, wide-legged with hands on her hips. Tara put her pocketbook down on the ground and punched Sha-Sha in the mouth. Sha-Sha fell back into the car and Tara pounced on her, raining blow after blow. Sha-Sha tried to fight back but she couldn't get a hit in. Tara grabbed her by her fake ponytail and slung her on the ground. She dragged her a few feet away from the car and started stomping her in the face.

"Bitch, I don't have no mothafuckin' mistress!" Tara yelled, as she kicked Sha-Sha in the eye with the square toe of her Joan & David boots.

Cheetah shoved Ozzy in the car and ran over to the fight. She grabbed Tara in a bear hug from the back and pulled her to the car. Sha-Sha lay on the ground, broken and bloody.

"Cheetah, bitch, you're gonna pay for this! On everything I love, you gonna get yours!" Sha-Sha yelled.

Cheetah put the key in the ignition and pulled off leaving Sha-Sha in a cloud of exhaust smoke. Tara was so hurt she didn't even look Cheetah's way. She turned her face towards the window and began to cry.

"Tara, please, baby, let me explain," Cheetah pleaded.

Tara kept her face planted on the glass, and said, "Cheetah, there's really nothing to explain. Either you were fucking her or you weren't."

"Ma, I can't lie to you. Yes, I did fuck her, but only once. It was when me and you first got together."

"So why the fuck did she say y'all been fucking for months

Cheetah?" Tara screamed, turning around to look Cheetah in the eyes.

"Baby, I swear she was lying. It was only once and I didn't even give that bitch no head."

No sooner than Cheetah got the words out of her mouth, Tara slapped her. Cheetah brought her hand up to her cheek where Tara slapped her.

"What the fuck…" Cheetah began.

Tara slapped her again, even harder this time.

"Cheetah, I don't want to hear anything else your trifling ass has to say. Just take me to my brother's house."

"Ma, please don't do this. Please, let's go home and talk about it. Don't leave me."

"Cheetah, I'm not leaving you. I just need some time to myself. I love you too much to leave you, but right now, I can't stand your cheating ass. I need to get away from you before I hurt you."

Tara turned back towards the window and made it clear that she was through with the discussion. Cheetah drove her to her brother's house then dropped Ozzy off at their home. She then called Naj and told her to meet her at the laundromat.

When Naj got to the laundromat, Cheetah broke down and cried on her shoulder like a two-year-old baby. Naj only saw Cheetah cry a few times before, but never over a woman. Cheetah cried like someone had died. Naj knew it was her first heartbreak and it wasn't anything that could be done. The only thing that could heal the hurt was time.

When Cheetah stopped crying, they talked for two hours straight. Cheetah wanted to call Tara, but Naj told her to just leave it alone for now.

"She said she wasn't going to leave you, man, so now you just got to give her space. Let her go through whatever she has to and she'll be back. She loves you. This is not the end okay?"

Cheetah went home and copped a bag of gank. This would be the first time in months she smoked. She smoked the blunt and didn't even get high. She was too hurt. She tried to call Tara, but she wouldn't accept her calls. Through the course of the night, she left thirty-six messages on her machine, all of them saying the same thing—*I'm sorry!*

The next morning she got up early and called Tara again. Still no answer.

She got in her truck and rode to Tyrique's house, but was too afraid to knock on the door. Cheetah rode down to Seth Boyden apartments and bought two bags of gank. She went back home and locked herself in her room.

She opened up two blunts, filling them with the gank. She rolled the blunts, lay back on her bed, and smoked them both, one after the other. The more she smoked, the angrier she got at herself for being so stupid. She missed the hell out of Tara. Without her, she felt lost.

Cheetah had never in her life felt the pain she was feeling at that very moment. Her whole body hurt, even the tips of her fingernails. How could she have been so stupid? Over a quick piece of ass, the love of her life had walked out on her.

She paced the room, back and forth, willing the phone to ring and Tara to be on the other end.

"Please, Tara, please, just call me," Cheetah said over and over. "I promise to never cheat on you again. Just please call me, baby."

Cheetah got out the photo album and looked at their pictures together—them in the Bahamas, at the parade, in New York at the wax museum, on a cruise ship to St. Croix. Every page held a picture of the two of them.

Cheetah closed the photo album and threw it across the room. She went to the closet, got her gun out of the shoebox in the back, and ran outside to the backyard. She found some empty beer bottles on the garbage can, lined them up on the brick barbeque grill, and one by one she shot them down.

She loves me?

Bang!

She loves me not?

Bang!
She loves me?
Bang!
She loves me not?
Bang!
She shot down six bottles and went to the can to look for more. Between the high of the gank and the state of her depression, Cheetah was completely out of control. She lined up more bottles and shot them down the same way she did the others. Fifteen more shots were let off before the police arrived.

Cheetah was arrested for having an illegal firearm. She went with the police willingly.

CHAPTER 21

Play or Pay

Sha-Sha couldn't believe Cheetah just stood back and watched her get her ass whooped. She was going to have to get grimey on her. There was no way Cheetah would get away with this shit.

Sha-Sha cleaned up her wounds, fixed her hair and made a phone call.

"Yeah who's calling?" asked a deep male voice.

"It's me Sha-Sha."

"What the hell you want? I ain't got no money so don't be asking me," Slick said nastily.

"Mothafucka, I ain't calling you to ask you for shit with your sorry ass. I take care of my son. We don't need you."

"Fuck you want then?"

"I got some info for you. I'm sure you want to hear it but I'm not telling you shit over the phone. Can you meet me later at the pizza parlor on Clinton Avenue?"

"Bitch, you better not be wasting my time with your silly ass games."

"Please, nigga, don't nobody feel like playing with you. Meet me at nine okay?"

"Aight."

Slick hung up the phone wondering what this bitch could possibly have to tell him. Sha-Sha was a slick ass hoe and he couldn't stand her. He regretted the day they ever met. When he found out she was pregnant, he wanted her to get an abortion. He knew she was just having the baby to try to hold on to him. The bitch was money hungry and as shiesty as they came. She better not be up to any tricks.

Sha-Sha walked into the pizza parlor wearing a pair of big ass Jackie-O aviator glasses to cover up her two black eyes. Even after just getting the beat down of her life she still managed to look good. She walked over to the table that Slick was seated and sat across from him.

"Fuck is so important Sha-Sha?" Slick asked wanting to get straight to the point.

"Damn, you can't even ask me how I'm doing? I am your baby's mother Slick."

"From the looks of you, I can see some sucka whooped your ass so I know how you doing. You must still be up to your same old tricks."

"Fuck you, Slick."

Sha-Sha hated him just as much as he hated her. She didn't even know why she dealt with his trifling ass in the first place. He wasn't no pretty boy, not with those watery eyes and long ass head. His pipe game definitely wasn't worth bragging about. He just had a real smooth way about him that lured a person to him once they got in his presence.

"Listen," Sha-Sha continued. "I got some information I'm sure you want but your sorry ass is going to have to pay me. Now, tell me just how much is the reward you got out for the names of the people who jacked your mule for all that cake?"

"Bitch, you know damn well I'm offering fifteen thousand, why? What the fuck do you know?"

"I know who did it, but I ain't telling you shit until I get my money and I want twenty thousand not fifteen."

"Bitch, don't play with me. How I know you telling the truth?"

"Because you know I wouldn't have called you for any other reason."

"Aight, I'll give you the money, now give me the names."

"I'm not playing, Slick, I want my money."

"I just gave you my word. You'll get your money, now who the fuck was it?"

"You know that chick, Cheetah, who's making all that money up on Avon Avenue?"

"Yeah."

"Well, that's who did it."

"So you're telling me my money was jacked by some bitch."

"Not just some bitch, the same bitch you jacked got your ass back. How 'bout that?"

"How the fuck do you know?"

"Because she hangs out with my cousin, Qua and I heard them talking about it."

As soon as the words left her mouth, Sha-Sha realized her mistake. She didn't mean to mention Qua's name, but she had and Slick caught on.

"Your cousin and this bitch are the ones who jacked me? That's what you sayin'?"

"No, my cousin didn't have anything to do with it," Sha-Sha lied. "It was Cheetah."

"Bitch, four people jacked Sa'mone in that cab. Whether your cousin was one of them or not, I don't know, but I will find out," Slick said as he got up to leave. "I'll call you later to and you could then pick up your money."

"Slick, my cousin wasn't involved!" Sha-Sha yelled to him but he continued to walk out the door. Slick knew of the "L.L. Camp". He knew there were four of them and he knew who all four were. The bitches were well respected in the hood, and they made more money than he did. They also had a shit load of young soldiers repping for them. Slick was going to get his revenge though. One way or the other, all four of them would pay.

Naj bailed Cheetah out of jail later on that night. When she saw how Cheetah looked, her heart ached for her misery. Cheetah's eyes were bloodshot and her clothes were disheveled. Cheetah had to pull herself together.

"Yo, what's really good man?" Naj asked Cheetah as she climbed in the truck.

Cheetah looked over at Naj with dazed eyes.

"Naj, I can't take it without her. I need her. We had a great relationship and I fucked up on my half. I knew better but I just had to lay the wood on that hoe Sha-Sha. I feel like half of my heart was torn out. I can't do it without her man. I need her back."

"I thought we discussed all that, Cheetah? She's not gone forever. You dealt those cards yourself, man, now you got to finish the game. Whether you win or lose you should have thought about that before bangin' Sha-Sha. Come on, man up and stop acting like a wuss. The holiday is coming and this is the last one we all will get to spend together. I'll tell you what, I'ma call Tara for you. I'll get her to holla at you. If she still don't want to, then you just gonna have to deal with that, okay?"

"Yeah, man, aight."

"Good. Now let me take you home. Get a good night's rest because you look like shit."

It took every bit of will power Tara possessed not to call Cheetah back. She felt like someone cut her left arm off. Wasn't Cheetah the one who asked her not to cheat? Wasn't she the one who brought up all that loyalty and honesty shit? How could she do this to them? How could she taint their love this way? Tara missed her but she had to teach her a lesson. Tara was just about to go to bed when her cell rang. She looked at the picture ID and recognized Naj's face. She answered.

"What's up, Naj?"

"Hey, Tara, you okay, Ma?"

"Nah, I'm not. I'm hurting like I've never hurt before."

"Yeah, I'm sure you are and I'm not calling to take no sides, but I do want you to know that Cheetah is hurtin' too. Tara, this shit happened right when you and Cheetah met," Naj lied. "Cheetah loves you, Tara, and she wouldn't hurt you intentionally."

"Naj, whether it was intentional or not, I'm still hurt. She should have told me, that way that bitch wouldn't have been able to run down on us the way she did. I would have already known and I wouldn't have been left looking stupid, nah mean?"

"Yeah, I feel you. I understand, Tara, but do me a favor, Ma, call her. Please. I just had to bail her out of the county. She was in the backyard busting shots at some cans and she was high off of gank."

"Gank?" Tara asked surprised.

"Yeah, gank, Tara. She used to smoke it all the time before you guys met. She stopped when y'all got serious. I don't want her going back to that shit. Just holla at her okay?"

"Aight, Naj. I'll call her."

"Thanks, Tara. I owe you one, babe."

Slick met Sha-Sha back at the pizza parlor and gave her the twenty thousand he promised to her. He didn't need to check on the authencity of her words. He knew the bitch was telling the truth. It all fit together too well.

Around the same time Sa'mone got robbed, the LL. Camp came up out of the wood work as the big ballers in town. Now all he had to do was investigate their movements. There was no doubt that they would get dealt with. If he didn't seek his revenge he would be labeled a sucka, and one thing he was not was a sucka.

Slick began hanging out on Avon Avenue. He didn't affiliate himself with the cats on the block, he just sort of hung around, catching bits and pieces of the activity. He would go into the bars and listen to tidbits of conversation. That's how he found out Cheetah was the big Kahuna on this end of town. Mothafuckas were praising her like she was a God! He found out she drove a white Yukon and owned a laundromat on the other end of town. The best news he received was on day three of his investigation.

She was throwing a Memorial Day Block Party, and he planned on being an uninvited guest.

Tara called Cheetah later on that night. Just the sound of Cheetah's voice sent chills through her body.

"Hey, Cheetah."

"Oh, Tara, I miss you, Ma, and I'm sorry. I'm so sorry. Please come home."

"Cheetah, I love you. I love you more than I've ever loved anyone else in my life. Baby, it's killing me to be apart from you, but I can't have you thinking it's okay to just do what you want. You feel me?"

"Yes, I do. Baby, I wanted to tell you, but I didn't know how you would react. Can you come home so we can talk face to face?"

"Not right now, Cheetah. I need a few days. I'll see you this weekend at the block party, okay? Do me a favor baby and stay out of trouble."

"Aight, I will. I can't wait to see you. I love you, Tara."

"And I love you too, baby."

CHAPTER 22

Memorial Day 2003-Block Party

The sun was gleaming through a crack in the curtains; a kaleidoscope of colors danced around the room. Cheetah drew the curtains open a little wider. Even though it wasn't noon yet, the smell of barbeque ribs seeped through the cracked window. Cheetah raised the window pane and breathed in the aroma. Her stomach instantly growled. She lingered a moment longer before she walked back to her bed. Gathering her things, she called out to Esh.

"Come on, Esh. Hurry up and get that lil' nigga dressed. You gonna make me late!"

The smell of barbeque spread all through the room and Cheetah was hungry as hell. She had three different barbeques to attend before going to tonight's block party. The sooner she got started, the better. She still had to meet up with Naj, Nissan, and Qua at IHop on Bergen Street in thirty minutes.

Cheetah was taking Ozzy with her. He was clinging close to her since they moved in. He always wanted to be under Auntie Cheetah. Esh was a procrastinator. You could always count on her to be the last one dragging her ass to an event. Sometimes she moved so slow that when she finally arrived the event would be over. Cheetah wasn't about to allow Esh to slow her down anymore than she already was.

"You better at least be done with his hair by the time I get out of the shower!" Cheetah said as she walked past Esh, heading toward the bathroom. "Damn! Why you gotta be so slow?"

Esh had just started oiling the miniature locks that were evenly spaced all over Ozzy's head. She didn't even look up at Cheetah when she passed by. She was used to Cheetah acting a fool when she was pressed for time.

"Stop rushing me, Cheetah. He'll be ready when you get ready. You act like you really going somewhere important with your greedy ass. You'll get there on time," Esh replied as she rubbed more oil between her palms.

Cheetah stopped in front of the bathroom door and shot Esh a look that could cut through diamonds.

"I done told you about your mouth. Stop getting so smart and put a little more oil on the back. I swear, one of these days you gonna make me smack the shit out of you," Cheetah said as she walked in the bathroom and slammed the door.

Esh sucked her teeth and continued at the same pace. She paid Cheetah no mind. Her threats were hollow and harmless when it came to family.

Cheetah turned the shower on, letting the bathroom steam up as she looked at herself in the mirror. The past year had definitely taken its toll on her. The cold, hard look in her eyes accentuated by the dark rings underneath, hinted at the hardships she faced but survived this past year.

Cheetah stepped into the shower, and let the water beat down on her body. She washed as quickly as she could.

"Esh, you got that little nigga ready yet?" Cheetah hollered as she turned off the shower.

"Damn, Auntie, I'm putting his clothes on now, stop tripping!" Esh yelled back.

Cheetah wrapped herself in her robe and opened the bathroom door. Walking towards her room, she looked at Esh and said, "Girl ain't nobody tripping but your ass. He better be dressed when I get my clothes on and I'm not playing."

Cheetah walked in her room and plopped down on the bed. Glancing towards the window, she noticed that it was a beautiful day outside. Perfect weather for the beige Kenneth Cole linen suit she'd bought from the mall yesterday. She also bought an identical suit for Ozzy, Steve Madden sandals and straw hats. Macy's was having one of their famous one day sales and Cheetah bought shit like she was at a garage sale. She and her little nigga was definitely going to shine today.

Cheetah stepped out of her robe and walked over to the closet doors. The entire front of the closet was mirrored. Cheetah grabbed a bottle of lavender scented baby oil and rubbed it all over her still damp body. This was something she did every time she took a shower. It made her skin feel nice and smooth. She took the towel, dried off, and got dressed.

Fixing her locks into a ponytail, Cheetah thought about driving her '67 Chevy today. It was fire red, in mint condition and pimped out. She just bought it a few weeks earlier and had only driven it twice. It was more of a show piece than anything else. After a minute of contemplation she dismissed the thought. The haters would truly hate if she pulled up in the engine. She would just have to take the Yukon. It was a 2003 white on white, fully equipped monster with 24-inch Sprewell rims, and a DVD player and Xbox mounted in the headrests. Needless to say, the truck was butta!

Cheetah put on some Escada cologne and admired herself. Satisfied with what she saw, she grabbed her keys, wallet, and headed out the room. When she walked into the living room, Ozzy was ready. He looked just like a mini Cheetah. His twists were oiled and shining like stars. He had his hat hanging on a string down his back. Cheetah straightened out his shirt and grabbed his hand. Esh had just started to get her other two children ready and Cheetah was not about to wait for her.

"Look," Cheetah said, reaching for her wallet. "Take this money and meet me at Mom's house. I don't have time to wait on you."

219

Cheetah handed Esh one hundred dollars and left the house. She had ten minutes to make it to the IHOP, which was on the other side of town.

She helped Ozzy get settled in the backseat, then walked to the driver's side. Once inside, she stuck the key in the ignition and cued number three on the CD player. DMX's "*Ain't Killing Nothing*" flooded through the speakers.

DMX was her dawg! She didn't care what new artist came out. They could never compare to the D. She loved this nigga's music. He was the illest, realest rapper on the mic. Even though he hadn't dropped any new shit in two years, she still thought he was the best. She had just finished reading the autobiography of his life and felt she could relate to him. She could definitely identify with the hardships he endured growing up in the hood. He was a thug and so was she. He was thorough as hell, and so was she. He didn't give a fuck about nothing but family and friends, and that's exactly how Cheetah felt. In a nutshell, they were just alike.

Cheetah pumped up the volume, causing the truck to vibrate. Her system was ridiculous. The shit pumped so loud, you thought you were in an Usher and Lil' Jon video. You had no choice but to bounce with the beat. She looked over toward Ozzy and smiled. He was used to the music. He had already tightened the straps on the seatbelt and was singing along.

Ozzy was already a mini thug. Cheetah loved that about him. Some may think that he was out of control or even a little mannish, as the old people would say. Even though she was showing him the ways of the streets, she would make sure he got a formal education as well. She had already taken the initiative of raising him as her own. Her motto was to raise him tough, because the streets were crazy and wild. He would not grow up a sucka.

When Cheetah pulled into the IHOP parking lot, she saw Naj's platinum Durango parked right next to the door. Naj's truck was just as hot as Cheetah's, with spinning gold rims and gold piping. The interior had soft, charcoal grey leather with all the extra gadgets, an Xbox and televisions in the head rest like Cheetah had in hers. If one was flossing so was the other. Naj was her peoples for real. Cheetah would give up her right hand for her.

Cheetah reached in her ashtray, pressed a button, and the secret compartment under her dashboard popped open. Not too flashy with her jewelry, she kept it simple. She wore a three karat diamond stud in her ear, Ice Man watch with a platinum band, and a platinum link chain with a diamond medallion of a cheetah. Her prized possession was the five karat diamond pinky ring. Cheetah took all of it off, and placed it into the secret compartment. Ever since the robbery, she kept her jewelry in her safe or her truck. She never wore 'em when she was hustling or running minor errands.

Naj saw Cheetah getting out of the truck and walked to the door to meet her.

"Yo, Cheetah, what's up?" Naj asked, waving at her.

Cheetah went to the other side of the truck and helped Ozzy down. Together, hand-in-hand, they walked over to Naj.

"What's good, my nigga?" Naj asked, extending her fist out to get a pound.

"Nothing much. You know, same shit, different day," Cheetah replied, pounding Naj's fist with her own.

"I see you got your little man with you," Naj said, acknowledging Ozzy's presence.

"Yeah, this my dawg, you know that."

"Aight, well let's get in and wait on Nissan and Qua to get here."

They walked into the IHOP and sat down next to Ja'nise and her six-year-old son, Malik, and seven-year-old daughter, Malikah. They ordered some drinks and ice cream for the kids. With the three different picnics they were going to there was no need to get any food.

Sharing casual conversation, Cheetah saw just how excited Naj was about moving in a few weeks. Between the four of 'em, they had eight million dollars saved up. That was two million a piece. Just last month that Ja'nise found out what the four of them had been really doing in the streets. She gave Naj an ultimatum, either her or the streets. Without hesitation, Naj chose her family. They have been together for nine years and that was too much to throw away.

Nissan and Qua were running late because Nissan couldn't decide on what to wear. She wanted to put on a Dana Buchman sundress she'd gotten off a sale rack at TJ Maxx, but her stomach had gotten so big that she thought she looked like a beached whale. Qua watched her change into four different outfits before deciding to wear the sundress anyway.

Nissan looked beautiful pregnant. Her skin was glowing and her hair was healthier. She gained weight in all the right places, even though she already had a "ka dunk ka dunk" ass. She now had a "bump ba bump ba!"

A week earlier, the ultrasound let them know they were expecting a girl. They decorated the spare bedroom into a nursery. Qua hand painted it pink and white with flowers all over. She bought an antique bassinet that cost two thousand. Stuffed animals crowded the shelves and floor. She went out and spent two thousand on diapers, bottles, T-shirts, socks, and everything else a newborn baby would need. The baby was due in three weeks and everyone was anxiously awaiting her arrival.

By the time they made it to IHOP, everyone was there except Tara. Cheetah saw them pull up and everyone went out to their cars. Their first stop was Mrs. Johnson's house. A couple of the tenants were barbequing in the front of the building. Cheetah parked the truck and spotted her mother over by the grill. Mrs. Johnson looked up, saw them all and smiled.

"Come on over here!" she yelled, waving her hand. "Come on and taste some of this five alarm sauce I got on the ribs."

Cheetah greeted her mother with a tight embrace and a kiss on the lips. Naj, Qua, and Nissan all followed suit. Ja'nise had only met Mrs. Johnson twice before, but she couldn't help but to admire and love her. She was such a strong woman. No matter what trials or tribulations came her way she overcame them through the strength of Christ.

"Where is Esh and the rest of them younguns?" Mrs. Johnson asked as she piled some baked beans on a plate for Naj.

"She'll be here soon; you know how slow she is. She wasn't ready when I was so I left her," Cheetah replied munching on a cob of corn.

"Well, have you seen Dana?"

"No, mom, I haven't," Cheetah lied.

Cheetah had just run into Dana a few days earlier. As always, she hit her off with some money, which Dana took, and walked away without saying a word.

"Well, if you see her before I do, tell her to get her butt here to see me."

"I will."

They stayed there a little over an hour. Esh was just arriving as they were leaving. She was dressed in red, white, and blue Iceberg jeans with a matching fitted top. She had on a pair of red stilettos and was carrying a Dooney & Burke clutch bag. Her hair was cut so close it looked like she had waves but she actually had small curls.

"Damn, you took all that time and you still look the same." Cheetah joked with her as she walked past with the kids.

"Please, maybe if you would have taken time you wouldn't be looking like that."

"Whatever. You coming to the block party?"

"Yeah, I'll be there."

"Good. I want you to see Ozzy when he gets onstage for the talent show. He's gonna tear that shit up with the new dance moves I showed him."

"Don't be having my son up there acting a fool, Cheetah."

"Girl, this ain't your son no more. There's a new sheriff in town and just like they say on the Maury Show, 'you are not the mother'," Cheetah smacked Esh in the back of the head and ran to the car.

223

The next stop was Ra'dee's house. They ate some more and bullshitted with him before they drove to Ja'nise's parent's house. By six that evening they were pulling up on Avon Avenue. Cheetah barely had enough time to park before twenty or so children ran up to her waving their report cards.

"I got two."

"I got four."

"I got three."

"Hold up, calm down. Let me see," Cheetah said grabbing a handful of the papers. Cheetah had promised all the children she ran into on the block, five dollars for each 'A' they showed her on their report cards. Cheetah handed them back their papers and looked around. Slim was standing over by the DJ booth.

"Slim! Yo, Slim! Come here."

Slim put down the album he was looking at and walked over to her.

"Hey, Cheetah, what you need?"

"I want you to take this money and give each kid five dollars for every 'A' you see on their report card. If you need more just holla, okay?" Cheetah said, handing him two thousand dollars worth of five dollar bills.

"I got you. Aight, all you rugrats form a single file," Slim yelled out to the children.

Avon Avenue was blocked off between 11th and 12th Streets. Cheetah hired a DJ and a magician for the kids. She had people walking around dressed up like Dora the Explorer and Boots. There were all types of food tables and arts and crafts booths. Everything was free! There were so many people out, you could hardly move. Cheetah had banned everyone from hustling that night. If she caught somebody making a sell she was taking them off of the payroll.

At nine they were going to have a talent contest where the winner would win five hundred dollars. Everyone and their mother were at the block party. They were having so much fun nobody noticed Slick standing in the cut. Everywhere Cheetah went, he followed close behind. He was itching to shoot the bitch right then and there, but he knew that he wouldn't make it far if he did. This was her turf and he was a stranger among her people, but he would get her soon enough. He would get them all.

"Excuse me. May I have everyone's attention?" Cheetah was standing on the stage with the microphone in her hand. "Please, may I have everyone's attention?"

In a few moments, a hush fell over the crowd.

"How is everyone enjoying themselves?"

The crowd yelled out like fans at a Lakers game.

"Aight! We about to get this show on the road, but before we start the talent contest, I want to give a shout out to some very important people in my life. First, is my nigga Naj! I love you, man. You've watched me grow from a little snotty nose teenager to the woman I am today. You always had my best interest at heart and for that I got forever love for you, man.

"Ja'nise, I love you too, big sis. Family for life, ya heard? Ra'dee, nigga, if you out there, you need to know I've never loved a man in my life until I met you. To the grave, baby! Nissan, we all run around you acting like we are the men, but I got to give you your props, Ma. You are definitely the strongest one of the clique. You struggled your entire life and look where you are now. On top, baby! I love you, girl. Quayanna Harris, please could everyone just give this girl a hand?"

The crowd applauded long and hard. Cheetah raised her hand to quiet them down and started talking again.

"Qua, we all know you're the true brains in the bunch. I'm the most proud of you, baby. Just three more weeks 'til you get that degree. That's what's up! Y'all hear that? My dawg is graduating from Seton Hall University on June 19th. Y'all come on down and show her some love, okay? Quayanna Harris, when y'all hear that name I want it to get loud as hell at that graduation."

Cheetah took a breath before she continued.

"Okay, last but certainly not least, the love of my life. Tara, baby, I don't know if you are out there in that crowd because I haven't seen or spoken to you in four days. I need to tell you that I love you and I'm truly sorry. I will do anything to make this right between us. If you're out there, please find me and come home. I miss you."

Cheetah was about to put the microphone down when she heard someone from the audience say, "Do you promise not to cheat anymore?"

Cheetah looked around but could not tell where the voice was coming from.

"Yes, I promise not to cheat anymore."

"And do you promise to love and honor your woman?"

Cheetah still couldn't make out where the voice was coming from, but she did recognize it, so she played along.

"Yes, I will love and honor my woman."

"And do you, Cheetah, promise to never ever lie again or keep any secrets?"

Damn, Cheetah thought, *this shit is straight out of the movie Mahogany.*

"Yes, I promise to always be honest from this day on. Please, whoever that is talking, could you step forward?"

At that moment, the crowd parted and Tara walked towards the stage. Cheetah bent down, and held her hand out. Tara grabbed it and Cheetah pulled her up on the stage. Tara was crying. She was so glad to be in Cheetah's arms.

"I missed you, baby, so much," Tara whispered in her ear.

"And I missed you, Ma," Cheetah replied before she planted a kiss on Tara's mouth. The crowd went wild. They kissed so long Naj had to come up on the stage and pull them apart so the show could start. Everything was all good!

Sha-Sha noticed Slick at the Block Party and was clocking his every move. She hoped and prayed he didn't pull any bullshit stunts out here around all these children. But then Sha-Sha got so caught up in Cheetah's speech that she didn't notice Slick slip through the crowd and disappear. When she did, she panicked and ran to the end of the block just in time to see his mint green

Jaguar bend the corner. Sha-Sha wondered for the millionth time if she had made a mistake by telling him about the stick up. Deep down she knew it was. She just had no idea how big of a mistake it was.

The party didn't break up till the wee hours of the morning. It was the best function that Cheetah had ever thrown. The next morning she paid all the dopefiends she could find a bundle of dope a piece to help clean up the mess. She still had fifty bricks of dope left. She called Ra'dee and gave him forty of them, and found Dana and gave her the other ten. She tried one last time to get her to go into another rehab but it was useless. Dana was a burn out. She told Dana that she wouldn't be able to give her anymore drugs because she was getting out of the game. She told her she would always be there if she needed her for anything else. Dana took the bricks and left the truck just as silently as she had gotten in.

Cheetah pulled away from the curb and her cell phone rang. She didn't look at the number. She just picked it up and answered.

"Yeah who dis?"

"Cheetah, it's me, Sha-Sha. I really…"

"Bitch, don't you ever call me again. If you even attempt some more bullshit, I'm gonna kill your ass."

"Cheetah, wait…"

Cheetah hung up and immediately called Tara and told her Sha-Sha had called. Tara told her to just throw the phone away. She wouldn't need it anymore anyway. It was basically a business phone and since she was getting out of the game she had no use for it.

Cheetah pulled the truck over and threw the phone on the ground. She jumped out and stomped on it till it broke into pieces.

Sha-Sha called back four times. When she didn't get any answer, she knew it was useless. She wanted to warn Cheetah about Slick. She knew he was going to do something crazy and regardless of how mad she was at Cheetah, she didn't want to see her dead.

CHAPTER 23

When It All Falls Down

Qua was a nervous wreck! She had studied four years to reach this point, yet she still couldn't believe she was graduating. She would now have a career, a title: Quayanna Harris, CPA. She liked the way it sounded. She had spent two hours at the barbershop. She got a wash, cut and a shape up. She went to the salon to get her nails manicured, a pedicure and a full body massage. Now she was getting dressed, waiting to meet up with the rest of the clique. They all planned on riding to the college together.

Cheetah bought Qua a platinum and diamond chain with a 2004 charm. She was going to give it to her later that night when they went to surprise graduation party at Bentley's in New York. She also planned to give Tara her ring tonight, and get her knees dirty proposing.

They all met up at IHOP. This was the official meeting place. Once everyone showed up they got in their cars and rode one behind the other to the college. The graduation was being held in the field behind the main building. It was as big as a football stadium. They found parking spots and Qua went inside as the rest of them found their seats.

Sha-Sha was trapped outside in a line a block long. She had seen Slick get in his car and knew he was headed here. She got in her car and followed him but once they got to the college she lost sight of him. She had to get to the front of the line. She had to warn Cheetah.

After the valedictorian gave her speech, they began passing out the degrees and diplomas. Qua had her own personal cheering squad. Lots of people from the block party had shown up and everyone was patiently waiting to hear her name called.

Sha-Sha pushed to the front of the line and got in. She ran through the chairs trying to get up to the front where she knew Cheetah would be. She spotted Cheetah's dreads and ran toward her. From the corner of her eye she saw Slick running up to the stage. The professor was calling out Quayanna Harris and the crowd went wild. Sha-Sha saw Slick pull out his gun and point it at the stage. As soon as the professor handed Qua her degree, he squeezed the trigger.

"Nooooooooooo!" Sha-Sha screamed.

The crowd was so loud, nobody even heard the gunshots.

Qua dropped her degree and grabbed her chest. She looked down at the front of her gown and saw blood stains appear on the white fabric. Cheetah saw the blood and was on her feet with her gun in her hand. She looked around wildly for the shooter. She was almost up on the stage when the second shot caught the left side of Qua's head. Her brains exploded and she dropped to the platform. Pandemonium broke; people were screaming, running and trampling each other to get away from the gun shots.

Nissan ran up on the platform and bent down towards Qua and Cheetah caught sight of Slick with the gun in his hand pointed at Nissan. Cheetah let off five consecutive shots. Three caught Slick high in the chest and threw him back on the ground. He lay dead; looking like someone had used him for target practice. The other two shots hit a student in a graduating gown. They dropped down next to Slick.

Naj grabbed Ja'nise, Tara and the kids and led them safely to the car. She ran back into the yard to check on the rest of the clique.

230

Nissan was sitting on the stage with what was left of Qua's head laying on her lap. She was rocking back and forth, clearly in shock.

Cheetah saw the police coming towards her with their guns and took off running. She ran out of the yard and headed towards the streets. When she was away from the crowd, the police started busting shots at her. She dipped from side to side running in a zig zag line. She ran like she was at an all state track meet back in high school. She was hauling ass!

She heard sirens in the background and ran harder. She ran through two apartment complexes, jumped a gate and wound up on Barclay Street. She ran inside building number 114 and sprinted up the seven flights that led to the roof.

She left the two cops chasing her so far behind, they didn't know what building she went into. She hid behind an air duct and changed the clip in her gun. She sat back quietly, waiting on the war that was about to come. She knew the day would come when she would have to hold court in the street. She was not going to jail. It was live or die! Them or her! Cheetah was ready for either one.

Within fifteen minutes, the entire complex was barricaded and swarming with police. They were going in all the build-ings checking each apartment. Cheetah heard the police enter building number 114 and pulled out her cell. She pressed the number two in her phone and dialed Naj.

"Naj, it's me Cheetah," she said in a whisper.

"Cheetah, man, where you at? You okay? You safe?"

"Nah, I'm on the roof of building number 114 on Barclay. They got the place surrounded and they just walked in the building. I'm not going to make it out, Naj."

"Cheetah, stop talking like that. Don't do nothing stupid or crazy. You can get out of this, just hold on, man."

"It's over, dawg," Cheetah said as the tears cascaded down her face. "It's over. I'm not going to jail for murder. I'll never come home. I gots to battle this out. Where's Tara? Let me speak to her."

"Cheetah, I'm not with them. I took them home and I'm headed towards you. Just hold on, please."

"Naj, tell my mom I love her, okay? Would you do that for me? Tell my family I'm sorry and I love them. I love you too, man."

Cheetah hung up the phone and dialed Tara's cell. Tara saw Cheetah's number and quickly answered.

"Cheetah, where are you?"

"Tara, I love you," Cheetah said.

The roof door exploded open and six officers came up on the roof. Cheetah dropped the phone and ran towards the edge of the roof. The first bullet hit her in her back and threw her to the rooftop. She saw Tara's face. She got up and fired back. The second bullet hit her in the chest. She saw her mom's face. She squeezed the trigger and emptied her clip. The third bullet hit her in the stomach. She fell back to the rooftop. She saw Dana's face.

She crawled to the edge. She struggled to her feet and the next and last bullet caught her in the neck, sending her over the edge of the roof. On the way down she saw Esh, Ozzy, Naj, Qua, Nissan, Ra'dee, and Ja'nise. She smiled just before hitting the pavement.

Naj had just rounded the corner when she heard the shots. She stopped the car, jumped out and ran through the police barricades. She got to building number 114, just in time to see Cheetah fall from the roof.

"Cheetah, noooooooo!" Naj screamed, but it was too late.

The cell phone was lying on the roof, with someone screaming on the other end. One of the cops stepped on it, and kept on walking.

The Funeral

One week after Cheetah and Qua were killed, they were laid to rest. Best friends to the end, their families decided to give a double funeral. To say that the funeral was packed would be an understatement. People came for hours to view the bodies. The line was so long at times that it went all the way around the corner. The whole hood came out.

Naj and Ja'nise sat with Cheetah's family, and Nissan sat with Qua's. Mrs. Johnson sat attentively, listening to the sermon the preacher was delivering. After every few words she gave a nod and a few amens. Even though she heard every word spoken, she couldn't help but to think of the daughter she hadn't been able to save. So many nights she knelt down on her knees asking the Lord to save Cheetah from the streets, but the good Lord says that everyone must reap what they sow. The Old Testament states that if you live by the sword, then surely you would die from the sword. She just wished she could have saved Cheetah in some way, maybe even gotten her to give her life to the Lord.

Mrs. Johnson let the tears flow freely down her face as the preacher spoke about the young men and women getting killed over senselsss acts of violence. The sermon lasted almost two hours.

After the bodies were taken to the gravesite and lowered into the ground, the humongous crowd, headed back to the church.

Naj, Esh, and Nissan sat at the table with Mrs. Johnson. Esh's children, Ozzy, Nu-Nu, and Malaya, sat with Janise's children, Malik and Malikah. Naj sat in a daze. Sadness poured out of her skin like sweat. The lost of Cheetah and Qua was like losing two-thirds of herself. Shattered soul and all, she still held it together enough to give Mrs. Johnson the strength and support she needed.

Esh was a total wreck. She cried continuously without even trying to shelter it. She missed her aunt more then anyone could ever fathom. Nissan controlled her emotions. Why? That was still unknown even to her. She just felt that she had to be strong for the sake of her sanity and her newborn child. She gave birth to a healthy, eight pound girl soon after Cheetah and Qua were killed. She named her Quayanna.

No one saw Ra'dee at the funeral. He came several hours before the funeral started and sat alone in the church. At the burial site, he stood behind a cluster of trees and saw the bodies being lowered. Emotionally distraught, he felt that a true thug mourned alone, and besides that, he had become obsessed with finding out the cause of Cheetah's death, and avenging it at all cost.

Ra'dee's Revenge

Ra'dee sat at the bar with an untouched shot of absolute vodka in front of him. He had already downed four of the same drink. He was in deep thought and oblivious to everything going on around him. Today was the one month anniversary of Cheetah and Qua's deaths. As he sat there thinking about the loss of the only best friend he ever had, somebody tapped him on the shoulder.

"Is this seat taken?" A bad ass bitch dressed in an electic blue Chanel sundress with matching sandals asked him.

"Nah, Ma," Ra'dee answered snapping out of his daydream. He picked up his drink and took it to the head, drinking it all in one shot. Sha-Sha sat in the seat next to him and ordered a cherry kiafa and orange juice. Turning to the side, she looked Ra'dee over again.

Damn, he's a fine ass black nigga. She thought to herself.

Ra'dee caught her staring and stared back. For a moment they both looked deep into each others eyes without blinking.

Ra'dee, who had never cheated on Michelle, felt strongly attracted to Sha-Sha for some strange reason. Something inside of him was saying, "Put your mack down dawg!"

R'adee blinked, causing Sha-Sha to smile.

"So, I guess you got to pay for my drink. You lost." She said as she flashed her most seductive smile.

"I lost what?" Ra'dee asked. "I didn't know we were playing anything," he said as he stared at her cleavage.

"Oh, you don't know about the staring game? I know you played it in school," she said.

"I never went to school. The streets taught me."

"Oh really?" Sha-Sha asked as the bartender brought her drink to her.

Ra'dee dug into his pocket and pulled out a twenty. He gave it to the bartender and ordered another drink.

"So now that we got the games out the way, what's your name?" Ra'dee asked.

"I'm Sha-Sha and you?"

"I'm Ra'dee" he said and he gulped down his drink. Sha-Sha looked at him for a moment.

"Damn, why you drinking like that? When I walked over here you were drinking like you lost your best friend. You want to talk about whatever is on your mind?"

Ra'dee didn't want to talk about his problems with this chick. He just wanted to take her somewhere and hit that ass.

"Nah, Ma, I'm good. Just thinking about someone that's all."

"Damn, she must got you turned out!"

"Look, let's forget that shit. What you getting into, you wanna chill?"

"Damn, you don't waste no time do you?"

"For what? Tomorrow ain't promised to neither one of us."

"You're right about that."

They both sat silent for a moment and both of their minds were flooded with thoughts of Cheetah. Sha-Sha finished her drink and got up off the stool.

"Okay, let's go."

Outside, Ra'dee got in Sha-Sha's car with her and they drove to the nearest cheap hotel. They spent four hours fucking and sweating. Over the next two weeks they saw each other as much as possible. It wasn't like Ra'dee was digging her or anything, he just couldn't stop seeing her. On their seventh date, Sha-Sha took Rad'ee to her house. Sitting in the living room, Ra'dee noticed a picture on the corner of the mantle that looked familiar. He got up and picked it up. The picture was of Qua at the graduation walking up the steps to the stage. Sha-Sha walked in with two drinks in her hand and stood behind Ra'dee. Sensing something, Ra'dee played dumb and asked who that was in the picture.

"Oh, that's my cousin Qua. She got killed two months ago. Her and her friend. Remember that shooting at the college grad-uation? That picture was taken right before she got shot. My aunt

235

had copies made and gave them to everyone in the family."

"Word?" Ra'dee asked feigning ignorance. "Who was her friend?"

Sha-Sha walked over to the couch and sat the drink down on the table. Feeling comfortable with Ra'dee, she decided to tell him about the role she played in her cousin's death. She needed to tell someone. The secret had been driving her crazy. Patting the spot next to her she motioned for Ra'dee to come sit next to her.

"Ra'dee, I need to talk to you about something." She let out a sigh. "My cousin got killed on the same night as her best friend, Cheetah. My son's father killed Qua and the cops killed Cheetah. You see, Cheetah and I used to fuck around. She's the only girl I ever dealt with, and she played me like a whore after I set my son's father up so they could rob him. I only told him about Cheetah. I just really wanted him to hurt her, not my cousin. I never thought he was going to kill Qua. Do you know how it feels everyday to know I was the reason my cousin got killed?"

Sha-Sha was crying so hard her face was soaked with tears. Ra'dee sat on the side of her shocked by the news. Sha-Sha leaned her head on his shoulder and he flinched.

"What's the matter?" she asked, as she straightend up. It was at this moment that Ra'dee heard Cheetah's voice loud and clear.

Not now dawg, don't react. You know what to do, but not in her house. Act normal and play it cool. I lead you this far, now you handle the rest, aight?

"Aight!" Ra'dee said aloud.

"Aight what?" Sha-Sha asked, clearly confused.

"No, I said I'm alright," Ra'dee said as he stood up. "Look, I got to go. I'm sorry but I got some important business to handle."

"Are you sure?" Sha-Sha asked. "You just got here."

"Yeah, I'm sure. I'll holla at you this weekend. I'll call you later."

Ra'dee kissed her on the cheek, and left. Outside in his truck Ra'dee put in the CD of *Set It Off* and cued track four. Gladys Knight's voice filled the air with *"Missing You."*

Ra'dee rode all the way home with thoughts of his next move deeply embedded in his brain.

Later that night

Ring…Ring…

"Hey, this is Sha-Sha. Sorry to miss your call. Leave a quickie and I'll get back."

Beep!

"Yeah, this is me Ra'dee. This Friday at nine, meet me in Elizabeth at the train station on the New York to Trenton side. We going away for the weekend. No need to bring nothing. I got you, alright? One!"

Friday night in Walmart

"Let me get one of those in a large and one of those in jet black. Also the specs, the big ones."

Ra'dee paid for his things and hit I-95. Reaching his destination in one hour forty-five minutes, he parked his truck on a deserted road behind an old chemical plant. Walking half a mile to the nearest town he found a shopping center and stole a white Honda Civic. Back in Newark, he took the liscense plates off the Civic and removed the inspection sticker. Placing temp tags in the window, Ra'dee went to his grandmother's house and sat in the basement, smoking blunt after blunt until 8:30.

9:00 Friday Night

Ra'dee saw Sha-Sha's car pull in the lot. He knew she wouldn't notice him, so he honked the horn at her when she got out. Sha-Sha walked over to the car and turned around to leave once she looked inside.

"It's me, Ra'dee," he said, with the window slightly cracked.

"Come on, get in."

Ra'dee was fully disguised with a hat, fake beard and glasses. He was dressed in a black dickie outfit and had on black leather biker gloves.

"Why the hell you dressed like that?" Sha-Sha asked, looking at him like he was crazy.

"Because I got mad beef with some niggas out here and I don't feel like the rowdy shit tonight."

11:00 Friday night

The ride to New Rochelle, NY was driven in silence. Sha-Sha had no idea what was going on. It wasn't until they pulled behind the chemical plant did she start asking questions.

"What the hell we doin' back here?"

"Oh, I got a stash out here. Come on and help me get it and we can leave. Here take this flashlight."

Sha-Sha got out and turned the flashlight on. It was dark as hell and besides the sound of crickets, it was quiet. Radee removed the beard, hat and glasses and got a shovel out of the trunk.

"Come on, it's over here."

He led Sha-Sha to a small clearing not far away.

"Right there, hold the light right there." He said pointing under a bush.

Sha-Sha bent down a little and flashed the light. When the light hit the area, she saw what looked like a baseball card. She picked it up and saw a picture of Cheetah and Ra'dee standing in front of the laundromat. Astonished, she looked up just in time to see the shovel coming at her head. Wham! Blood splattered every direction as the shovel smashed into the side of her head. Sha-Sha flew back and Ra'dee brought the shovel down again, this time breaking her knee caps.

"I lost my best friend, BITCH!"

WHAM! A hit to the chest.

"And it was all your fault."

WHAM! Another shot to the head!

Ra'dee beat Sha-Sha with the shovel for five minutes. When he was done, Sha-Sha's body was a bloody pulp. He walked back over to the bush, reached between the leaves, and grabbed the can of gasoline he had hidden. He poured it all over Sha-Sha's body, pulled a pack of matches out of his pocket, lit the whole pack and threw them on her body.

Looking up to the sky, Ra'dee blew a kiss. "For you, Cheetah. Loyalty to the grave."

Cheetah Epilogue

T ara had a nervous breakdown the night Qua and Cheetah was killed. She heard the shots through the phone and freaked out. She was taken to Anne Klein Psychiatric Hospital for observation and couldn't attend the funeral.

Naj moved to Atlanta the day after the funeral. She opened her clothing store and vowed to never step foot in Newark again.

Nissan moved her entire family to Florida where she enrolled back in college, this time majoring in Accounting.

Mrs. Johnson and Esh tried to find Dana to tell her about the murder. She was nowhere to be found. A month later, a partially decomposed body was found in an abandoned house with a hypodermic needle still in her arm. Dana had overdosed the same night Cheetah was killed.

A READING GROUP GUIDE
CHEETAH
MISSY JACKSON

ABOUT THIS GUIDE

The suggested questions are intended to enhance
your group's reading of this book.

DISCUSSION QUESTIONS

1.) Do you think it was careless for Cheetah to walk to the
bus stop with a large amount of money?
2.) Do you think Tara was already curious about the the
lesbian lifestyle since she contacted Cheetah so quickly?
3.) Just because Cheetah was robbed, was it justifiable for
her to go out and commit robberies?
4.) Just because Cheetah "gave back" to the community, do
you feel it was okay for her to sell drugs?
5.) Do you feel that Dana gave up on her addiction too
easily?
6.) Do you agree with Nissan going to meet her ex-boyfriend
alone? If so, why?
7.) Do you think Ja'nise should have given Naj the ultimatum
to quit selling drugs as soon as she found out?
8.) Why do you feel Qua was so attracted to the street lifestyle when she already had everything going for herself?
9.) Do you believe Sha-Sha should have handled her infatu-
ation with Cheetah in a different way?
10.) Do you feel a sequel should be written, even though
Cheetah is dead?

Coming June 2010

Excerpt from
THE JUMP OFF

CHAPTER 1

"Emergency face count ladies. Everybody to their assigned areas...now!" the fat CO yelled to the girls in the day area.

Fuck is going on now? Jinx wondered as she put the weights back on the floor.

Everyday it was something new in this county jail. She couldn't wait until she got the hell out of this place next week. This would definitely be her last time coming through these doors. She had big plans for when she hit the bricks, and none of them involved ever coming back to jail.

Jinx grabbed her towel and water bottle off the floor. She wiped the sweat from her eyes, and laid the towel across her shoulders. She took a sip of water as she slowly walked towards her cell.

"Jordan, put a little pep in your step. Get to your cell!" the CO warned as Jinx passed the control booth.

"Don't fuckin' rush me. I'm going. This is probably a bunch of bullshit anyway," Jinx said, continuing at a slow pace.

"Jordan, what I tell you about your mouth? You got one more time before I write you up on an infraction."

Jordan was Jinx's government name. The Correctional Officers were the only ones that addressed her in this manner. Jinx stopped and turned around. She stared at the CO as if looks could kill.

"Write it now, bitch! It's still not going to stop me from getting out of this hell hole."

Jinx was maxing out on a one hundred eighty day sentence she received for shoplifting. She would have served one hundred twenty days if she hadn't constantly gotten into trouble. Since she'd been to solitary confinement four times, she had to do the full one hundred eighty days. This terminated any chances of getting parole.

There was nothing the correctional officer could do, but put Jinx back in the hole for seven more days, Jinx could care less. She wasn't a people person anyway. Solitary confinement gave her peace of mind; time to get into herself and put more thought into her plans for when she got back out on the streets.

Jinx reached her cell and walked in, slamming the steel door behind her. Her roommate Kristy, a white chick from Manville, New Jersey, was in the cell, lying across the top bunk, reading. When the door slammed she jumped, startled by the noise.

"Damn, Jinx, do you have to slam the door every time you come in here? You scared the shit out of me," Kristy said as she placed the book on her pillow.

"I can't help it if I'm buffed," Jinx replied, flexing in front of the steel mirror that was bolted into the wall over the toilet seat.

"Buff or not, you can learn how to close the door like a normal person."

Jinx turned around and looked at Kristy with crossed eyes and a twisted mouth.

"How many times I gotta tell you that I'm not normal?" she asked, making a grotesque face.

"Everybody on their bunks for a count!" yelled the CO over the intercom.

"Yo, what's up with this cunt? You got any idea?" Jinx asked.

"Nah, you know how they do. They probably got their pop sheet wrong or somethin'."

A pop sheet was a log correctional officers used to keep track of inmates on their tier. It wasn't unusual for an inmate to turn up missing, causing their count to come up short. This would cause an immediate recount or even a lockdown of the entire jail.

"Yeah, they dumb as hell," Jinx stated, "but always trying to degrade us like we some kind of derelicts."

Jinx sat down on the bottom bunk, stripped out of the gray county issued sweatsuit, and laid back on the bunk, wearing a sports bra and boxers. She was hot and sweaty from the hour long workout she just endured, but her workout wasn't done yet. She placed her feet flat on the bed, raised her knees up to her chest, put both hands behind her head, and proceeded to do her daily sets of crunches.

She had gone through five sets of ten by the time the correctional officer made it to their door.

"Face forward, Jordan. I need to see your face," the CO demanded.

"Bitch, you know who I am. Go on to the next room."

"Why you always got to be a wise ass, Jordan?"

"You wanna see a wise ass?" Jinx asked. "Here, look at this." Jinx turned to her side and faced the wall. She stuck her hand down the side of her boxers and pulled them down to her thighs, then said, "I got your wise ass, fat ass."

To Be Continued....August 2010

COMING
AUGUST 2009

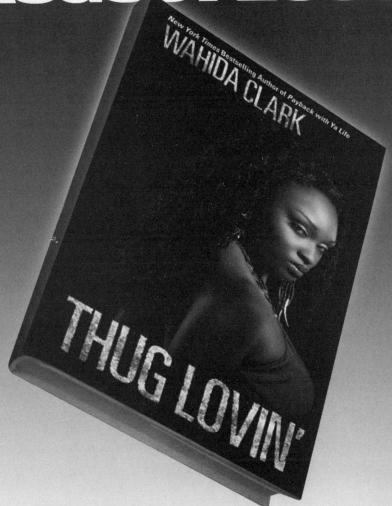

New York Times Bestselling Author of *Payback with Ya Life*
WAHIDA CLARK

THUG LOVIN'

Best Selling Author
Wahida Clark

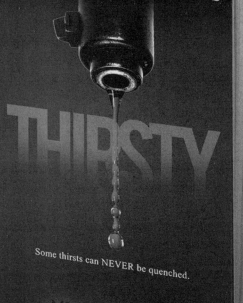